NATIVE DECEPTION

A Zeb Hanks Mystery Book 13

Mark Reps

This book is a work of fiction. Names and characters are products of the author's imagination. Any similarities between the good people of southeastern Arizona and tribal members of the San Carlos Indian Reservation are purely coincidental.

NATIVE DECEPTION
ISBN: Paperback 9798378990665

Contents

Chapter 1

OCTOBER 24, 2022

ECHO HAD HIKED THE hidden trail to and from the sacred place of the Knowledge Keeper hundreds of times and the nuanced markings of the trail had become as familiar as her own breath. The six-mile route was a brisk ninety-minute walking meditation. When Echo trotted the path at a steady pace the time was reduced in half and became both a physical and mental experience. Today as she hiked back to her truck she chose to use the full ninety minutes to cover the distance.

The two prior evenings had been spent in a sweat lodge in the sacred place preparing for her role in leading the White Painted Woman ceremony for the young women of the San Carlos Reservation. As a result, with each stride her physical body reacted with a curious combination of strength and fatigue. The very same steps led her mind and spirit to the crystal clarity of dawn's first light. Consumed by the bestowed blessings of the Creator, Echo radiated beauty and love.

Two nights without sleep made traversing the numerous arroyos and twist-backs tricky. To keep her mind sharp Echo sang the songs of White Painted Woman.

The Creator of all things directed the flowers to feed the White Painted Woman with pollen and commanded the clouds to burst forth with rain so that she might grow. It took the Creator a mere eighteen days to create her. Yet she was without life until the wind filled her lungs with breath. The sun, taken by her beauty built her a home amidst the four sacred mountains.

The White Painted Woman, filled with gratitude, danced on each of the mountaintops. Her actions created rain from the east, jewels and beautiful fabrics from the south, plant life from the west and all the animals from the northern mountain. From the first woman, the White Painted Woman, love and plenty abounded.

When White Painted Woman first rested she stood tall and vigorously brushed off parts of the outer layer of her skin. As these flakes touched the ground they created human beings. These were the First People.

Taking a rest in the morning sun Echo sustained herself with water, dried fruit and nuts. She could only wonder what the White Painted Woman must have felt when she created the First People. Why had the Creator chosen the Apache as the First People?

Echo stilled her heart so that she might better understand the purpose of her own journey. The quieter Echo became the closer she came to understanding why the White Painted Woman also rested and rejuvenated after creating rain, plants, animals and beautiful things for mankind.

Echo envisioned the White Painted Woman as two goddesses within one. The first woman was a youthful maiden, fertile and replete with vitality. The second was old and infertile with sagging skin, softening bones and weakening vision. The goddesses were the bookends of life itself.

As Echo prayed and sang, the memory of another great Apache woman, Lozen, legendary Apache warrioress rose from the depth of her mind. Lozen with her strong spirit performed the rites of the White Painted Woman for hundreds upon hundreds of Apache girls. The elders, recognizing her supernatural abilities, made her a spiritual tribal leader when she was only a teenager.

Lozen's supernatural powers grew over time and came to include the ability to locate the enemy and know their number and location. Using this power she saved hundreds of women and children from the United States Cavalry. As well, Lozen fought side-by-side with Geronimo during the savage forty-year-long Apache-U.S. Cavalry wars. Singing the heroic songs of Lozen to all of nature uplifted Echo's tired body and enhanced her spirit.

Reinvigorated and rich with newly found vitality Echo stepped up her pace, realizing how much she had missed her children and Zeb. With each step she neared the hidden exit from the six-mile path leading to the secret place of the Knowledge Keeper. As she climbed the final steep arroyo and her eyes popped level with the desert floor a warning song of a Canyon Wren circled her head, stopping her dead in her tracks. Knowing the wren's alert was meant for her ears, Echo ducked low. Her eyes searched all that surrounded her.

Echo strained to see the exact origin of the cascading birdsong of the Canyon Wren. Its subtle coloring made it difficult to spot. This strange bird that drank no water obtained the necessary liquid to survive from eating insects. Yet no swarming insects were in sight. The bird's song amplified elusively as it bounced from canyon wall to canyon wall before disappearing into the atmosphere.

A ground squirrel raced across her line of vision. It stopped only to drop the nut from its mouth and chirp braggingly to its mate about what a delicious dinner it was bringing home. Echo listened as the chatter faded into the distance. Holding her nose in the air, only familiar smells entered. Moving to a nearby tree Echo hid herself while remaining upright thereby expanding her view. Her already heightened senses sharpened further.

In the distance something caught her eye. A pile of clothing? Someone sleeping on the ground? Echo knew there was no way to approach it without giving herself away. The senses that are unnamed but known by all whispered to her that something was amiss. Instinctively she checked herself for a weapon she knew wasn't there. Because this had been a spiritual journey Echo had chosen to carry only her throwing knife.

Viewing her surroundings with great intent she was certain there was no way to get to her truck without passing the clothing pile which was only a few hundred feet from where she stood.

Echo tightened and readjusted her backpack. She'd witnessed how an ill-fitting rucksack could slow someone and interfere with their actions. Knife tightly in hand she chose to walk the opposite canyon wall to her destination. The path put her within fifty feet of the clothes. Overhead, the solitary Canyon Wren seemed to have multiplied into many. By the time she'd walked a further ten steps they were joined by a murder of crows circling ominously. She followed their movements. They spoke to what she already surmised.

Edging closer to what she'd spotted, Echo's instincts shifted into an even higher level of vigilance. Experience had long taught her that when her senses became alarmed the only action was to attempt calmness. Creeping ever closer she now clearly saw the clothes contained a human being. The body lay atop the butt of a rifle. Its barrel pointed in her direction. In combat this circumstance was known as the dead man's trap. Inching closer she could see the body's panted legs and hiking boots. Moving stealthily she crept ever closer.

Almost unconsciously her mind laid out an escape route. Slowly Echo flattened herself against the ground. If the person under the pile had designs on killing her, she needed to be prepared for anything.

She waited. The only discernable movements were created by wind flowing down the canyon. The breeze rippled the arm of Echo's shirt. Tamping it down with a finger and tucking it under prevented further movement. Echo focused her vision on the hands. They belonged to a woman. A ring on the right hand shimmered in the sunlight. Echo did her best to merge into the landscape as her mind considered a myriad of possibilities.

Fifteen minutes passed. The body under the clothing did not move despite several small creatures crawling over it. Knife in hand, hugging the ground Echo approached with the stealth of a wolf. The woman made no motion as Echo sneaked in within touching distance of the body. A body which she could now tell was deceased.

The cause of death abruptly became clear. The woman's carotid artery had been severed. The blood, in draining from her body, pooled almost artfully. A closer look showed what appeared to be a second knife wound on the underside of the arm. Enough blood had flowed from this cut to suggest the brachial artery had been sliced open. The combination of these two incisions assured a quick end of life. Death had come in a surgically precise package. The killer was well trained.

Echo's eyes followed the direction in which the barrel of the gun was pointed. Her eyes landed on a fallen tree. Was the woman aiming at someone when she'd been murdered? Unlikely, unless this killing was a two-person job with the cohort of the blade wielder using diversionary tactics to distract the dead woman.

Common sense told her someone had sneaked up behind the dead woman, grabbed her by the jaw, pulled her neck to the left and used the knife with precision on her right carotid and brachial arteries. This was an efficient killing.

The body of the woman was not warm enough to be a truly recent slaying and not fetid enough to be more than a few days old. Since she hadn't noticed the body upon entering the trail to the sacred place, the killing could only have taken place within the last forty-eight hours.

There was nothing Echo could do to help the dead woman at this point except say a quick prayer for her eternal spirit.

Echo put on a pair of gloves before grabbing the dead woman's rifle, a Henry .30-.30 with a shell already chambered and no ejected shells nearby. Rifle in hand Echo moved stealthily toward the fallen tree. Though she could see nothing of consequence in the open space she knew how well a person might hide were they bent on distracting someone.

Hearing crunchy shuffling of leaves as she neared the tree, she instantly became one with the dirt and sand of the desert floor. She landed, rifle in hand ready to fire. Echo instantly flashbacked to her first firefight in Afghanistan. It lasted no more than thirty seconds but each fraction of each second was an agonizingly elongated eternity. The volume of the crackling dry leaves increased. From her position on the ground she could see eye to eye with a desert ground squirrel that was simply scavenging for a bite to eat. She allowed herself an easy breath and waited as the creature scrambled off, leaving her in silence.

She recalled overhearing a lesson Song Bird had been teaching Sawni. He taught her that when someone plots the murder of another human being, regardless of how they'd killed, a fatal flaw was always present. Let your mind see that flaw and you will find your killer, were Song Bird's words of wisdom. Echo held her hands in the way of Lozen. She sensed the vapor trail of someone long since gone. That person may have been the killer. She was uncertain. Echo moved back toward the body of the dead woman.

Examining the body for identification she found a bear tag with an accompanying bear hunting license. Both were covered with dried blood. Not wanting to tamper further with potential evidence, she left them alone. Echo pulled out her cellphone and took pictures of a small tattoo of the letter Z on the inside of the right ankle just above the ankle bone, a tiny discoloration on the right wrist that might be a birthmark, the dead woman's weapon, her boots, the bear license, the bear tag, the ring on the fourth finger of the woman's right hand and a photo in the direction of the fallen tree where she imagined the killer's possible accomplice to have hidden. Lastly she zoomed in on the woman's face. Echo noted perfectly ponytailed hair and even in death, her chiseled musculature. Putting the phone in her pocket, Echo rolled the dead body onto its side. Light shined off the edge of a highly sharpened knife blade. Moving closer she immediately recognized the knife to be an Emerson CQC6, identical to the one she carried in Afghanistan. Hers had been a gift from a departing Seal Team 6 Special Forces soldier. Looking more closely at the knife her jaw dropped when she saw ES1 etched into the open, bloodied blade.

"What the...?" It took everything Echo had not to reach down and grab the knife. She knew that tampering with what appeared to be the murder weapon would only bring the worst kind of trouble. When Echo brought her eyes to within six inches of the weapon she recognized each nick and scratch. There was no doubt. It was her knife. Echo knew where and how she vaulted her weapons. There was no way her knife could be here unless someone had broken into the house and opened a safe that only she and Zeb knew the combination to. Echo hesitated but took a picture of the knife as her mind raced with anxiety at the thought of someone breaking into her house in the last forty-eight hours.

Echo gently rolled the body back on top of the knife before tapping 2 on her cellphone. Zeb answered her call halfway through the first ring. She knew he only picked up that fast when he truly was missing her.

"Zeb."

"What's up darlin'? I was thinking about you just this very minute. You on your way home? Get done what you needed to get done?"

"No and yes..."

"Sounds like there is a but in that sentence."

"I'm fine. But we've got a little problem on our hands."

Chapter 2

STRANGE TRUTH

"*WE* HAVE A PROBLEM on our hands?" asked Zeb. "As in the both of us?"

"Yes, *we* do."

"What might our problem be?"

"Our problems begin with a dead female body that I'm currently standing directly over," said Echo.

"I take it from the tone of your voice there's something other than a dead woman's body that *we* have a problem with?"

Zeb was a breath away from instructing Echo on the handling of a dead body but stopped himself. Her skill level was far above someone who might muck up an investigation scene. His only concern at that moment was for her well-being. Still when she said *we* and the way she said it created an aura of weirdness.

"Everything we have an issue with involves the dead woman."

"Nothing other than that?"

"You'll know soon enough."

Whatever she was being so cryptic about had Zeb bewildered.

"Send me your GPS coordinates. I'll be there in thirty minutes or less. You're sure you're safe?"

"I'm safe."

Echo's simple response was so minimal Zeb was certain something else wasn't right.

"What's really going on?"

"Where are Elan and Onawa?"

Zeb never liked it when Echo answered a question with another question.

"With your parents."

"Did you talk with them this morning?"

"Yes. Why?"

"Did you sleep at the house last night?"

"Yes."

"The night before?"

Zeb chuckled. "I know better than to cheat on you. That might be the death of me."

When Echo didn't laugh at his joke, Zeb knew something was seriously wrong.

"What's going on?"

"I've told you what you need to know. I'll explain the rest when you get here. I'd rather not do it over the phone. You never know who's listening. Just get here. Please."

"Are you certain that you're safe?" They had a code word, *truth*, worked out between them should either be in serious, immediate danger and unable to talk. Whatever was going on it didn't rise to the level of the code word.

"Yes."

"Be careful. You're in close proximity to a dead body. God knows who or what may be lurking in the area."

Her mind made a beeline to something Zeb had told her about professional killers. They were patient, checked their work and did not make foolish mistakes.

"Zeb, honey, I know what I'm doing."

It sure as hell wasn't her first rodeo. That didn't matter one iota. If it were her first or her one hundredth there was always an increased possibility of danger near a dead human.

"I know you know what you're doing. But I'm also a sheriff who's seen more than his share of weird shit."

"The murder weapon is secured. She was carrying a Henry .30-.30 with one chambered bullet and no ejected shells. I have protection."

"Hmm. Spoils of war?"

Zeb's joke wasn't funny to a combat veteran.

"Protection. If necessary. I've also got my throwing knife."

Zeb chuckled knowing there was no one better with a knife, up close or at a distance than Echo. He was certain that whomever she turned her knife on would come up on the short end of things.

"One more thing?"

"Yes, Sheriff Hanks?"

Zeb smiled. He loved Echo in more ways than he had words to describe.

"Any ID on the body?"

"Yes, a bear hunting tag and license. Something about them feels fishy."

"Fake?"

"I don't know. It's just a gut feeling."

"Okay. Call if you need me."

"You're number two on my speed dial. See you in thirty."

Zeb clicked off his phone, got out of his chair, pulled up the sock in his left boot and made a beeline for the front door, stopping only at Helen's desk where he ever so briefly detailed her in on the situation.

"You want me to send Kate or Rambler in that direction for backup?"

The Sheriff of Graham County just shook his head no, offering no further explanation before jogging to his truck. As he ran Helen noticed her nephew was getting a bit thick around the middle. Too thick for a man of his age and in his occupation.

At the scene of the crime Echo knelt near the dead woman. What struck her, outside of the fact that the killing weapon was her personal knife, was that whoever did the killing left it behind. It must have been placed under the body for the sole purpose of making her look guilty of murder.

Someone knew too way much about her. Was it another veteran from her PTSD group? Was it someone with a personal vendetta against her? Was it someone wanting to set up Zeb because of his position as Sheriff of Graham County? She stopped herself from thinking when she recognized her thoughts were spinning out of control. There were too many options. The only thing she was certain of was that she didn't kill the woman. Yet with her fingerprints and DNA likely all over the murder weapon, her being the first on the scene and the location of the body, it was going to be difficult to prove otherwise. She was almost beginning to feel guilty or that she'd lost her mind. Echo took three deep breaths to calm herself. That did the trick.

With her gloves still on, Echo examined the dead woman more closely. She focused on her prominent cheekbones and grey-green eyes. They gave her an Eastern European-looking face. Echo loosened the woman's shirt and found a necklace. Softly holding it between her finger and thumb she gave it a thorough examination. In a circular amulet made of silver someone had carved a hunter aiming his bow and arrow at a stag. Something more was etched above the stag's head. She held the talisman in the shadow of her body, blocking out the sun to give her a clearer view. Her original impression had been correct. There was a crucifix cleverly inserted between the stag's antlers. She eyed some writing across the bottom arc of the pendant. Though Echo didn't recognize the language, the letters appeared vaguely Cyrillic. She looked around, sensing that she was being watched. Nothing. With great care she replaced the amulet. She then stopped the world, taking time to say one final Apache prayer for the spirit of the dead woman.

Echo wrapped her boots in two pairs of extra socks she pulled from her backpack. Making certain her footprints wouldn't disrupt the crime scene she carefully moved through the area by doubling back in her own steps. She also marked her path with sticks. After checking the soles of the dead woman's boots she followed those footprints back to the north, the direction Echo assumed she had come from. She followed them for a hundred feet before returning. Retracing her steps to where the dead woman's gun had been pointed she did a second search for boot prints. Though she wasn't seeing much, her instincts were telling Echo to head west from the downed tree. The desert ground was little more than hardened dirt and tufted grass until she rounded a rock ledge. There the soil turned sandy. She found prints both leading toward the dead woman and away from the site. She marked three of them before following them until the dirt became solid rock.

The spirit of Lozen whispered in her ear. The wind-driven murmur stopped Echo in her tracks. Retracing her steps one more time she crisscrossed back and forth covering a twenty-foot section.

Returning to the boot prints she had previously marked, Echo could readily see where the brand name on the heel should have been pushed into the sandy soil. Whoever was wearing the boots had no intention of being identified. All trademarks had been cut off the soles of the boots. She was dealing with no fool. The person who did this was clever and no doubt trained in the art of disappearing without leaving a trail behind. Zeb was going to have his work cut out for him.

In the distance she heard Zeb's footsteps. In her head she scolded him. When was that man going to learn to walk in silence? Just making love with her for these last eight years should have put some Apache blood into his brain. He was still hundreds of feet away and she could hear him as though he were a mere ten feet from her.

Lifting her eyes from contemplation of the nearly innumerable possibilities regarding someone clever enough to hide their steps the way the potential killer had, her skin tingled. The pronounced prickly sensation was a recurring premonition of the presence of a nearby human being. As inconspicuously as possible she rotated in a three-hundred-sixty degree arc searching the surrounding area for the eyes of a human. At a dead cactus her gaze landed on a ferruginous pygmy owl. Echo knew from Song Bird the owl to be an omen of destruction and possibly even death.

"Echo. Echo?"

"Over here Zeb."

Zeb was calling to her while standing over the dead woman's body.

"Come over here."

Once again acting with caution so as not to disturb any part of the crime scene Echo made her way to Zeb.

"I assume you've done some preliminary work on the scene already?" asked Zeb.

Echo, hands on hips, nodded.

"What've you got?"

Echo pointed to the ground just behind where she assumed the dead woman had been standing when she was attacked. Zeb bent down and put his hand in the imprints made by boot toes compressing into the soil and twisting, exactly the motion a killer slicing a neck from behind its victim would take.

"I see."

"Her carotid and brachial arteries were severed by a single cut each from a highly sharpened knife. The weapon is under the body. It appears to have been placed there. The cut appears to have come from behind by a right-handed person. They apparently went specifically for the right carotid artery and the right brachial artery."

"Overkill?"

"Certain death was the obvious goal. My best guess is the killer was highly trained."

"I agree. The killer knew what they were doing," replied Zeb. "But I'd never rule out a nut job who watched one too many YouTube videos or read one too many CIA murder mysteries."

"I'll stick with highly trained."

Echo removed her leather gloves and took a pair of crime scene gloves from Zeb.

"Then there's this..."

Echo showed him the necklace and its details.

"Curious. Can't be a ton of these around. Should be traceable with any luck."

She pointed to the ring on the dead woman's right hand. Zeb eyed it closely. Even with his glasses on and the light from his phone the details were so small as to be impossible to decipher exactly what they were.

"Obviously not a wedding ring," said Zeb. "It must be ornamental or a traditional ring of some sort."

"It's delicate. I'm certain it's hand carved, but I don't know how someone could sculpt such fine detail. I can barely make out anything on the face of the ring."

Echo pointed out the blood-soaked bear tag and license she had set to the side.

"I think we can clean them up and get useable information."

She respectfully turned the body and pointed out the knife. Zeb reached in and began to check it over.

"You'd think a professional would have cleaned up the scene a little better," said Zeb.

"Maybe the killer was interrupted, spooked or something. Which would make him or her not a professional," said Echo. "Or the killer wanted the murder weapon to be found."

"It's odd no matter how you look at it."

"And if it was all they left behind, they had a reason for doing so."

"Agreed," responded Echo.

"This knife looks familiar. Don't you have one like this one?"

"Remember when we talked and I said that we had a problem?"

"Of course. What's our problem?"

"That happens to be my knife."

"What? How?"

"I can't explain it at the moment. But unless someone wiped it clean it has my fingerprints and DNA all over it."

"Did you know the dead woman?"

"That's the first question I'd ask me too. No, never saw her before..."

Echo took a long moment to study the dead woman's face.

"...that I know of. Yet, she somehow seems familiar."

"Any idea how this particular knife, your knife, might have ended up under a dead body?"

"I grabbed my throwing knife from the safe before I left. But I know I locked it up when I was done. I remember seeing this knife in there at that time."

"So, your theory is that someone broke into our house and the safe since you left?"

"That's the way I see it," replied Echo. "It's the only thing that makes any logical sense."

"And at the same time it doesn't make any sense."

Zeb thought for a moment before responding a second time.

"Damn it. I went in the safe the evening of the day you left. I'm certain I shut it but maybe I didn't. I got an emergency call when I was standing in front of the safe. Maybe I got distracted and didn't shut it completely."

"What was the emergency?"

"Drunken tourist in the southern part of the county who was harassing some people, some religious people. Weird situation. In the end everyone simply apologized and no one pressed charges."

"So, you think maybe you didn't shut the safe?"

"I pushed it shut with the heel of my boot as I turned around to leave. I was talking on the phone at the time but swear I heard it click shut."

"You're certain of that?"

"I was. Now I'm not."

"Doesn't make our little problem any easier to deal with, does it? When you were in there did it look like someone had gone through our stuff?"

"Not that I noticed," replied Zeb. "But I didn't have a reason to look through the safe that closely."

Echo was too steamed at Zeb's foolhardy mistake that it took her a moment to chill out.

"Would you have noticed?" demanded Echo.

Zeb was already working the scene and didn't directly reply to her question. The answer was obvious. Echo quickly gathered herself. Being angry at Zeb was pointless. There was work to do. The deed was done. Zeb would have to learn to be more careful or one of the kids could get hurt.

It took Sheriff Hanks, with Echo's help, just over fifteen minutes to work the scene and gather all the pertinent evidence. With everything bagged and tagged Zeb called for an ambulance.

Killing time until it arrived meant an opportunity to make a second sweep of the scene of the crime to look for additional evidence. Zeb and Echo each marked a half-dozen potential points of interest. By the time the ambulance arrived they were waiting mutely by the dead woman's body. Zeb recognized the driver Sahara by her tattoos and nose rings. Her assistant was a tall, skinny dude who everyone called Porky.

"Hey Sheriff Zeb."

Sahara had worked with Zeb a dozen times at crime scenes and interacted with him with an easy familiarity. Porky on the other hand was standoffish. Zeb knew he had a long history of misdemeanors. They all happened before his nineteenth birthday and Zeb thought little of it. Sahara, inhaling deeply on a cigarette, stepped up to Zeb and Echo.

"Sahara."

"This your better half or do we have a new deputy sheriff that I ain't heard about just yet?"

"Pardon my manners. Sahara, this is Echo Skysong Hanks, my wife and the mother of our children."

Sahara pinched off her cigarette and slipped the remaining half into her leather jacket pocket.

"These ain't cheap. Not gonna waste one."

Sticking out her hand she greeted Echo with a firm squeeze that Echo returned.

"Pleased to meet you ma'am. Looks like we'll get along just fine. My partner here is Edward, but he goes by Porky."

As unusual looking as she was for Graham County, her handshake was welcoming, her smile friendly and her voice warm. Echo took an immediate liking to her. Porky nodded, remaining frozen in place. Echo nodded back at him. He lifted a single finger in response before quickly looking away.

"I've seen you around, Echo. It's okay if I call you Echo, right? I've met your folks. Good people. Real nice."

"How'd you happen to run into them?"

"Your mom helped me change a flat tire 'round three months back. She had a bagful of dried venison sticks. Meat of her own making I believe. She gave me a handful. I don't mind telling you, they were dee-licious."

"I'll pass the word on to her."

"No need. I wrote her up a thank you note, being that she was so kind to a stranger and all."

"In that case I'll greet her for you."

"Much obliged. Now what have we got going on here?"

"Female, likely in her 30s, deceased from a bleed-out after having her carotid and brachial arteries severed," explained Zeb. "I'd like her taken directly to the morgue."

The information seemed to bring Porky to life or at least loosen the wag of his tongue.

"Unaccompanied death. Most likely murder. An autopsy is required by state law. Sahara, with all the blood, even though it looks dried, let's double glove and mask our faces."

Sahara turned to Zeb and Echo uttering a single word. "Paranoid." Then she put on a smile and responded.

"Excellent ideas, Porky. Let's do this one by the book."

Zeb and Echo helped them carry the body on a portable stretcher the half-mile to the ambulance which was parked at the end of a tertiary dirt road. Helping Sahara and Porky carry the dead woman strengthened the bond between the ambulance crew and the sheriff's department. Sahara thanked them profusely. Porky, who remained mute on the trek, almost imperceptibly nodded his head for the second time before disappearing into the passenger's door of the ambulance.

Zeb reached in and grabbed the evidence bags he had placed on top of the body. Once again he asked them to take the woman's body directly to the morgue.

"Doc Yackley is expecting you and the body."

"I know he likes to sign personally for possible murder victims," said Sahara. "I'll see to it that it gets done his way."

"Thanks. Good to be working with a pro."

Sahara tipped her head forward as she relit the half cigarette she'd pulled out of her jacket pocket.

"I'm always at your service, Sheriff Hanks."

As the ambulance headed down the road Echo watched Zeb place the Henry rifle, along with the bagged evidence, in the rear seat of his truck. Echo noticed immediately the knife was not among the evidence.

"The knife?" she asked.

"What knife?"

"You know what knife. My knife. The Emerson CQC6. The one we found under the body."

"What knife are you talking about?"

Echo's mind was awhirl. Did the little problem of her knife being found at the scene suddenly become a huge one? Or did the huge problem of her knife being a likely murder weapon suddenly become a nonexistent one? Was Zeb protecting her in a massively unethical fashion? Was it something else altogether? She had to know. After all it was her life that hung in the balance.

"Zeb?"

"The knife?"

"Yes?"

"What's going on with it? Shouldn't it have been bagged with the rest of the evidence?"

"Echo, there's the letter of the law and then there's the intent of the law."

Chapter 3

15 MONTHS AGO: JULY 24, 2021—LUHANSK, UKRAINE

BRONYA KARPENKO AND TAVISHA Karpenko, identical twin sisters by blood and religious Sisters of the Order of Saint Eustace, knelt silently in prayer at the side altar sanctified as holy in the name of their blessed saint. It was the closest side altar to the high altar at the Eastern Orthodox Church of Afan.

The women of rare and seductive beauty had been training for their missionary trip to the United States for more than a decade. They had not dared to dream that the social justice mission they been training for since their twenty-first birthdays was nearing its moment of reality. The timing, much to their pleasure was exactly the date they had been told it would be nearly two years earlier. To Tavisha it was the will of God, not part of a devious plot hatched inside the walls of the Kremlin. Yet, Bronya was dubious of the politics involved. Luhansk, while technically part of Ukraine, was administered by Russia.

Sister Bronya, whose name when translated meant warrior, moved her lips as she prayed for the success of their mission. Her hope was that the one month additional training period in Belarus would go by quickly. In her mind the nuns she had been training with were weak and lacked dedication to the cause of true social virtue. A decade of training in solitude had taught Sister Bronya the Divine Truth and how to go about achieving it for a greater cause. Sister Bronya, even though she knew it bordered on blasphemy, considered Mother Russia and the Mother of Christ to be on an equal par. Sister Bronya after a decade of devotion and training was now deemed a missionary of the highest order. She had but a single mission to complete before being made the head of her own Priory where she would train others like herself. Joy filled her heart at the thought of the changes she could bring about.

Sister Tavisha, whose name meant heavenly, prayed with wholeness of heart to Saint Eustace. She found it no small coincidence that in one month she would be leaving for the recently established Eastern Orthodox Priory in Arizona near the Mexico-U.S. border. The timing would be perfect in terms of giving them the time they required to prepare for the planned activities of September 2, the Holy Day of Saint Eustace.

Tavisha's mind bounced from image to image as she prayed and vividly recalled the history of the life of her beloved Saint Eustace. Thrown in the lion's den by Roman Emperor Hadrian with his entire family, they all escaped untouched. The lions had simply refused to attack them. Only a direct miracle sent by the hand of God Himself could have made that happen. She wept as she remembered the artists' renditions of the horrifying death of Saint Eustace with his family. Emperor Hadrian had them placed in a Brazen Bull torture device. While the device had indeed killed them, the flames the Brazen Bull had been placed over never touched the bodies of the Saint and his family. Were she to die while performing her mission, Sister Tavisha felt secure in the fact that she would be blessed by the Almighty as had Saint Eustace.

Lost in contemplation Sister Tavisha jumped when Sister Bronya tapped her on the shoulder.

"The time has arrived. We must leave. Have you completed your goodbyes?"

"Mostly. I imagine we shall return within the year. I don't like to say goodbye to the younger acolytes as it may frighten them about their own futures in the missionary world."

Sister Bronya had long known that Sister Tavisha, despite all that she knew, was naïve. Perhaps her innocence would serve her well with all that was headed in her direction. For the moment it was best for Bronya that Tavisha remain as virtuous as possible. Martyrs, after all, were a necessary part of the scheme.

Chapter 4

BELARUS—AUGUST 26, 2021

SISTER TAVISHA WAS AS surprised as much as Sister Bronya was not that their destination in Belarus was not a religious community at all. Rather it was a darkly secreted military base hidden deep in the forests of Mayak Mountain.

At the edge of a dense woodland, seemingly in the middle of nowhere, Sisters Bronya and Tavisha were greeted by General Alexey Vadim and his entourage. He eyed them lasciviously, a point of view that excited Bronya and frightened Tavisha.

"Sister Tavisha, Sister Bronya, you look so much alike that you could be twins."

The two eyed each other and softly giggled in an identical fashion.

"We are rent from the same seed," replied Bronya.

"It was the will of God," added Tavisha.

In the quiet moment that followed the sisters gazed upon the General's uniform. The mere presence of the highest Belarusian military award on his chest spoke to extreme acts of bravery and an unwavering commitment to the Republic of Belarus, a satellite nation of Mother Russia. His presence spoke directly to the gravity of their journey, a do or die mission designated Code Red Square.

A few exchanged words and the Sisters quickly surmised General Vadim was not the head of the mission. It was apparent that responsibility fell to Vladimir Vladimirovich Putin, the President of the Russian Federation himself.

General Vadim, ever the ladies' man took Sister Tavisha's hand and kissed it before brushing his lips with the lightness of wind against each of her rosy cheeks.

"You are a beautiful woman, Tavisha."

The nun took a fraction of a second to firmly correct the General.

"Sister Tavisha."

"Perhaps you would like to stay here in Belarus and work directly with me? I have a place for you on my staff. The pay is good and the benefits are excellent. You will want for nothing. I have the ability to put you in powerful places that other women can only dream of."

While another woman might have been flattered by being highly praised by a man of great stature, Tavisha was angered by Vadim's insolence. She had been trained and was being sent as a missionary to the United States of America. In her heart and mind she believed it to be nothing less than God's will and President Putin's command.

By the grace of the Almighty she had suppressed her sexual desires and human cravings since flowering as a woman. Not even the sweet seductive words of a handsome, powerful man who could make her life easy could speak to her heart the way her Lord God had. Tavisha's sole loyalty as well as her soul's dedication was to the Lord and to Saint Eustace, a true martyr and true saint who had suffered for Christ. Her President gave the earthly commands.

"I am most flattered General Vadim. But at this time I must complete my mission. Perhaps when that is done our paths shall cross again?"

The General's steely grey eyes turned hard. How dare the young woman deny his implied command? He returned his words with a threatening, gravelly whisper.

"Staying with me may be your only salvation. If you're as smart as you are beautiful, you will think it over."

Sister Tavisha bowed her head, lowered her eyes and made a broad Orthodox Sign of the Cross before taking one step back. The General shook his head, making no attempt to hide his disgust as he spoke.

"Success to your missionary endeavors, Sister Tavisha."

Sister Tavisha nodded politely as the General brusquely side-stepped her and moved to Sister Bronya. Sister Bronya, while a spitting image of her twin sister, oozed sexuality. However, she found the General, even with his power and lustrous career to be off-putting, an emotion she hid well.

"You will be leading this missionary endeavor, no?"

"Yes, my General. I am the commander of the missionary operation."

"Are you sufficiently prepared?"

"With the final month of training under your command I feel that I shall be sufficiently prepared for all that need be done."

"Be wary of those under your command. Some will be very clever and others devious."

"I have been so instructed."

"Allow nothing to get in the way of the success of your mission."

"Yes sir, General Vadim. No one will stop this mission."

"Not even those close to you?"

"No one will prevent me from leading this mission to its successful conclusion."

The expression on Vadim's face was stern.

"Did you train Sister Tavisha?"

"Yes. Do not mistake her reaction as one of disdain or mistrust, General. She has a single guiding principle, that of Saint Eustace. As an information gathering specialist there is none better. Still, her mind is capable of seeing only the small picture."

"Is she celibate?"

The General's question took Bronya by surprise.

"Of course, sir."

"Does she like men or is her sexual persuasion otherwise?"

"She is inexperienced in such matters. Presently she is guided only by the divinations of her God, Saint Eustace and her President."

"She is still a virgin?"

"I can only imagine that she must be. She has been in the nunnery since prior to becoming a fully blossomed woman. Her constant training has involved little contact with men. I believe she will have no sexual desires until her mission is complete."

"That explains it then."

"General?"

"Her lack of desire for me."

"Of course, General Vadim. Were she to be attracted to men I am certain she would find you most desirable."

"Could you see to it that she visits my quarters in the evening?"

"Yes, General. But..."

"Yes?"

"But you may find her quite unsatisfying sexually because she has no experience. I believe she also may have no thoughts of male companionship."

General Vadim swirled the ends of his mustache in his fingers and smiled.

"Send her to me this evening at seven."

Chapter 5

7 PM

Tavisha gently tapped on Vadim's door. Her body felt strange and uncomfortable adorned in the seductive dress that had been left on her bed. The General's adjutant answered her knock.

"I am here at the invitation of General Vadim."

"You are Tavisha?"

"Sister Tavisha, Order of Saint Eustace."

"Follow me."

The adjutant marched across the outer chamber, knocked once on a massive oak double door, entered without an answer and announced the General's guest.

"Sister Tavisha, Order of Saint Eustace."

The room she stood in carried nothing less than the imagined opulence of a Tsar's castle of old. Tavisha curtsied as if before royalty. The slightest of hand gestures from the General directed her to rise. Still quite uncomfortable, the sound of her own voice helped clear her mind.

"Reporting as directed, General Vadim."

Sister Tavisha was surprised to see the man in charge of the military base dressed in civilian clothing. She was even more shocked to see General Vadim clad in the latest western-style apparel. She had been expecting *avtorskiy gonorar*, the dress-wear of military royalty. The casual nature of the evening caught her completely off guard. General Vadim eyed his faithful adjutant who responded by silently backing through the double doors and disappearing from the lavish surroundings.

General Vadim approached Tavisha with a horse-like strut. His cocksure maneuvers appeared nothing short of foolish to the sexually inexperienced woman. Her eyes fell upon the hair forest that rose through the top of his half-unbuttoned shirt.

Vadim brushed lightly against Tavisha as he passed by her to a table of alcoholic beverages.

Tavisha turned slowly and watched as he lifted a carafe and poured the contents into two goblets. Krambambulia, the national Belarusian drink, comprising red wine, rum, vodka, gin, honey and various spices, filled their chalices. The beverage had never passed the innocent sister's lips. Others she knew raved about it and the numerous myths that spoke to its erotic potency. Never did she imagine herself drinking Krambambulia, especially with an honored national hero of one of Mother Russia's satellite nations.

The pseudo-suave General Vadim handed one goblet to Tavisha and lifted his own to propose a toast. Tavisha lifted hers as well, keeping it slightly lower than the level of the General's.

"To you my dearest Tavisha and to your mission."

Slowly the sexily clad nun brought the drink toward her lips. The stimulating aroma of the drink pleasured her nose as Tavisha began to tingle and come alive in her womanly places. Every ounce of her flesh and every thought in her mind fought this strange, new feeling. Yet she felt herself yielding to the temptations of the flesh. The harder she fought the feeling of lust, the more it swelled inside her.

A few sips of the exotic drink later her head swooned with an air of erotic titillation. The classic image of an American movie actress with loosely flowing hair falling head over heels in love floated into her mind.

Understanding the American cultural way of thinking had been part of her training. Although it had been only a small part of her education, watching American movies and television taught her how to fit in, how to be an American. However, the behaviors of beautiful women falling in love was quite different on the movie screen than in real life. None of it had ever made sense until this very moment.

Tavisha, lightheaded, turned to admire a painting she knew as *The Ninth Wave* by famed nineteenth century Russian artist Ivan Aivazovsky. The General, never taking his eye from her innocent beauty posed a question.

"You are impressed by my art collection?"

The royal atmosphere and the distinguished art combined with the Krambambulia to quite literally steal the breath from her body while simultaneously dropping her inhibitions.

"It is stunning. Much more beautiful than I had imagined."

"As one who herself is filled with rare beauty, I am delighted you recognize the exquisite nature that accompanies a magnificent piece of art."

The Krambambulia altered her mind and swirled her thoughts more quickly than she imagined anything could. Or was it General Vadim's smooth words that swayed her away from a long held desire to maintain her virginity? What did it matter? For a decade she had been training for an American mission. Her hard work and training now felt like a dream within an entirely new reality. Tonight her overbearing sister was not controlling her. What more could she possibly ask for? Perhaps General Vadim was her God-given destiny.

Chapter 6

THE NEXT MORNING

WHEN TAVISHA AWOKE THE next morning General had already departed. A handwritten note and a small bouquet of purple flax, the national flower of Belarus, was left on the nightstand by the four-poster bed in which she had given herself to the General. Still tingling from the previous night's encounter she gracefully unfolded it and began reading.

When you arise the beauty of the morning rises with you. Wear the flower in your hair and think of me. We shall dine tonight. I have made reservations at Kukhmystr at 7. I will have Natalia Zhuk choose your dress and bring it to you at 2 p.m. today. I will be honored if the dress is as beautiful as your smile.

Tavisha spread herself over the bed as she sighed in disbelief. Natalia Zhuk was the most celebrated dressmaker in all of Belarus. Her fame had come from adorning the celebrated and renowned elites in Minsk. And the Kukhmystr! Tavisha had read about the restaurant in international fashion magazines used in preparation for her mission.

That evening from her central table, Tavisha saw that the Kukhmystr with its wooden beams, tiled fireplace and antique *objets d'art* was everything she dreamed it might be. It was considered to serve the most authentic Belarusian food in the world and she was surrounded by the city's elite.

The reasons behind her decade of preparation for this mission were becoming readily apparent. She had been chosen to be one of the *crème de la crème*.

After dinner and still floating on air, Tavisha sighed happily. Adorned in the most beautiful dress she had ever seen and dazzled by the combined effect of delicious food and the attentions of the General, Tavisha was a changed woman. Later, when

General Vadim was called away by an emergency, his final words were a simple vow to see her again in the immediate future.

Returning to the room she shared with Bronya, Tavisha felt the heated vibration coming from within before even touching the handle of the door. Deeply trained in the psychology of human interaction and the importance of reading facial features, the sisters could hide nothing from one another. Stepping across the threshold it took but a single glance at Bronya to see that rage coursed her veins and hatred stewed in her heart. Her sister's vocal intonations, try as she may, could do nothing to hide her fury.

"Pleasant evening I presume, dear sister?"

Sister Tavisha closed the door before responding. Although she knew the room was likely filled with listening devices of the most sophisticated variety, her words were not for those passing by in the corridor.

"Excellent. Thank you."

"Is General Vadim all they say he is?"

Bronya's interrogative was laced with pity for herself and indictment of her sister's behavior.

"Yes. And more, my dear. Much more."

Tavisha was physically moved by the wrath emitting from Bronya. How strange and unanticipated her sister's reaction. The pair had been trained for years to disguise negative emotions. Yet Bronya seemingly could not will back her rising resentment. A turn of the screw might just tell Tavisha how Bronya would react under extreme duress. It was imperative that she knew.

"My actions with General Vadim seem to make you ill at ease, Bronya."

"They do nothing of the sort, Tavisha. I am most certain this interlude was but a mere fling for the General, one in which your body was defiled. I'm certain it was nothing more than something that the General, despite his lack of genuine desire for you, managed to carry out as part of the greater mission."

Bronya, unable to hide the devastation of not being the one to be seduced by the famed General, flashed a flame to her cigarette. In her irritation, Tavisha glared at her sister.

"When are you going to stop that filthy habit?"

As Bronya blew smoke in her sister's face her mind was watering the already planted seeds of a plot to which she had spent the previous night writing the coda. Tavisha could read the tale in her sister's eyes. There was no hiding it. Now, were she to be the survivor, she must lay larger plans of greater consequence.

"We have work to do. They have moved up our departure date," stated Bronya.

Tavisha well knew that their exodus to the United States was by design directed through Bronya. Such was the nature of the scheme.

"When do we leave?" asked Tavisha.

"I suppose you have plans with General Vadim for this evening?"

"I do indeed. Nothing short of my immediate departure will have any effect on them whatsoever."

The women, each for their own reasons, glared with fierce animosity at one another.

"We leave at five a.m."

"Five a.m. tomorrow morning?" asked Tavisha.

"Yes. The arrangements have already been made and approved by Moscow. Authorized by President Putin himself. It is not within General Vadim's power to change them."

Smiles of hatred crossed between the sisters. Tavisha knew that she would have to make an eternity of her final night in Minsk. All the while she could see that Bronya was plotting to despoil all that Tavisha now held dear.

"I'm sorry to have wreaked havoc with your plans," said Bronya.

The lies that crossed Tavisha's lips sparred an equal duel with Bronya's words.

"What we are part of is much larger than what I desire for myself. War is coming. We must do everything within our power to safeguard the mission. We must remain loyal missionaries. We can let nothing come between us and our mission."

Chapter 7

JANUARY 2022 – PREMONITION OF WAR

ELAN AND ONAWA WERE laughing loudly in the television room as Echo made pancakes in the kitchen. Her ears were sharply attuned to Arizona public radio that was playing in the background. Zeb sneaked up behind Echo and kissed her on the neck. She reacted by flipping a pancake that only half reached its intended destination before finding its way to the griddle.

"Looks like you've lost your touch."

Echo turned to her husband. A foreign look lived on her face.

"Sorry. I was lost in thought."

Echo put down the spatula, placed her arms around Zeb and kissed him. He knew his wife well enough to tell her heart wasn't in her lips. She turned back to her pancakes without any of her usual additional caressing touches. Something was definitely distracting her. It became readily apparent what it was.

"Zeb, do you think there is going to be a military invasion of Ukraine?"

"I hope not. The world doesn't need another war."

"Do you think Russia is being run by a sane man?"

"I don't know President Putin personally," replied Zeb.

"You always choose to play the role of the neutral sheriff, don't you? Don't you at least have some sort of opinion to share with me?"

Zeb could see he'd said exactly the wrong thing. He gently braced Echo by the shoulders and burrowed deeply into her eyes. His gaze was met with an unusual combination of fear and compassion. The realization that her thoughts were of the men and women soldiers of both Russia and Ukraine as well as the entire population of Ukraine who were likely soon going to be locked in a probably vicious ground war that could kill tens of thousands of them made Echo's reaction understandable.

"There might not be a war. It might just be a military exercise like Putin claims."

"When was the last time you trusted a politician of Putin's ilk who said something like that as they amassed thousands of troops and weapons along the border of a country they want to be sovereign over."

Zeb paused for half a second even though he didn't need to.

"When you put it like that..."

"Right. Putin already has ninety-two thousand troops amassed in Belarus and other places near the border of Ukraine."

"It could be a military exercise. I've heard on the news where he's done this kind of thing before."

Zeb noticed a slight tremor in Echo's hand as she flipped a couple more pancakes. He made an attempt to calm her by placing his hand on her own.

"Mmm. They look good."

Echo pulled her hand away and slapped the spatula down hard on the stove. The muscles in her neck became visibly taut. Stress lines instantly appeared on her face.

"Pretty soon people are going to die, Zeb. Probably lots of people. Citizens and soldiers alike will lose their lives. Not to mention the children who will be casualties of something they have no understanding about. I don't like it. In fact, I hate it."

"The pundits on the networks are predicting that if Russia invades Ukraine it'll be over in three days, a week, tops."

Echo placed her hands firmly on her hips and gave Zeb the straight eye.

"Zeb Hanks. What sort of fool are you?"

"What? I'm only quoting the experts."

"How long did the experts predict we'd have fighting men and women in Vietnam? Afghanistan? Just about anywhere we've sent troops in the last sixty years the so-called experts have always said the wars would be over in weeks or months. Have they ever been close to being right? For God's sake we were in Afghanistan for twenty years. The Russians were there for a decade before we were. We've had troops in Germany and Japan since the end of World War II. That's eighty years. Once a conflict begins it just never ends."

Zeb retreated into silence. What could he say that would be
helpful? He didn't feel like engaging in any sort of argument that
not only could he not win but would dampen a day off with his
family. He poured himself a cup of coffee and listened to Echo
vent on the developing situation in eastern Europe.

"Russia is going to invade and destroy the infrastructure of
Ukraine. They are going to kill as many people as they damn well
feel like. They'll torture people by the thousands. It's going to be
a bloody massacre. They've got the massive weapons and feel
they have right on their side. They're even claiming that Nazis
have a foothold in Ukraine. What sort of crazy talk is that?"

Fortunately, Zeb was in the middle of a sip of coffee or he
might have attempted an answer. He wanted to reassure Echo
that it might not be as bad as she was projecting. But she kept
on rolling at full speed.

"Nazis? Good lord above. What is that all about? When have
you heard anything about Nazis having a foothold in Ukraine?
Or Nazis even being in Ukraine for that matter? Never! That's
when you've heard about it. Never!"

"Maybe there are some fringe groups with Nazi socialist beliefs in Ukraine? There are kooks all over the world. You know
that. Christ, we've got fringe groups right here in Arizona that
use the *Sieg Heil* salute."

"C'mon, Zeb. Putin is using nationalistic nonsense as a reason
to invade and destroy Ukraine. We had Ukrainian soldiers as
support in Afghanistan. They're good people and damn good
soldiers. They didn't run and hide like some did. But they are
going to be outgunned and outnumbered. I fear they're going to
get slaughtered by the tens of thousands."

"If it's over in a week, tops, how is it possible to kill that many
people?"

"It's not going to be over even a year from now. There is
going to be siege warfare. The infrastructure of Ukraine is going
to get blown to bits. The Ukrainian economy is going to tank.
People are going to starve because Ukraine is the breadbasket
of Europe. There's a damn good chance Putin and his thugs will
blow up a nuclear power plant, or worse, use tactical nukes."

"Echo..."

"Women and children are going to pay a heavy toll. Europe gets its natural gas almost exclusively from Russia. Strange alliances will be made. The military-industrial complex will grow ever stronger and get everything they want and a lot more than they need. There's no getting around it. Jesus, Zeb, it's going to affect the entire world."

"You think the Ukrainians will rise up against the Russians?"

"Oh, they will. Never underestimate the power of people protecting their homeland. My own people fought to the bitter end with the United States military. I saw it all the time in Afghanistan. But unless someone sticks their nose under the tent and starts arming Ukraine, it will be nothing short of a slaughter."

"And the camel you think that will stick its nose under the tent is exactly who?"

"The same arms brokers that always do and they'll be funded by U.S. taxpayers. That means you and I are going to be supporting another war with our money. I'd bet my bottom dollar that we already have dozens of special advisors, likely even operatives, on the ground in Ukraine and by the time it's over we'll have troops there."

"I..."

Echo handed the spatula to Zeb.

"You finish the kids' breakfast. I'm going for a run. Feed the kids and do the dishes. You can probably bribe the kids into helping."

Chapter 8

NSA

TWO DAYS AFTER THE dead woman was found Zeb greeted every-one at the front desk of the hospital before finding his way to Doc's office. The door was open. Zeb peeked in. Zeb had known the old country doctor as long as he could remember. In fact, Doc had quite literally brought him into the world. When he witnessed the peculiar expression on Doc Yackley's face he knew something wasn't going his way.

"Knock, knock."

"I see you out there Zeb. I heard you clomping down the hall. Geez you make more noise than a barrel half-full of marbles."

"You sound like my wife."

"Well, if she's talking about how noisy you are when you walk, she's ain't wrong. You're walking on your heels. Throws your back out. No damn wonder you got to go see the chiropractor all the time."

Zeb arched his back and a few vertebrae in his lower back popped and snapped. How in hell was he going to learn to walk differently than he had his whole life? May he should get some new boots with softer bottoms?

"I'll think about changing the way I walk. I might even invest in some new boots."

"You should. Try some orthotics, too. Now come on in here and have a seat. I've got something to tell you that I promise you won't make your day."

"Something other than criticizing the way I walk?"

"Don't be so damn sensitive. I was just giving you a bit of medical advice free of charge. Take it or leave it."

Zeb spun the wooden chair placed in front of Doc's desk and proceeded to make himself comfortable. He took his hat off and placed it on the edge of Doc Yackley's cluttered desk.

"What's going on, Doc?"

"The body you brought in day before yesterday? That's why you're here, right?"

"Yup. Kind of wondering if it's still on ice or if you've found the time to look it over."

"It might be on ice somewhere for all I know."

"Wait. What are you saying?"

"I never got the chance to look her over."

"No autopsy?" asked Zeb.

"That's right. I never had the opportunity to do a post-mortem analysis of any sort. Barely had time to sneak a peek at the body itself."

"Too busy?"

"Kind of. Sort of. But that ain't it. I didn't get right to it because I had a couple of minor surgeries to do and had to set a broken leg. A mule kicked the oldest Iverson boy. Then I got really busy."

"Yeah? Tell me what's going on with the body."

"So the staff went through the usual procedures with the corpse; pictures, fingerprints, blood typing, DNA and the like. You know the drill."

"I do."

"They had the body all set for an autopsy. They did their job. A damn good job at that."

"All sounds routine to me. So you're taking a little more time than usual to get the autopsy done. So what? You work your ass off. Everyone knows that. I don't blame you for being behind schedule. Happens to the best of us."

"No need to blow hot air up my skirt, Zeb."

"I wasn't."

Doc began turning red and blue in the face.

"What's going on, Doc? What the hell's up?"

"When you brought that dead woman in, one of the first steps demanded by law and very basic procedure includes entering the fingerprints of the deceased into a federal data bank."

"Yup. I know that. I did the same."

"Well one of us triggered some stinkin' bureaucrat somewhere."

"What? How do you know that?"

"Because before I had a chance to do anything a couple of NSA agents showed up at five this morning with a signed warrant for the body."

"A warrant?"

"Yessiree."

"Where was the warrant from? Who signed it?"

"A federal judge in D.C."

"What the hell is a judge in D.C. doing sticking his nose into this? Was a name attached to the dead woman in that paperwork?"

"Nope. It was a Jane Doe writ of habeas corpus from the federal bench. The warrant allowed the NSA agents to take the body and they did just that. Bastards. Abusive SOBs."

"Why? On what grounds did they claim the body?"

"You think those bastards ever give anyone even a half-assed reason for what they do? They took it because someone signed an order for them to do it. Someone no doubt pretty high up the food chain would be my guess."

"You got a copy of the warrant?"

Doc reached into his desk, pulled out the legal document and tossed it to Zeb.

"It's legit. I checked it and all the i's have been dotted and t's have been crossed."

The sheriff briefed it. Everything was cookie-cutter. It was the kind of boiler plate federal warrant that gave away very little information as to why the body was taken or who took it. Reading it Zeb had no doubt some branch of the federal government had decided the body was theirs.

"I actually know the judge who signed off on this."

Zeb pulled back as he noted Doc speaking through gritted teeth.

"You know a sitting federal judge in D.C.?"

"He was an Arizona judge about twenty years back. We tippled a few together at the Coach House Bar on Indian School Road in old Scottsdale at a federally sponsored convention for autopsy specialists. Back in the day the Feds wanted docs who would follow orders military style."

"They wanted the doctors to do what the Feds asked and not ask any questions?" asked Zeb.

"Got that right. They wanted docs to jump at any and all federal orders."

"I don't imagine that went over so well with you?"

"Hell no. Needless to say I told them they could kiss my ever-lovin' ass if they expected me to bow down to their sorry rear ends."

Zeb chuckled. Doc's mien remained angry.

"What do you remember about the judge?"

"Unless he's found the Lord, he's most likely a drunken asshole who does exactly what anyone with higher authority tells him to do. He was the type that never questioned a thing when it came from someone higher up the ladder. Dumb as a mud-covered stick made from soft wood. I also know him because his name has crossed my desk on legal documents for the U.S. Border Patrol. Like I said, he does what the man or woman above him tells him to."

Doc paused, reached into his top drawer and pulled out a pipe. He stuck it in his mouth without lighting it. He set his sights on the judge's signature.

"Whatcha thinkin', Doc?"

"At first I wondered if this thing has something to do with the border. Then I thought about it differently."

"Yeah?"

"I began to wonder what the NSA wanted with a random woman who was killed in the middle of nowhere while hunting bear."

"Doc. I went back and checked over the scene. From what I could gather it was a close-up cold-blooded murder most likely done by an expert."

"Doesn't matter. What matters is those dirty stinkin' rats didn't even give us a chance to do our jobs. I don't much cotton to that kind of business."

Zeb tapped his own memory, recalling what he could about the NSA. He knew they were responsible for collecting and processing information for both foreign and domestic intelligence as well as counterintelligence purposes. Echo had told him they did a lot of work in signals intelligence in Afghanistan while protecting U.S. communications networks and their information systems. What any of that had to do with the dead woman was beyond his grasp, at least for the moment. In the same instant he realized he hadn't responded to Doc's statement.

"Didn't think you would."

"Didn't think I'd what?"

"Be a lackey for the Feds."

Zeb noticed how Doc, when he was angry, looked older and even more tired than he usually did. The Vietnam veteran had probably seen his better days already slip by him, yet he was still vital and the best damn physician the county had ever seen. To him slowing down might equal death.

"Can I get a quick look and a copy of the data you have on the dead woman?" asked Zeb.

"I'd like to say yes..."

"Yeah?"

"But I can't."

"Say what?"

Nothing was making sense. Even if the NSA had given Doc a legal writ to not share any of the evidence, he'd pay no heed to such a thing. Zeb leaned forward, rested his right hand on the brim of his hat and drummed his fingers.

"One of the agents must have been a computer tech expert because all of the information has been erased from our database as well as our backup drives. I got no proof that the body of the dead woman was ever in our possession."

"The video cameras must have caught something."

"The agent was thorough. Professional. She wiped everything clean as a whistle."

"How do you know it was a woman agent?"

"The night shift security officer was the one who had to let her into the tech room."

"What on earth is going on here?"

"Whoever that dead woman was, the NSA wanted her to disappear completely from everyone's radar."

"Wait, I've got pictures from the scene on my phone."

"I doubt it," replied Doc.

Zeb pulled out his phone and pulled up his photo files. The images he'd taken at the crime scene had somehow been erased from its memory.

"Son of a bitch. Wait, I've still got the weapon locked up in my office."

"From the way these agents acted, I doubt it's still there. I assume you did all the paperwork on the gun?"

"I did."

"Good. It would have been a bad time to make a mistake with the Feds doing whatever it is they're doing."

"Helen would have called me ASAP if someone had come demanding to take evidence."

"There's a damn easy way to find out, Zeb."

"Yeah, yeah. I'll call her right now and find out if they've been by."

Zeb tapped the office number into his cellphone. Helen answered on the first ring. Her voice was flooded with anxiety.

"Zebulon P. Hanks! Why are you not answering your phone? I thought you might be dead."

"I'm still alive and well, but I haven't received any calls from you this morning."

"I've called you thirty times if I've called you once."

Zeb scrolled down his recent calls. There were none from Helen. In fact, since he'd been awake the only call listed in his recent call history was the one he had just made to Helen.

"If you called me a bunch, none of them came through."

"You heard me. I did call you. Those federal agents from the NSA did something to my phone," said Helen. "I just know it."

"What? What do you mean, Helen?"

"That woman agent, the one with the dark hair and the little scar on her cheek."

"Doc Yackley told me a couple of them showed up here early this morning at the morgue and took the body. I didn't personally see any of the agents."

"Doesn't surprise me one bit. That woman, that agent, did something to the office phone lines and my personal cellphone."

"How do you know that?"

"First she took my cellphone and hooked it up to a small box. I checked when she gave it back and it erased my recent phone calls. Then when she left I saw her fiddling with the telephone junction box. The one just outside the back door."

"She must have blocked your outgoing calls."

"I don't think so. I used it after that and I've been able to get ahold of everyone but you," said Helen.

"It must be that she just blocked any contact between our phones. Try me right now."

Zeb's phone rang. It was Helen.

"Call Shelly and tell her everything."

"Consider it done," replied Helen.

"Good. Have her get hold of me the second she's got anything figured out."

"She's not stupid Zeb, so don't you be," said Helen. "You know that's not something I need to even mention to her."

"Right. I'll be in shortly. Good-bye."

Zeb put his phone next to his hat and turned to Doc Yackley.

"Somehow those agents blocked any phone contact between me and my office for the last few hours or so. My guess is they blocked contact between my office and the deputies as well."

"Obviously, they didn't want you to know they were stealing your evidence. Smart move on their part."

"They've erased every single photo I took at the scene from my phone."

The worldly-wise physician and long-time observer of human behavior smiled.

"I already had that figured out," said Doc.

"Wait a second. If I know Echo she has pictures on her phone and there's no way the NSA knows that."

"Call her before they make that connection if they haven't already. I assume you mentioned Echo in your report?"

"She never wants her name connected to anything the Feds might touch. Doesn't trust what she calls the three-letter agencies. She knows too much to want them sniffing around."

"Use my phone in case they're tracking yours."

Doc, who loved his roleplaying with his old medical school chum, Doctor Zata, as Watson and Holmes, immediately changed into the detective tactician who enjoyed the cloak and dagger routine that the NSA was up to.

Zeb rang up Echo. She'd been behaving unlike herself and it all had to do with the ongoing Russian invasion of Ukraine. She was adamantly vocal about the potential American military response to such an event. Zeb couldn't help but believe her reaction was linked to her PTSD.

"Echo?"

"What do you need, hon?"

The tone of her voice told him the war was on her mind.

"Those pictures you took of the dead woman the other day?"

"Yeah? What about them?"

"Would you check your phone and see if they're still there?"

"They're there. I didn't erase them."

"There's a chance the NSA might have erased them for you."

Her voice softened when she next spoke.

"The NSA? That's not good. What's going on?"

"Please look."

Echo scrolled through her phone. The pictures she'd taken were all present and accounted for.

"I've got them. All of them."

"Can you do me a huge favor?"

"What's going on, Zeb? I don't like the sound of this. Why on earth is the NSA sticking its nose into a local murder?"

"I'll explain everything once you do what I ask."

"Okay."

"Print five copies of the pictures. After you've done that, you know that burner phone in the lower right-hand drawer of my desk?"

"Untraceable Betty?"

"That's the one. Send the pictures from your phone to that phone and from the burner phone send them to Shelly. She's #3 on Betty. She'll be expecting them. When you've done that remove the SIM card from the phone and destroy the card completely. There are some extra SIM cards in the safe. Got all that?"

"Yes. Of course. Now what is this all about?"

"The body of the woman you found has been confiscated by the NSA."

"Why?"

"No idea."

"SOBs."

"Any trace of her is being quickly and completely eradicated. If you need to, and maybe you should anyway, write down notes regarding everything you remember from the time you first found the body until you were no longer with it. Put them somewhere safe, like in case we have a burglary at our house again."

"Consider it done."

"Any idea who the woman is/was?"

"Not a freaking clue," replied Zeb. "Not a freaking clue."

Chapter 9

MEETING

ZEB CALLED HELEN AND politely asked her to call Deputies Rambler Braing, Kate Steele-Diamond, Clarissa Kerkhoff and computer genius Shelly Hamlin for a round table meeting at the office ASAP.

"I'll get right back to you. Give me five minutes."

In less than the time promised, Helen the ever-efficient office manager had put in her calls and received responses. Rambler was fifteen minutes out. Everyone else was closer. She called the sheriff back.

"Meeting in fifteen minutes. Don't you be late, Zeb."

Helen hung the front desk office phone back in its cradle and set out to prep the meeting room just as Kate walked in. Kate helped her put the room in order as she got an earful of information that instantly brought her up to date.

"I know exactly where the scene of the crime is, and so do you and Rambler and Clarissa," said Helen.

"You're right, I do know exactly where it is," said Kate. "Sometimes I think that place was meant to be stayed away from."

"I know just what you're talking about and I can't disagree with you," replied Helen. "But we both know if almost anyone heard us talking like that they'd say we sound like a couple of superstitious old biddies. Well, you're not so old as me."

"Helen, you are aging like fine wine and always young at heart. That's all that really matters."

"I know. I know. But Kate, we both know that we have to put some level of trust in our instincts. I understand it is easier to make a mistake by believing that something you feel is real when it's really just coincidence. But somehow this has a completely different feel to it."

Kate's skin rippled with gooseflesh.

"How does one know when to truly trust their instincts?"

"Excellent question," replied Helen.

By the time Zeb arrived sixteen minutes later his deputies Rambler, Kate and Clarissa were being given a close-up guided tour of the crime scene courtesy of Shelly and Google Maps. Their comments were amazingly consistent. The Pinaleño Mountain area near the U-Loop and Skinny Creek, which ran right through the center of the incident site, had been nothing but a repetitive thorn in everyone's side. The deputies and Shelly looked up only when their boss, Sheriff Zeb Hanks of Graham County entered the room. He cleared his throat. Anyone who ever worked for Zeb knew this was his universal request for quiet.

"Let's not let confirmation bias lead us down a snake hole. I'm guessing you're all thinking place, not crime. Think crime first. Let go of your feelings about the location."

"That place is full of bad juju," said Kate.

"I think it's an electromagnetic vortex of some sort," added Clarissa. "The spooky kind."

"Spirits linger there," suggested Rambler. "Don't ask me how I know that or why. I simply know it to be true."

"The place is part of the solution. It's not part of the problem. Remember that as we begin to cut this thing into smaller bites and start chewing on them. That place can be one of the pieces of the puzzle but let's not start there. Is that alright with all of you?"

Zeb counted on his staff to be not only independent thinkers, but team players. They were going to think however they chose and do whatever their brains told them to. Still, he had to speak his piece. None of them were totally up to date with what was going on, even though he imagined Helen had more or less filled them in. His words were an implied order and he waited for none of them to answer.

"Okay, good. Listen up."

Zeb explained what he knew about how the woman died, the exact location where she died, Echo's having found the body after an Apache pilgrimage for the preparation of the White Painted Woman ceremony, and of course the missing evidence courtesy of the National Security Administration. Then he asked

Shelly to pop up the pictures Echo had taken at the scene of the killing.

"Where'd these come from?" asked Clarissa.

"How did they survive the NSA purging?" asked Rambler.

Zeb explained that by a stroke of good fortune Echo had taken pictures at the scene.

"If the NSA was involved and wiped your phone clean, how did they miss Echo's?" asked Rambler.

"I don't know the answer to that one," replied Zeb. "Shelly?"

"A long time ago, roughly six months, I did some fractionalized looping of the interface of all of your phones."

Her response was met by four blank faces.

"I installed the frac loop just in case one of you was hacked, then the others wouldn't be. Does that ring a bell?"

When she put it that way, memories were triggered. The sheriff and his deputies all breathed a sigh of relief that they hadn't lost their minds or at least their memories.

"I also included Echo, Elan and Onawa's phones. Just a basic security measure. But you had to activate it. I sent out a memo. Remember?"

To a person they all avowed they had installed the measures on their cellphones.

"How'd the NSA get the pictures if you took that particular security precaution and everyone installed it on their phones?" asked Zeb.

"If all of you truly installed the frac loop correctly they could have bypassed it only with some special knowledge. But if you didn't install it correctly...or at all..."

Everyone hemmed and hawed just enough so that Shelly walked them through the one-minute installation process.

"If they did bypass my measures I'll figure it out and correct it and in the process throw a little jab at them for messing with me, with us. That they failed to target Echo's phone turned out being a stroke of good luck for the good guys."

Heads nodded. Zeb spoke.

"Bring up the photo of the right ankle, Shelly."

On a fifty-inch screen appeared the right ankle of the dead woman with the letter Z tattooed in red and blue ink.

"Odd coloring for a tattoo," said Kate.

"Anyone familiar with this tattoo or its meaning?"

Everyone except Zeb jumped on their phones.

"Z stands for the atomic number in chemistry and physics. Z is the number of protons found in the nucleus of any particular atom," said Shelly.

"Maybe the dead woman was a chemist or a physicist?" suggested Zeb.

"Z also represents the complete set of all integers," injected Kate.

"Maybe she was a dedicated mathematician?"

"Z on Russian tanks stands for victory if the Russians put it there. On the other hand if some Ukrainian kid has balls enough to tag a Russian tank, it means losers."

"Tagging a tank is some ballsy shit," said Rambler.

"Who has that kind of death wish?" asked Clarissa.

"That's the weirdness of war," said Zeb. "Same thing happens in all wars according to what Echo has told me. The most famous example is from WWII."

"Kilroy was here, right?"

"Right."

"Here's another Russian meaning. Z stands for *zveri* or animals."

"Z was a movie about the assassination of a Greek diplomat."

"Z is the de facto symbol for support of Russia's war in Ukraine," said Shelly. "If you really want to find the hundreds of meanings of the Z just google it. There are a thousand or so different conjectured meanings based on what I've found."

"And Z was my nickname as a kid and A is for apple," added Zeb. "So what of it?"

The others had heard about the kidding Zeb took when later his older brother changed his nickname from Z to Zipperhead. No one chose to pursue that any further.

"Okay. It's also the last letter of the alphabet. Dig deeper on all of those and anything peripherally related that might be linked somehow, God knows how, but look anyway," ordered Zeb. "And keep looking. I don't see any immediate link to anything meaningful other than maybe if she was seriously into physics and mathematics she might have worked at one of the telescopes on top of Mount Graham."

"I've got a private security list of all their employees," said Shelly.

"Should I ask how you came to get that piece of information?" asked Zeb.

"I didn't get it. The office receives an updated employee list annually. I simply read it over before inputting it into our database. The scientists who work up there are susceptible to agencies of foreign governments seeking to gain specific information that is only available through them."

"Can you check and see if anyone has come up missing, quit, disappeared or for some other reason not shown up for work recently?"

"I'll check it now and in a day or two, as well as intermittently over the next month. If the dead woman did work up there she could have been on vacation. They have a unique vacation system of giving extended days off at a time. Hence the recheck in thirty days."

"Good deal if you can get it," replied Zeb.

Those sitting around the sheriff all had the same thought. Zeb had never taken more than a few days off in any given year. The same was basically true for everyone who worked for the sheriff's department.

"I'm also going to do a wide search for recently missing scientists, even though we actually have no idea if the dead woman was one or not. I'll tightly cover the last sixty days and the next sixty days. If something pops up I'll let all of you know," said Shelly.

"We're casting a mighty wide net on the scientist thing simply because of the Z," said Zeb. "Let's not get hung up on that."

"What about all the Russian and Ukrainian connections?" asked Rambler.

"There's a Russian Orthodox all-female Priory headed by Prioress Anna Nichinka on a tertiary road between Solomon and Artesia. It's been there about three years," said Rambler.

Everyone had heard of it but for the most part no one at the meeting had much knowledge or even an opinion until Rambler offered something up.

"The women from the Priory come up to the San Carlos every six weeks or so and volunteer. They help out with whatever needs helping. They don't preach, don't ask for money, don't seek conversions or anything for that matter. They simply do good deeds."

"Have you had any interactions personally with them?"

"One."

"Yeah?"

"This is going to sound a bit odd but they came up to teach and certify young girls in gun safety."

"Nuns and gun safety? That does seem odd," said Clarissa.

"Anything in particular about them that sticks out in your memory?"

"I certainly don't mean to sound sexist ladies, but these nuns, and there were seven or eight of them, were some of the prettiest women I've ever seen in my life," said Rambler.

"Do you realize how sexist that sounds?" asked Kate.

"I said I didn't mean to sound sexist. What if I'd commented on how ugly they were?"

"That'd be even worse," said Shelly.

"Perceived beauty when properly described in a non-sexist manner is a legitimate identifier," replied Rambler.

"What the hell are you talking about?" asked Clarissa.

"It's a quote from the United States Identification Manual for Identity Validation."

"I call bullshit on that one," said Clarissa.

"No. Wait. He's right. I just pulled it up," said Shelly.

"Regardless, let's all act like grownups here. Did you notice anything else about the nuns?"

"They were doing manual labor and not dressed in their habits. Dressed in civvies they all looked to me like they worked out. I mean they were muscularly fit and they could shoot the bullseye out of a target almost every time."

"All of that doesn't leave us anywhere by and large. And we're getting off track. Next image please."

The right wrist of the dead woman's hand appeared with the discoloration highlighted.

"I've got an answer for this," said Shelly. "I blew it up 100X and I believe it's almost certainly a birthmark."

"Anything else it could be?" asked Rambler.

"A color stain from something as simple as a pen, marker or something like that. It's difficult to tell exactly."

"Okay. What do we have next?"

The victim's scoped .30-.30 Henry rifle appeared.

"I've got this one too," said Shelly. "Most of you probably already recognize it as a Henry .30-.30. What's harder to tell is that the scope is Leupold VX Freedom 1.5-4X20 with the latest in optical instrumentation."

"I'd say it's pretty obvious she was hunting something reasonably large. Like a deer or a bear."

"I wonder why she didn't use it to defend herself," said Rambler. "A gun usually does pretty well in a knife fight."

"You'll see soon in one of the images that she was most likely killed from behind, indicating someone probably sneaked up on her."

"If she had been hunting, she wasn't very successful. But we can't rule it out. I checked out her rifle as did Echo. We both agree there was a single bullet in the chamber and no evidence of it recently being fired. This gun is no longer in our possession because our friendly federal counterparts from the NSA took it away a few hours ago."

"NSA?"

"You heard right," replied Zeb.

"Did they have a warrant?"

"Yes, a generic seizure warrant," replied Zeb. "But they had one. The warrant also gave them the ability to take the woman's body, which, as you all know, they did."

The aura of the room turned dark quickly. Not a single person there liked what they were hearing. But they all knew at this point there was little they could do to fight the Feds. Zeb could feel it and asked for the next slide.

"This is her hunting license. We didn't get around to cleaning off the blood so we didn't get a positive identification. Next image. And this is her bear tag. All easily included in the seizure warrant as potential evidence."

"Maybe she really was bear hunting?" suggested Kate.

"Maybe. Here is another picture that might lead to that conclusion."

Up popped a picture of the woman's hunting boots, complete with the brand name cut off the soles of both boots.

"These are the boots she was wearing. Standard hunting boots, found in any good hunting store. As you can see someone went to the trouble to cut off the brand identification from the soles. My assumption is that this was done for a simple reason. In case boot prints were found elsewhere, especially nearby, they couldn't be matched to those of the dead woman. When Echo and I noticed that the brand name had been cut out we took a closer look. The cut was smooth but didn't appear to be recent. These boots had been well worn."

"Assumption being the killer didn't cut off the brand identifier."

"Correct."

"Maybe they were stolen," said Rambler. "If those boots are special enough to be individually numbered, the missing brand name/number would make them less traceable."

"Whoever follows up on the boots, show them around to experts and see if they are specially designed, limited edition or something that makes them different than just a regular pair of boots."

Zeb's order was directed at Kate whose husband Josh sold sporting goods at Diamond Gun and Ammo. No doubt he could be the source of potential leads.

Chapter 10

WHO DO YOU TRUST

"Next, please."

"Here is a picture of the dead woman. It is easy to see that she was dressed appropriately from head to toe for hunting."

Up popped what had once been a lovely-looking woman in blood-soaked clothing. The slice on her throat was readily apparent.

"Doc Yackley, as I earlier pointed out, saw the wounds and noted the cuts were specific to the carotid and brachial arteries," explained Zeb. "The cuts, per his examination, appear to run from left to right. This is consistent with a right-handed person attacking the woman from behind."

"Is that it?" asked Kate.

"No," said Zeb. "Next please, Shelly."

The next image was a piece of art. Someone had created an icon of a deer hunter aiming his bow and arrow at a stag. As Shelly zoomed in they could all see a small crucifix carved between the deer's antlers. Letters from some foreign language completed the piece.

"The victim was wearing this when we found her. Any ideas? Anyone?"

"The lettering I think I recognize as Cyrillic," said Shelly. "I can check, but I know I've seen it before."

"The hunter is killing a deer who bears a religious icon in its antlers," said Clarissa. "Perhaps the deer is symbolic of ridding oneself of one's enemy while taking their food."

Clarissa's statement quieted the room. They all stared intently at the image. What did it mean?

"The deer is often a spiritual messenger. Perhaps this is symbolic of killing the messenger," suggested Kate.

"Sometimes the deer is an omen of death, often sacrificial death," said Rambler.

"It could mean a lot of things. What you all bring forward is what you personally know. We need to find an expert in the field of art that covers this kind of image."

Everyone agreed. All eyes turned to Zeb.

Zeb glanced at Shelly. She knew there was one more image. He hesitated for a long few seconds before nodding in her direction.

"One more. This is the knife that I believe was used to kill the woman. It was found under her body. It appeared to have been placed there by the killer. It's an Emerson CQC6. It was commonly used by American GIs in Afghanistan and Iraq."

"Zoom in please," said Clarissa. "What's that marking on the knife?"

Shelly hesitated as she already knew what the etching was. She even considered blurring it out for Echo's sake, but she knew she couldn't.

"ES1."

"That must be significant. It looks as though it was etched into the knife for ID purposes. That should be helpful if we can find where the knife was purchased," said Rambler.

"There won't be any need for that. We all know the owner of this specific knife."

Kate caught his insinuation immediately. A second or two later the rest of them put ES1 and Zeb's cryptic statement together.

"Yes, it's Echo's knife. And yes, as you already know she was first on the scene and the first to work the scene," said Zeb. "And yes, she was by herself when she came across the dead body."

"Is she our primary suspect?" asked Rambler.

"I think we are all reasonably certain she's not the killer. Still, she's our number one suspect at this point. At least on paper. Please keep all of these pictures as well as today's meeting under your hats. We can't show her any favoritism. We need to rule her in or out using our standard procedures and practices. Please put your biases in your back pockets and if you find anything that links her to the murder it's important to share it with me first. I'll decide if it goes further than me. Is everyone okay with that?"

"Are you sure you can remain objective?" asked Rambler. "I mean, after all she is your wife and the mother of your children. You're the last person on earth who would want to see her go to prison."

"I have reason to believe that the knife was stolen from our safe several days ago," said Zeb. "Kate, I'm going to have you work that evidence with me so we do not appear prejudicial should this evidence end up in court."

"Got it."

"What do you mean by reason to believe the knife was stolen from your personal safe? How can you not be one hundred percent certain?" asked Rambler.

"Maybe a better way to put it is that I have a possible explanation of how the knife found its way to the crime scene."

Zeb explained that after Echo had gone on a two-day retreat he had opened the safe and although he thought he'd shut it, he later realized that he might not have.

"You're standing on pretty shaky ground with that explanation," said Rambler. "Don't you have a security camera aimed at your safe?"

"I don't. No excuses. I simply haven't gotten around to it."

"Zeb, how many times am I going to have to tell you to add security cameras?" asked Shelly. "We've talked about this a dozen times."

"I did add cameras. I didn't have one pointed directly at the safe. Even if I had I don't believe it would have done us any good because it looks like my security system was tampered with in such a way that put it temporarily out of use. But I can't prove that."

"Why not?" asked Rambler.

"I don't have the skill set. Shelly, I'd greatly appreciate it if you would check my home system as well as check into all local security cameras in the area from that time. I'll give you the specific hours and dates that the safe could have been broken into. Please see what you can find."

"Yes, sir," replied Shelly. "Consider it done."

Zeb quickly assigned a specific task to each of them and backup assignments on everything. Setting up a plan of action that involved doublechecking everything up front was a new way of doing business for the staff. They all knew it had to do with Echo's potentially precarious position in the murder. A minute later all were out of the sheriff's office and hoping to make quick work of a case the NSA had pushed them out of.

Rambler lingered as the others departed.

"Zeb?"

"I don't believe Echo had anything to do with the murder. It's just not her style."

"Agreed."

"But protecting a possible suspect is also not your way of doing business."

Zeb felt heat rising under his collar as his ire grew. How dare Rambler question his motives.

"Is there a question in that statement, Rambler?"

"No questions. Just an observation. I've seen it happen with the Rez police force. More than once the police chief has pushed evidence in a direction in order to keep his or her force from looking where he didn't want them to. I don't want that to happen here."

"You're concerned I'd cover for Echo?"

"I would if I were in your position."

"Well, you're not me, are you?"

"No Zeb, I'm not you. But I know you and I know how you operate and how you think."

"I don't think you do, that is if you're questioning my motivation."

"I'm not questioning anything you're doing. But you know as well as I do when the Feds, especially an agency like the NSA which has a budget seven times bigger than the CIA, steps in out of nowhere and takes your case from you that something big is up."

"You think I don't know that?"

"No, I think you do. I also think it's why you're going to protect Echo to the degree that you can."

"I'll pull no favors for her. But I will protect her."

"If you cross a line with the Feds and they don't find the killer quickly, they'll go after Echo simply because she's your wife and you've crossed them. If you play your cards wrong they'll bury both you and Echo. Don't you see how nabbing a county sheriff's wife for murder would and could make someone's career? They'll put a damn target on your back. This is the kind of shit they pull."

"What makes you so certain that's what they have in mind?"

"I've seen more than one career made by using an Apache or a member of some other tribe as a scapegoat. I can give you a list of names if you'd like."

"No need for that. I have no doubt you've seen exactly how they operate. Anything else, Deputy Rambler?"

"Yes. As a matter of fact there is."

"Go on."

"How well do you know the newly appointed San Carlos police chief, Gabriella Cocheta?"

"I've met her three times. Echo invited her and her boyfriend over to the house for dinner about two months ago. Why?"

"Word is that she's jealous of Echo."

"Who told you that?"

"A woman I'm dating. She's Gabriella's ex-office manager."

"What'd she say? Do you remember exactly?"

"No. She mentioned it in passing a while back. Before the murder. I do know that Gabriella was a hot-shot analyst for the DEA before she took the appointment as police chief on the San Carlos."

"That's a step down. Why would she do that?"

"Politics."

"What?"

"She wants to be the first female Native American Senator to serve in D.C."

"Didn't what's-her-name from Massachusetts...Warren...claim to have Indian blood coursing her veins?"

"A lot of politicos claim a lot of things. The Senator from the great state of Massachusetts lied about her bloodline. But you know how it goes. Repeat a lie often enough and people believe it's the truth."

"Right."

"She did successfully use her story to get into Harvard Law School."

"Was her ancestry ever proven or disproven?"

"Funny you should ask and even funnier that I know the answer. A Stanford professor of genetics showed that Warren's DNA sample contains five genetic segments, spanning 12.3 million DNA bases which are Native in origin."

"That being said, what does it all have to do with Gabriella's jealousy of Echo? Even more to the point, what does it have to do with this case?"

"I'm just saying politicos will go to no ends to get what they lust after. Taking down Echo would be a huge feather in Gabriella's bonnet. Plus, I heard via the grapevine that Gabriella had phone contact with the NSA recently."

"Strange."

"I suspect it's going to get even stranger."

"Then we'd better get on with the show. We've both got work to do."

"Right, Sheriff Hanks. We've got a lot to get done to keep Echo safe. Let's go to work."

Chapter 11

EVIDENCE

KATE HEADED TO HER husband's shop, Diamond Guns and Ammo. She wandered the shop straightening up a few things while Josh finished with a customer. She was standing in a far corner when she felt his hands around her waist just as the entry/exit bell clanged as the customer departed through the front door of the business. She backed herself into Josh's hands as he sexily curved his hands around her waist.

"Can I help you with something, ma'am?"

"You can help me with a lot, but that will have to wait. I'm here on official business."

Kate pulled out her sheriff badge and flashed it to Josh, who promptly kissed it, then her.

"What sort of official business may I help a beautiful young woman like yourself with?"

Kate grabbed him by the collar and pressed her lips firmly against his.

"There. That will have to hold you for the time being. More to come, I promise."

Josh straightened his shirt.

"It will and I can wait because I know you never break a promise. What do you need?"

Kate pulled out the printed pictures of the dead woman.

"You ever seen this woman before?"

"No. But that's a pretty nasty amount of blood."

"It is."

Kate tapped the photo near the neck wound.

"Ouch," added Josh.

"She didn't buy this hunting clothing here, did she?"

Josh looked closer, taking an extra moment, as anyone would, to familiarize himself with the arterial wound, before checking out the clothing.

"No, but I recognize the brand. It's an expensive brand with all kinds of hidden pockets. Here's the cool thing about it, this clothing has the ability to keep you warm in cold weather and cool in warm weather."

"Kind of like a thermos?" asked Kate.

"That's an appropriate analogy and it's also their marketing tool. It's mostly used by a few elite foreign military mountain divisions. It's expensive, too expensive for the U.S. military. Or should I say the U.S. military has enough money to buy them but refuses to dress their soldiers in the best way possible?"

"I would bet I know one sheriff's wife who would agree with you."

"Touché. I imagine you'd have to order it online or go to Tucson or Phoenix to find a boutique military store to buy it."

Hearing her husband's reference brought a chuckle to Kate.

"Do you find that there are boutique military clothing stores at all odd?"

"No and yes. Some people are seriously into hunting fashion."

She handed him the picture of the gun that was found with the dead woman.

"How about the gun?"

"Standard Henry .30-.30. Definitely an older-generation model."

"Older generation?"

Josh pointed out several details including the loop lever, stock and several other parts that dated it back to the 1940s before walking over to the counter and pulling out a magnifying glass to give it a brief but detailed once over.

"The scope is a Leupold VX Freedom 1.5-4X20. It's much newer than the gun. Want to look at an old Henry much like this one up close? I happen to have an original 1894 version of this gun. It's my pride and joy when it comes to all the Henrys I own."

"Not necessary right now, but thanks. I may need to have a look at it sometime in the future."

"That's cool."

"With what I've shown you, any thoughts you'd like to share? I mean based on the clothing, the Henry and its scope. What do you think?"

"What you have here is probably a hunter with high quality gear. Nothing unusual about that in these parts. Where was the body found?"

"In the Pinaleños. Want me to show you more precisely?"

Josh pointed to a county map that hung on a nearby wall. Kate rolled a finger across the map until she landed on the precise location.

"I know that spot. It's near the U-Loop and Skinny Creek. I've had the dogs out there a number of times. It's a great place to hunt bear and this is the season. But it's got a strange vibe. The dogs always act weird out there."

"Speaking of which, take a look at this."

Kate handed Josh the pictures of the bloodied hunting license and bear tag.

It took him all of two seconds to conclude both were fakes.

"Fakes? How can you tell?"

"If you cleaned the license up you'd be able to tell in a second. The corners are squared. They should be slightly rounded. I can't believe one of you didn't spot that. Plus look at the shade of blue. It's way too light to be legit. The tag, you should have caught that one."

"No one did. So I wasn't the only one who missed it."

"The state changed bear license tags this year so I suppose none of you have seen the new ones. This is a copy of an older style one."

"Why would someone make their own license and tag?" asked Kate.

"Usually they do it to save money."

"Odd, considering the expensive clothing and good quality gun and new scope," replied Kate.

"I guess some people are just cheap when it comes to giving the government their due."

"Can you think of any other reason someone might do something like that?"

"Not really. Maybe they didn't want anyone to know they were a hunter. Or maybe they were just a rule breaker or someone who doesn't like state rules and regs. Tags and licenses also require a form of ID. Maybe the person is an illegal?"

"Want to take a look at what else we've got?"

"Sure."

"These are the bottoms of the boots she had on," explained Kate.

"She went so far as to cut off the brand insignia. I know this boot."

Josh pressed a few keys on his computer and up popped an image of the exact women's boot. It was a Meindl Women's Explorer 400. He pointed to the ad writeup on the boot.

"Made in Slovenia. Sold primarily in Germany but probably sold all over eastern and western Europe. It's a good boot. Pricey. I'd guess someone cut the brand off the bottom because they were sold on the secondary market..."

"Stolen, you mean?"

"Yeah, maybe. Or maybe just manufacturer's rejects. The dead woman won't be able to tell you, that's for sure."

She showed him the picture of the Emerson CQC6, the murder weapon.

"Ironic."

"Ironic? What do you mean?" asked Kate.

"Echo Skysong owns a knife just like that one. She had me fix the blade on it about a year ago. I cleaned it too."

"How was it damaged?"

"I don't know for sure. She was rather evasive about what happened to damage it. I figured she'd done something stupid and was too embarrassed to tell me."

"Do you remember having any thoughts on how the knife may have been damaged?"

"That's a funny question."

"Did you? Have any thoughts on how it might have been damaged?"

"As a matter of fact I did. In fact I joked with her about it."

"What'd you say?"

"I asked her if she'd jammed it into someone's ribs. I remember thinking that because it was right around the time those two Mexican drug dealers were stabbed to death on the Rez. I think I joked around about her and Zeb having a knife fight. Why?"

"Was there any blood on it when you cleaned it?"

"No. What's with all the questions about Echo's knife?"

"This is Echo's knife. It was found under the body of the dead woman. To make matters even more interesting it was Echo who found the body and the knife. We also believe it is the murder weapon."

"Oh. Wait just a second. You don't for one minute believe Echo killed this woman, do you?"

"We're just following a trail of evidence, that's all."

"I can't believe that Echo is even capable of such a thing."

"Me neither. But if any Feds come snooping around and asking, you'd be doing her and us a favor if you didn't know much, especially about the knife. They don't know we have it."

"Gotcha," replied Josh. "Am I to be expecting them anytime soon?"

"No idea."

"I can handle them," replied Josh.

"I love you, Josh. Now I've got to go prove Echo isn't a cold-blooded killer."

Chapter 12

PINALEÑO MOUNTAINS

ZEB OFFERED NO EXPLANATION as he ordered Clarissa to come with him.

"Where we headed, Zeb?"

"The Pinaleños."

"I know the area where the body was found like the back of my hand."

"That's why I'm having you come with me."

"How much ground are we going to cover?" asked Clarissa.

Zeb patted his belly.

"I'm not in the shape I used to be, so I don't know how much turf we'll cover in one day. I got maybe three-four hours in me. You?"

"I can run up and down those mountains all day and all night."

Zeb stepped back and gave the once-over to the youngest member of his team. She was in excellent shape, far better than himself. As he imagined her effortlessly traipsing around the mountains a twinge of envy ran through him.

"I have no doubt you could run those mountains all day," replied Zeb.

"But if we're smart we'll stop by my folks' ranch and pick up a couple of mountain-experienced horses. That okay with you?"

"I haven't ridden a lot lately, but I should pick it up again for the sake of my kids. They've already asked us for a pony, which I don't think they're going to get any time soon."

"If you get one, I'm sure you can board it with my parents' animals. I think you should get them each one. My brothers and I all had our own horses. Some of my best childhood memories are riding around these mountains on horseback. It's a good way to discover the world, test your limits and figure out who you really are."

"Has Echo been talking to you about this? You sound exactly like her. You have been discussing this with her, haven't you?"

"She might have mentioned it in passing. Turn left up there. It's a shortcut to our ranch."

Thirty minutes later Zeb and Clarissa were pulling a horse trailer and heading up Diego's Wash toward the flatland path that led directly to the U-Loop and Skinny Creek, close to the scene of the crime.

"Why do you think the killer left Echo's knife under the dead body? I mean other than obviously trying to make her the fall woman?"

Clarissa's words were the first time he'd heard anyone say fall woman instead of fall guy. Political correctness was everywhere it seemed.

"I've been thinking about that ever since I saw the knife lying there under the dead woman's body. It seems so foolish for a killer to have left the murder weapon behind. As sheriff, I have to look at all of the evidence. That includes ruling evidence both in and out. Whoever used that knife, for that matter whoever stole it from the safe in our house, knows that Echo didn't commit the murder. But they do intend for her to be set up, as you said, to be the fall woman."

"I imagine they were banking on the notion that you couldn't prove her innocence," replied Clarissa. "I mean it's obvious that you're going to do everything you can to protect your wife."

"Which could make some of the steps that I might take to prove her innocence look like I'm acting in a prejudicial manner."

"I have no doubt that it will appear that way to some folks. I guess there's one thing the bad guys don't know, though."

"What's that?"

"Just how far you will go to prove Echo's innocence."

Zeb turned away from Clarissa as he wondered exactly what she thought about his handling of Echo's knife, the murder weapon that he had removed from the crime scene and left out of all official reports. He knew Clarissa's history. To maintain the law, she had killed her brother in a legitimate gun fight. As someone willing to go to such extremes what might she be thinking about Zeb removing evidence from a crime scene?

From the sounds of it, she seemed to believe there were no limits to what he would do to protect Echo. She wasn't wrong. Nor did she seem to be judging his actions. It was difficult to read between the lines with Clarissa. Zeb felt that when push came to shove, she'd be on his side. Still, if he didn't eventually reveal that he had the murder weapon in his possession, someone else might. That would make things bad for him and even worse for Echo. For the moment, his position was unbending.

"You know full well that I will do anything and everything to prove Echo's innocence."

"None of us who know you would expect anything less."

Zeb pulled the horse trailer to within a quarter mile or so from the spot the ambulance had parked when it picked up the dead woman's body. The horses were quickly unloaded and the pair mounted up.

Clarissa's horse took off at a medium-paced trot, circling around to approach the scene from a fresh direction. Zeb followed closely but after a few minutes his back and legs were cramped and aching like bolts of electricity had been shot through them. Middle age was somehow sneaking in without his knowledge or permission. Zeb Hanks wasn't at all fond of what he knew to be inevitable.

It took half an hour to reach an open approach to the crime scene since they were coming from the opposite of the usual direction. When Zeb began to become familiar with the surroundings he shouted out to Clarissa.

"Whoa!"

Clarissa reined in her horse, stopped and turned. Zeb was in the middle of a dismount. She was surprised to see him slide off English style.

"Slick," she said. "Where'd you learn that?"

"Echo's dad. He claims it saves on the back."

"It does. Most men won't use that kind of dismount. Vanity, I suppose."

"When it comes to pain, I'm not going to be embarrassed."

Clarissa laughed and glided off her horse in the same fashion. Only she dismounted with a whole lot more style and flair than Zeb had.

Clarissa watched as it took Zeb a moment to get his land legs.

"You okay, Sheriff Hanks?"

"Been way too long since I've journeyed this far on the back of a horse."

"Then for your own sake as well as Elan's and Onawa's, it's time to get some ponies for the kids and maybe even horses for you and Echo."

"Like I said, I'm thinking about it."

"Be a good dad and teach them to ride," said Clarissa. "You won't be sorry you did."

"Okay. It's on my mind. Let's leave the horses here and walk in. Echo and I marked a dozen or so possible sites that indicate people had been there. Let's check those out first. The first one is over there against the canyon wall. We marked the spots with small yellow flags."

Near the first marker were a set of smaller footprints, indicating either a woman or a smallish man. They found twenty-five or so prints leading toward where the body had been found. Another fifteen or so of the same prints were intermixed over the top of those steps, this time leading away. Clarissa and Zeb both saw them as an indicator someone had reversed their footsteps. The distances between the steps going away from where the dead woman had been found were greater than the distances between the approaching steps.

Zeb and Clarissa examined the footprints closely. Zeb knew exactly what he was looking for, the presence of or lack of a marking on the heels indicating the brand. In checking all the prints it became obvious the brand markings had been removed, just like the victim's had.

"Curious, wouldn't you say, Zeb? I mean what are the odds both victim and perpetrator would have done the same thing to their boots?"

"The first thing that pops into my mind is that they may have known each other."

"That's one way of looking at it."

Clarissa took some pictures on a digital camera. Zeb had instructed everyone to not use their phones to take pictures based on the fact that earlier images had been erased, presumably by the Feds. Making the same mistake twice was something Zeb keyed in on preventing.

Zeb walked to the west paralleling the footprints for about fifty feet before reversing his steps. Then he took off at a right angle and trotted fifty feet, stopped and walked back.

"What are you doing?" asked Clarissa.

"Checking the distances between footprints using a running pace and a walking pace. Based on both walking and trotting it appears the killer walked into the scene of the crime and hightailed it out."

"How far can you follow the tracks?"

"I lose them when they enter a crossing path for hikers at the small creek just over the hill."

"What do you have in mind now?"

"Let's follow the other three directions and check for fresh tracks. I want to see if anyone else may have been in or out of here. If we find nothing else, we'll go back to the creek and see what we can find. You up to snuff on tracking?"

Clarissa had just downed a handful of trail mix. She almost choked, coming close to regurgitating it back up through her nose at Zeb's question.

"Hah! I hunted rabbits and ground squirrels while riding on horseback by following their tracks. If I can track squirrels, human tracks are easy as A-B-C."

Clarissa mounted her horse and waited patiently as Zeb struggled slightly in remounting his steed. Once steadily seated on his horse Zeb smiled.

"Clarissa, take the lead."

Dutifully the deputy headed north, following the route the victim had come in from. The dead woman's prints were exactly as Echo had described them. In no time Clarissa found a half dozen sets of boot prints. All of them were easily distinguishable from the tracks they were looking for. More importantly, none of them were what they were hoping to find. The same proved true as they trekked to the south and east.

"Back to the creek," said Zeb.

Clarissa was already heading in that direction. Fifteen minutes later she was directly on the presumed killer's tracks that had been found near the dead woman. While Zeb could barely spot them, Clarissa trotted her horse at a good clip westward before stopping at a pile of horse manure. Next to the manure was the butt of a cigarette with the imprint, NPIMA. She hopped off her horse, bagged the butt in one bag and a scoop of horse manure that Zeb had asked her to bag up in another evidence bag, before quickly remounting.

"There's your answer."

"The killer rode in on a horse."

Clarissa sat tall in the saddle and checked her line of sight in all directions.

"Maybe they smoked NPIMA cigarettes?"

"Never heard of them," said Zeb.

"Me neither."

"Come on, let's follow the horse tracks and see where they go," said Zeb.

"I think you're going to be disappointed."

"Why?" asked Zeb.

"Half a mile up that way is a well-used horse trail. I'll bet anything the tracks will blend in with those of a lot of other horses."

"Who uses the trail?"

"Some locals. But mostly rent-a-horse tourists who want to play cowboy or cowgirl for a day."

"We've got to look anyway," said Zeb.

"Good day for a ride, but I'm afraid you're going to be sore in the saddle before we're done."

Four hours later with little to show for their efforts, except for painful muscles on Zeb's part and a pair of well-used saddle strings that Clarissa had found, Zeb and Clarissa unsaddled the horses before trailering them for the ride back to Clarissa's parents' ranch, the Lazy J. Her parents walked out to greet them.

"I owe you folks for letting us borrow the horses," said Zeb. "I'm sore as I've been in ages, but we could have never covered the ground we did without being on horseback."

Clarissa's dad did the speaking for him and his wife.

"Always glad to help out the sheriff's department. Think nothing of it, Sheriff Hanks."

With saddles stowed away and the horses backed safely out of the trailer Zeb and Clarissa headed down the back road with a large baggie full of peanut butter cookies. Zeb drove as Clarissa

munched on a cookie and looked at the few things of interest
they had collected.

"These road apples?" asked Clarissa. "What do you have in
mind?"

"They seemed fresh enough to possibly be from the killer's
horse. At least they were in the right location to be. I'll send
them to a lab and maybe we can break down what type of horse
feed the horse had been eating. It's a long shot connecting the
horse droppings to anything, but it's worth a shot."

"Sort of like shooting craps, eh, Sheriff Hanks?"

The pair laughed. The manure was probably a foolish notion
but leaving no stone unturned was a necessary part of the job.

"The cigarette butt? I assume you're hoping for fingerprints."

"Another long shot. Especially since it was near the main trail.
But you never know unless you do the work."

"Another long shot," said Clarissa. "But like you say, they do
come in."

"Yup. They do come in. Not often. But they do."

Clarissa held up the saddle strings so the sunlight shined on
them.

"About these..."

"I do believe they're our best bet," said Zeb.

"Why do you say that? Every saddle has saddle strings."

"These look hand braided to me," said Zeb.

Clarissa ran them through her fingers. Though faded, it was
easy to tell that they were once significantly more colorful than
regular saddle strings. In looking at them she had concluded that
unless someone really knew what they were doing, they were
machine made, not hand made."

"I've probably seen more of these than you."

"No doubt."

"These are tightly woven and made of hand dyed leather. But
they are almost too perfect to be anything but machine made."

"Even if they are machine made we might be able to figure
out where they're from. From looking at them, and I agree they
appear almost flawless, I saw something that caught my eye.
Take a closer look at the end of the strings."

The ends of the strings were well worn. Clarissa put on her
glasses and looked them over closely. Sure enough, there were

markings burned into the last quarter inch of each of the strings. The markings were slight indentations that were barely visible.

"There's a magnifying glass in the glove compartment," said Zeb.

Grabbing it, Clarissa took a close look.

"Is that what I think it is?"

"What do you see?"

"I can barely make it out but I think it's a stag with a cross in the antlers."

"That's what I thought too."

Clarissa eyed Zeb wondering how he could have possibly seen it without a magnifying glass. Zeb knew what she was thinking. He reached into his pocket and pulled out a pair of cheaters.

"I used these."

"A man without his tools isn't much of a man," said Clarissa. "My daddy taught me that one."

Zeb smiled. Clarissa was young, but she was a quick study and an asset to his department.

"I spotted it when the sun hit it just right. Then I felt it ever so gently. It's a trick Echo taught me."

"Show me," said Clarissa.

"Wet it with some spit and when it's starting to dry rub the tip of your little finger across the area very lightly."

The spit made the stag much more visible and the cross slightly apparent. Rubbing her fingers across clarified everything Zeb had said.

"Neat trick," she said. "I'll remember it."

"Good skill to have," replied Zeb. "We'll call it your lesson for the day."

"This matches up with the talisman the deceased woman was wearing."

"And there you go. We've got something that might link the killer and the victim. We just might be one small step closer to resolution."

Chapter 13

ELAN AND ONAWA

CERTAIN DAYS WERE EXHAUSTING for no particular reason. Some days exhaustion was physical while other days were mentally fatiguing. Today had had been strenuous for Zeb in every way. Each clue they'd found, all of which seemed difficult to come by, brought him only one tiny step closer to proving Echo's innocence. That was enough to keep a tired sheriff moving ahead.

Horseback riding had knocked his back out of kilter and he'd need to see the chiropractor before work tomorrow. He'd catch Doc Hechtor at the Town Talk before he opened his clinic and coax a before-work-hours spinal manipulation out of him.

"Honey, tuck the kids in and tell them a story, would you?"

Echo's request was not presented as an option. Zeb had just put his feet up and was relaxing in his recliner when Echo's command came through loud and clear.

"Is it bed time already?" asked Zeb.

"Did you forget how to tell time?"

Zeb lowered his foot rest, pushed himself out of his temporary comfort zone and trudged up the stairs to the kids' bedroom where he was greeted by a pair of smiling, loving children. Suddenly the day's fatigue was lifted from his body. Onawa began the pleading.

"Tell us a story, Daddy. About when you were little. Please?"

"I want to get a Mohawk haircut."

Elan's interruption caused both Onawa and Zeb to do a doubletake.

"A Mohawk? You're an Apache. Why in heck do you want to get a Mohawk?"

"They're cool."

"We learned about them in Native American history class," added Onawa. "Mohawk women chose their husbands. Did Mommy choose you?"

"You might say that," replied Zeb. "Or you might say we chose each other."

"Do you love Mommy?"

"Yes, of course. What makes you ask that?" said Zeb.

"She said you were working so hard because you were worried about her. What are you worried about? Are you worried that Mom doesn't love you?"

Zeb lay down on Onawa's bed and the kids immediately snuggled in against him.

"I love your mother and there's no need for you to even think about something as silly as her not loving me. As to getting a Mohawk haircut young man, we'll talk about it with your mother. I'm pretty sure she'll listen closely to your request with an open mind."

"Yes!!"

His answers were sufficient to move the conversation forward. In unison Elan and Onawa begged.

"Tell us a story, Daddy. PLEASE!!!"

"Okay. Okay."

"Yeah!!"

"I'll tell you a good story. But first I have to tell you that this isn't my story. This is a story that was told to me by an old Apache chief who used to sit in the park."

"The park near your office or the one by Roper Lake or the one by the swimming pool?"

"The one that's near my office. He sat there every day of the year."

"Even at Christmas?"

"I'll never get the story told if you keep asking questions."

"But you told us that if we want to be smart we have to ask questions."

"And listen to the answers."

"How old were you, Daddy?"

"I was just a kid, about ten years old, maybe nine."

"We're eight almost nine," said Onawa.

"That's right. I forgot that I was just about your age when this happened. The old chief..."

"How old is old?" asked Elan.

"Older than you and Mommy?" asked Onawa.

"Yes, he was older than Mommy and me."

"As old as GMa and GPa?"

"Yes, if I had to venture a guess I'd say he was about the same age as your grandparents."

"They're not old," said Onawa.

"They can still play with us."

"They can run and play games with us and they never complain about being tired. I love them."

"As well you should," replied Zeb.

"Story! Story!"

"Well this Apache chief played catch with me sometimes. So he could still play with children. That's how old he was."

"It's kind of hard to tell how old someone is when you're eight," said Onawa.

"Yeah," echoed Elan. "It is."

"What'd he look like?"

Zeb's mind tripped back in time to the Apache who sat in the park every day of his childhood.

"He had long hair and a handsome Apache ponytail. His hair was mostly black with some streaks of silver and gray mixed in."

"I still want a Mohawk."

"He dressed in deerskin clothing, the old-fashioned way. He looked very much like pictures you see in books from a hundred or more years ago."

"That's a really long time," said Elan.

"Yes it is quite a while when you think about it. Getting back to the story, the Apache chief was my good friend."

"Was he your best friend?"

"He was my best adult friend. Him and Sheriff Jake Dablo."

"I miss Jake."

"Me too."

"What was the chief's name?"

"I don't think I ever knew his real name. He'd been hurt in the war and lost three of his fingers. Some people called him Two

Fingers. Even though he only had two fingers he could throw a curve ball in baseball."

"Cool."

"Here's the story he told me."

Elan and Onawa lay on their stomachs with the palms of their hands propping up their heads. Their ears devoured every word their daddy spoke.

"He told me that once upon a time there was no town of Safford."

"What?"

"No town?"

"How could that even be?"

"There was only wide-open desert as far as the eye could see. There were all sorts of Indian tribes that lived along the river. Most of the tribes were what are now called Apaches. But back then they called them clans."

"What's a clan?" asked Elan.

"It's like a big family. It would be like if you lived with your grandparents, parents, aunts, uncles and cousins."

"That would be so cool."

"And so much fun."

Zeb rubbed Elan's head and kissed Onawa on the cheek.

"The various small tribes or clans generally got along and helped each other out. But occasionally they would fight each other."

"Why would they fight?" asked Elan.

"Usually if one family took something from another family who thought it belonged to them."

"They stole from each other?" asked Onawa.

"No, usually it wasn't like that."

"What then?"

"What do you mean, Daddy?"

"Each clan had its own hunting grounds. Sometimes the hunters from one clan would cross over onto land where another clan hunted. One clan or tribe would feel like the other clan or tribe was stealing their animals."

"But they didn't have fences back then did they?" asked Elan.

"No. There were no fences and animals didn't know tribal boundaries. Like all animals they simply roamed around looking for food themselves."

"It must have been hard to figure out whose animals were whose," said Onawa.

"It was hard to know. But no one liked someone taking their animals because it meant food would be harder to come by," explained Zeb.

"I don't suppose there were any grocery stores back then, were there?"

"No. But there were trading posts."

Elan and Onawa had all kinds of questions about trading posts that Zeb tried to answer before getting back to his story.

"So clans would fight one another over hunting grounds?"

"They didn't like each other, huh, Dad?" asked Elan. "Did they kill each other?"

"Most of the time they worked it out by talking to each other. And even though they would have arguments over hunting lands, when outsiders came along and tried to take their game the clans would band together and fight the outsiders."

"Like the *indaa*? Are you *indaa*? Are we *indaa*?" asked Onawa.

Zeb had heard the term *indaa* since he was a child. He knew it meant white person. He always assumed it might have a derogatory overtone but had never asked anyone. At this moment he wished he knew.

"Did you learn that word in school?"

"Yes. Our teacher said she is *indaa*. She's a White lady, not an Apache."

"I think it means white-skinned person," added Elan.

"I think it means someone who isn't brown-skinned," said Onawa.

"If that's what it means, then I am *indaa*. Your mother is Apache. You two are both Apache and White. These days when you are both you can identify with either or both, whatever you want."

"Am I a Mohawk if I get a Mohawk haircut?"

"No. It doesn't work like that."

Zeb looked into his children's eyes as they thought long and hard about whether they were Apache or *indaa*. He supposed they didn't want to disappoint either him or their mother and were wisely choosing to think it over. The color of their skin would lead most everyone to believe they were Apache children. What was in their hearts was what truly mattered.

"Should I go on with the story?"

"Yes. Yes."

"The old Apache chief with two fingers taught me many things but the one thing I remember now is that he taught that if I used my eyes, ears, nose, mouth and hands I could learn everything there was to know."

"Was he teaching you to use your five senses?" asked Onawa.

"That's right. He taught me to listen to the wind so I could tell if the weather was changing or if something was coming toward me or moving away from me. He also taught me that if the wind was blowing away from me I couldn't tell if something was coming toward me unless I saw it. He told me to use my ears to pay attention to what others said, including mother nature. He taught me to listen to water so I could tell which way a stream was flowing. He said that if I used my nose I could not only tell good food from bad food but I could tell if there was a fire, an animal in the bushes and all sorts of other important things. If I used my mouth I could say the right words to help others and tell if a plant was safe to eat. As you can see he wanted me to use more than one of my senses at a time."

"What about your hands? What did he say about them?" asked Elan.

"He said that if I learned how to touch the earth I would be in harmony with nature. He told me that to be in harmony with nature was to be in harmony with myself and that if I were in harmony with myself I could do only good things."

As the kids peppered him with questions to stave off bedtime, Zeb wondered if he was in harmony with nature and if he truly was, what would he learn from the horse manure, saddle strings and other clues gathered in the mountains on his horseback ride with Clarissa. He knew that the more he was in harmony with all things the easier it would be to prove Echo's innocence.

While tucking Elan and Onawa into bed he wondered if he was a good father, a good husband and right now, a good sheriff.

Even more so he wondered what would happen if someone was out to get Echo and if she might be pulled from their lives.

Finally, Zeb kissed his children goodnight. As he stood outside their door listening to their innocent chatter he wondered if he had done the right thing by omitting Echo's knife as evidence. He was definitely of two minds. In seeking the truth had he gone too far to protect Echo? Did he not trust the system to treat her fairly? Self-doubt was gnawing at him.

Chapter 14

RAMBLER AT THE REZ

As Rambler drove onto the San Carlos Reservation the very first thing that caught his eye was an oversized billboard with a picture of Police Chief Gabriella Cocheta. Pulling off on the side of the road he took out his phone and shot a picture of the advertisement. Never in all his years on the Rez had he seen such a thing, not even during election time.

Gabriella's image showed a beautiful but stern-looking no-nonsense woman. Although dressed in a traditional police uniform she was adorned with Apache jewelry and her hair was done Apache style. The words beneath her image promised to make the San Carlos a safe place for children and guaranteed a brighter future for all tribal members, young and old.

A lifelong friend of Rambler's, Baishan Hoazinne ambling easily down the roadside toward his trailer home spotted Rambler and gave him a thumbs up. Rambler called him over with a wave.

"*Da'a'the*, Rambler Braing. I see you're still carrying water for the White man."

"Baishan Hoazinne, it pays the bills."

The men fist bumped as Baishan tipped the brim of his hat skyward before leaning against Rambler's truck next to the open driver's side window and asked an inside joke.

"You still smoke sacred tobacco?"

Rambler nodded and reached into a pack of pre-rolls which consisted of half tobacco and half marijuana. It was an old trick the two of them learned when they played together in an Indian hip hop band, Tribu de Deux. Memories of their well misspent youth danced between them. Baishan took a long drag that ate up half the joint, crossed his arms and stared into space. Rambler pointed to the cigarette.

"Still bogarting, I see," said Rambler. "I guess some things will never change."

"You're working, Deputy Sheriff of Graham County Rambler Braing. You'd be derelict in your duty if you dabbled in the flower while in the White man's uniform, would you not?"

Rambler started chanting the Apache introduction to their personal hip hop version of 'Don't Bogart Me'. Rambler stepped out of his truck, took the joint from Baishan's fingers, took a deep drag and handed it back to his former bandmate. A moment later they were singing and dancing alongside the highway.

The men shared a belly laugh as they concluded the song. Several passing cars honked and waved.

"We've still got it," said Baishan.

"And from the sounds of it, we've still got a fan club," added Rambler.

After finishing the marijuana-tobacco spliff Rambler invited Baishan into his official vehicle. Baishan ran his hand over the shotgun that was racked in the window just behind his friend.

"This baby street legal?"

"Hell, no."

The men laughed some more as Rambler did a U-turn and headed to Baishan's trailer house.

"How are your folks doing?"

"Getting older."

"Aren't we all? How about your brother, Ryne?"

"He's a federal agent of some sort," replied Baishan. "In his head, he's a big shot."

"What sort of Fed is he?"

"He just got a new promotion. He was DEA. Right now I can't really say which branch of the government has a tight grip on his testicles. But at least I know who owns yours."

The men shared another good laugh over Baishan's friendly ribbing.

"Any of your kids still live with you and your girlfriend?" asked Rambler.

"They've all moved to the city. The oldest boy is a computer software architect. The younger two work odd jobs. The youngest also sings in a heavy metal retro band."

"Cochise is a singer? Better than you were? Better than we were?"

"Different kind of music. Hard to compare. He's getting better all the time."

With the words to a Beatles song coming from Baishan the pair went into a ballad version of 'Getting Better All the Time' before switching it up into a hip hop version of the same song.

"We really do still have what it takes, don't we?"

"Sure do. Probably should have stuck with it. We'd be famous. Traveling the world. Lots of pretty young gals. The best and latest drugs. All of it."

"Yeah."

"Yeah," sighed Baishan.

"Your young ones are still finding themselves I take it. Chips off the old block, eh?"

"I suppose. They're good boys. No sense rushing through life. They've got a lot of years to work and pay taxes. Their spirits are all healthy. They love life."

"As long as they don't get in trouble and stay alive," replied Rambler. "They should be just fine if they're anything like their old man."

"So far, so good. You can't worry about what you can't control."

"Speaking of control, how is the new police chief doing in keeping things under control on the Rez?"

"Hard to say," replied Baishan.

"What do you mean?"

"Seems like she spends as much time rubbing shoulders up in Phoenix as she does working on the Rez. Sometimes I think she lives to hobnob."

"Who's she hanging with?"

"You read the paper?"

"Headlines and the sports section. I stay away from politics and never read the social media page," replied Rambler.

"You ought to have a look at it so you can see who your next Senator in Washington, D.C. is going to be. Gabriella is raking in the big bucks. The story I read said she's raised over four million dollars already for the senatorial campaign and the election isn't for two and a half years. She's a real go getter."

"Is she running as a Democrat or Republican?"

"When people know you're what the Whites Eyes call Native American you can run in either party. The White Eyes are begging for us Indians to have one or two very small seats at a monstrously huge table in the nation's capital."

"You got that right. I have to say that I'd vote for one of us just because there are none of us in the United States Senate. Truthfully, there are way too few of us Indians making national decisions," added Rambler. "Especially when you consider a few hundred years ago all of this land was ours."

"Time marches on."

"Shit changes."

"Even if she's a real asshole, she'll get my vote."

"That being said, what is she up to? Other than glad handing up in Phoenix?"

"She's managed to get the money from somewhere, probably the BIA or individual donors to hire ten new police deputies on the Rez. Mostly military vets as far as I can tell."

"That's cool."

Rambler didn't mean a word he said. He wanted Gabriella to be the next Senator from Arizona because if she was the hell off the Rez he might get appointed to return to the position of police chief, his lifelong dream. Every word of praise that came out of his mouth for Chief Cocheta was nothing short of a lie.

"Yeah. She's also brought in money for schools, some good after school programs, a program that sees to it that no student goes hungry and a couple of new buildings are in the works. Hopefully, they'll be built in the next year or two. Apache-owned businesses, especially if they are a female-owned business get first dibs on all contracts. That's okay by me."

"She takes care of her own, I see."

"That's one way of looking at it."

"There's another way to look at it?"

"Apache smoke signals say she's pocketing more than one out of every four dollars for her personal treasure chest."

"Do you think she can be bought?"

"I've heard that depends on one thing and one thing only."

"What's that?"

"How much money you've got."

Baishan and Rambler now sufficiently stoned on weed began to chuckle uncontrollably. Amidst the laughter they again began singing hip hop songs.

"We really should get the old band back together," suggested Rambler.

"Make the big Benjamins."

"Always knew you wanted to be a big willie."

"Fo' shizzle. But remember, mo' money, mo' problems."

"420 that."

Rambler took out a new pre-roll and smoked it halfway down before passing it over to Baishan. Both men sighed as a calm quiet came over them. Baishan and Rambler stared off into space as their imaginations ran as wild and as far as those of the young men whose futures had not yet been determined.

"I know this real foxy red woman who sings and raps like the sweet bird of youth," said Baishan.

"Yeah?"

"She's maybe twenty years old, if that."

"Whoa there my good *ndeeń*. We don't want to be cradle robbers. Do we?"

The pair exchanged a smile of possibility.

"She's Song Bird's understudy. We're just a couple of old farts to her. But she's the kind of young woman who is into many things. I suspect she'd love to join together with the band."

"Let's run it by Song Bird. His moccasins carry some big feet whose toes I don't want to step on."

"We'd never do anything to cross him. You know that. Besides, he's teaching her about the world and how to live in it. I'm certain this would be just one more thing to put in her bag of tricks."

"What the hell? Why not give it a shot?"

An agreement was made over a pound hug, the traditional hip hop handshake they'd used in the past. Both men would separately approach Song Bird and make attempts to get his blessing. Then together they would approach Sawni.

"Tribu de Trois!"

One fancy handshake later they were dreaming of changing their futures.

Chapter 15

MISSING

SHELLY ZIPPED INTO THE parking lot of the Graham County Sheriff's Department in her latest toy, a 2022 Audi RS e-tron GT. The car's nearly noiseless engine and flashy exterior would have gone unnoticed by Helen had her eye not caught the sun shimmering off its stunning exterior. Helen, a long-time extreme car aficionado opened her office window and leaned through it. She emitted a whistle of admiration as Shelly hit the lock button.

"What've you got there, my good woman?"

Shelly caressed the freshly detailed machine to remove a solitary bug that must not have heard the car coming in its direction. Blowing the dead fly from her hand Shelly responded gleefully.

"Whaddaya' think?"

"I think I'm looking at beauty, the future and saving the planet all rolled into one."

"Take five and let me show you how this baby runs down the road."

Helen, although she knew exactly who was in the office and where they were, looked around anyway. She placed her purse in the lower right-hand drawer and locked it before practically jogging out to the parking lot.

"Tell me about your new baby."

Helen walked slowly around the car.

"Audi RS e-tron GT."

"I heard Wesley Wren on an episode of Autoweek's *Quick Spin* talking to Patrick Carone of Hearst Autos about this luxurious electric vehicle. He called it the latest attempt to masquerade a car as a present-day time machine."

"The man understands this thing of beauty, then, doesn't he?"

"I'd say so. What else you dig about this spaceship?"

"The dual electric motors that separately drive the front and rear axles."

"Cool beans," replied Helen.

"Magnetic motors with 590 horsepower and 612 pound-feet of torque."

"Quick off the line, I take it?"

"Zero to 60 in 3.1 seconds."

"Sweet. What about the battery pack?"

"Ninety-three kWh that can feed the motors for 238 EPA estimated miles."

"There's a whole lot to love about this baby, I take it?"

"You sure got that right."

Helen caressed the exterior of the car like it was a living being.

"What's your favorite thing when it comes to the GT, Shelly? Besides the beautiful interior?"

"This baby feels normal running down the road and the acceleration is relentlessly quick."

"Mileage?"

"I've been getting between 77 and 84 MPGe on the highway."

"Any complaints?"

"Not really. I'm tall so I'd appreciate a bit more leg room. If I'm carrying a lot of equipment in the trunk, well, it's tight. The next gen will have more battery range, as will all of them."

"What'd this girl set you back, if you don't mind my asking?"

"With taxes, title, fees, and delivery around 160k."

"You drove comparable cars, I presume?"

"I did. But in my mind there were no equivalents."

The two chatted and admired the car until Zeb stepped out the front door and asked if they were coming to work. Helen winked at Shelly and sang out her sassy response.

"Coming big boss man."

The women sashayed to the office, Helen feeling young at heart as she always did when she and Shelly discussed cars and Shelly feeling a bond like the one that she and her own mother never developed. Zeb stood next to Helen's desk and sneaked a glance at her work to see what she'd been up to.

"Morning Shelly. I must be paying you too much. I see you've got yet another new toy."

"No Graham County Sheriff's vehicle is ever going to catch me. On that you can rest assured."

Everyone laughed. They all knew that among Shelly's side jobs, patents that she held, apps she'd created and numerous streams of passive income, the pay she received from Graham County amounted to little more than chump change. Camaraderie was what kept her on the job.

Zeb held a neatly written note he had taken from Helen's outbox that had his name written on it. By the time he asked her about it, he'd already read it.

"What's this about?"

"I know Shelly is doing a broad search on missing scientists. She briefly explained to me the letter 'Z' on the dead woman and how it might be linked to the observatory. But she didn't need to tell me, no one shut the door to the meeting room. I overheard everything."

Zeb tossed Shelly a sideways glance. That information was supposed to be confidential. Yet he hadn't specifically excluded Helen from knowing it. And he was the one who forgot to shut the door to the meeting room. That Helen had the data was more or less inconsequential as she could be wholly trusted. However it was Helen's tendency to gossip that had Zeb ever so slightly concerned. In general she could keep lips zipped but you never knew what might accidentally pass through them.

Zeb read the note aloud so that Shelly could add her two cents worth. After all it was part of her assignment.

"Cleaning crew at MGIO. Bridge club last night. Missing? In love? Delayed? Have Zeb talk to Alma Link. Have Shelly check out Doctor Izdzán Proteus Gouyen."

When he stopped reading Zeb peered over the top of his glasses and spoke seriously to Helen.

"What is all of this in relation to?"

Helen pointed to the pair of chairs adjacent to her desk.

"Have a seat. This will be of interest to the both of you."

Zeb pulled back the chair for Shelly before taking a seat himself.

"Your note mentions Alma Link," said Zeb.

"She's your ladies bridge partner, right?" asked Shelly.

"Ever since my sister died, we've been Friday night bridge partners."

Zeb found it strange that Helen referred to his mother as her sister rather than by her name.

"Alma heads up the deep cleaning crew at MGIO. Mount Graham International Observatory has their own regular cleaning staff, but once a month Alma and six others make the trek up the mountain and do two solid twelve-hour days of deep cleaning. She's good at what she does, no doubt about it."

The explanation was anything but clear to Zeb.

"Yes, I'm sure she is excellent at her job. Helen, what does Alma Link have to do with Doctor Izdzán Proteus Gouyen?"

Helen's hair practically curled with excitement. She gasped out her answer.

"Maybe nothing. Maybe something. Even maybe something significant. I can only tell you what Alma told me."

"Yes?"

"Alma, like I said, heads up the deep cleaning crew at the LUCIFER telescope up on the Mount. She's been working up there for seven years now and she knows everyone and has all the gossip," explained Helen.

"Lucifer? I've heard that a dozen or more times. I know it has to do with the telescopes but I never asked anyone what it stands for?"

Shelly stepped in with an explanation of the acronym.

"Lucifer, or more aptly stated, L.U.C.I.F.E.R., stands for Large Binocular Telescope Near-infrared Utility with Camera and Integral Field Unit for Extragalactic Research. It's an imaging accessory for a telescope."

"That's a mouthful," said Zeb.

"The name officially changed to LUCI back in 2012, but everyone around here still calls it by its original name. Appropriate, I'd say, given the controversy it's stirred up."

"I remember all too well the trouble back in 2009 when it was dedicated," said Zeb. "I even recall who was involved in the set up. As I recall the creation of the Observatory involved the University of Arizona, the University of Minnesota, the University of Notre Dame, the University of Virginia, the Max Planck Institute in Germany and the Vatican in Rome."

"Good memory," said Helen. "Too bad you can't remember acronyms."

"Now if I could only remember to take out the trash on Wednesday nights, Echo would be a happy camper," replied Zeb.

His amusing statement was interrupted by a political point of Shelly's.

"The San Carlos Apache filed a lawsuit back then and it still goes on to this very day," said Shelly.

"Along with numerous other lawsuits regarding who owns the Mount," added Helen.

"Whether you agree with what happened regarding the property on the top of the Mount or not, the government used legal means to take what had been traditionally Native lands," said Zeb.

"Legally, they had every right to do that," said Helen. "But is what they did truly for the greater good? I'd say that question is up for debate."

"I don't think any of us would feel the government had any right at all to seize the top of the Mount if it was our privately held property," added Shelly. "And, it has been considered sacred land for hundreds of years."

The room quieted in agreement with Shelly's words. The three represented three separate points of view on many situations involving the Apache tribe. Helen, though compassionate, leaned toward the traditional old school method of interpretation of the law. Zeb was somewhere in the middle having married Echo, who was almost one hundred percent Apache in her beliefs. Shelly, because of her age and education was liberal when it came to all things that involved social issues regarding the Apache. They all well understood the need to agree to disagree.

"We were talking about something Alma Link told you at bridge club, weren't we?" asked Shelly.

"Yes. Yes. And yes."

"Go on," said Zeb.

"Alma knows every single employee of MGIO as well as all the gossip about every one of them. She overheard something and passed it on to me. I think she told me because I work here, at the sheriff's office."

"Makes sense to me. If there is a problem and Alma passed on the information to you so it would get here, that's called being a good citizen."

The interest on Zeb's face in conjunction with the expression on Shelly's face gave Helen more than enough impetus to carry the story forward. She even went so far as to radiate proudly for Alma's good work.

"This has to do with one of the research scientists who might be missing from MGIO."

Zeb and Shelly leaned in. Helen was in her zone, that zone being sharing factual gossip that might be helpful in finding the truth.

"Go on."

"One of the researchers, a woman, Doctor Izdzán Proteus Gouyen is a direct descendant of Geronimo. Technically that makes her a Bedonkohe Apache which is a branch of the Chiricahua tribe."

While Zeb figured her family history likely to be local lore, Shelly had a completely different take on it.

"Impressive," said Shelly. "That's a lineage to be proud of."

"What about Doctor Izdzán Gouyen?" asked Zeb.

"Six weeks ago she left the facility and headed out on a one-month vacation."

Zeb shook his head not certain he was following her point.

"Say what? Say that again."

"For goodness sakes, listen up or clean the wax out of your ears, Zeb. I said that she took off for a one-month vacation six weeks ago. In other words, she's late in returning back to work."

"Got it," replied Zeb.

"And neither hide nor hair has been seen or heard from her since."

"Does your friend, Alma, know what Doctor Gouyen looks like?"

"She does."

Zeb had a glimmer of hope that the dead woman, who clearly wasn't Apache, but was dark skinned enough to maybe pass as one, might now have a name attached to her.

"The description Alma shared with me was that of an 'early middle-aged Apache woman with light brown skin about thirty-five or forty years old.' Oh, and she said Doctor Gouyen was missing the tip of her left ear lobe. At least that's what Alma saw in a picture that was on the doctor's desk."

"Did your friend, Alma, ever see Doctor Gouyen face to face?"

"Oh, my yes. But she always wore her hair down, covering her ears. It was only when she saw the picture that she noticed the missing piece of earlobe."

Zeb nodded at Shelly who nodded back and tapped the secondhand information into her cellphone.

"Anything else? I mean did Alma mention anything else that you found particularly interesting?" asked Zeb.

"That was it. I thought it mattered because she might be missing and I know that no one has reported her missing, at least not to this office," replied Helen.

"You've done a good deed. We'll check into it. In the meantime have Alma come in and give us what she knows."

"Wait. Wait. There was something else. I remember it because Alma said one of those scientists up there said it. I hardly gave it a thought until I realized scientists don't speak like that."

"Yes? What did the scientist fellow have to say?"

"The scientist fellow was a woman."

"Sorry. What did the scientist woman have to say?"

"Alma said that she accidentally overheard the woman say that Doctor Gouyen was as skittish as a newborn foal right before she left on vacation. That's about the size of it."

"You've been a great help," said Shelly.

"You most certainly have," added Zeb.

"I'm grateful for being of help but I do have one request," said Helen.

"Yes, Helen?" asked Zeb. "What is it?"

"Will you let me know what you found out when you find it out?" asked Helen.

A long pause told Helen that possession of that sort of knowledge might be above her pay grade. But if something did come up, she knew she likely wouldn't be the last to know.

Chapter 16

DOCTOR IZDZÁN PROTEUS GOUYEN

A MEETING FOR COFFEE and tea at the Town Talk was set up by Zeb with Rambler and Echo. With plenty of evidence to pursue Zeb wasted no time in getting right to the point. Urging them to speak freely he extended his hands, palms up, in their direction.

"You two have long-term ties to the San Carlos. What do you know about Doctor Gouyen and her time there?"

Rambler politely waited for Echo to speak first.

"She's a little older than I am. The science teachers all talked about her like she was some sort of Einstein in the making. I never have liked the word brainiac. But in this case, from what I heard it is appropriate."

"She was good in science, I take it?"

"What we were told was that by the end of ninth grade she was far more advanced than any teachers in the science department. Her sophomore year she was a teacher's aide and during her junior and senior years she taught advanced classes in physics, math and chemistry to the other smart kids and at the community college," explained Echo.

"You read about people like that. It's interesting that more wasn't said around town about her and how brilliant she was," said Zeb.

"There's still a whole lot of people who believe Apaches are unintelligent and superstitious."

Zeb blushed at remembering his own youthful beliefs and prejudices. He had learned from his old man that all Apaches were the same, ignorant and superstitious.

"Any other general memories of her, Echo?"

"I don't really have any solid personal memories from school days. What I heard back in the day said she was a shy loner who was quiet and spoke barely above a whisper. I heard she didn't make friends easily, nor for that matter particularly try to create friendships. Of course that is all secondhand information. I can't prove any of it."

"It seems to fit the stereotype."

Zeb gulped. Had he stepped his foot into the hole of political correctness once again?

Echo said, "Sometimes there are stereotypes for a good reason."

Zeb sighed with relief.

"I did recognize her when we spoke at a conference for young women. We talked a few times after that. But to be honest, I really don't know that much about her. I do think I still have her phone number."

"Rambler? What do you know?"

"I never paid much attention to her. She was younger than me. I remember hearing she was a true genius, which I wasn't, so I sort of had her pegged as some kind of science nerd. I don't remember that she ever had a boyfriend. I remember seeing her around. She was always carrying a stack of books. I got the impression that she was her own best friend," added Rambler.

"Anything else you could add to that?"

"I checked her out one time."

Rambler stopped and looked at Echo knowing full well what his words sounded like.

"Even though she dressed poorly and her hair wasn't well kept, she had a way about her. You know. A weird kind of quiet confidence. It seemed to me she didn't give a shit what people thought of her because she probably really did know better. I kind of admired that quality I perceived in her. I thought about trying to talk to her so I'd understand how geniuses talk, ya' know. But I never got around to it."

"A little afraid of her, maybe, Rambler?" asked Echo.

An embarrassed Rambler hung his head.

"I've got some stuff, too. I had Shelly do a quick search on her," said Zeb. "Not like one a reporter would do, but one the government would do if they were doing a background check for an entry level position and wanted to make sure they could trust you."

Both Rambler and Echo agreed it was the right approach.

"As both of you have noted she was the star student in her class. After graduation she attended the California Institute of Technology on a full scholarship where she obtained a triple major in astronomy, astrophysics and physics."

"Makes sense," said Echo. "Very impressive."

"That's what people with giant-sized brains do, huh?" said Rambler.

"She was also involved in the Native American Women's Rights Movement. She and some of her cohorts took over a campus laboratory building with several other radical campus groups."

"Which ones?" asked Echo.

Zeb glanced at Shelly's report before answering.

"Along with the Native American Women's Rights Movement the other groups were The Animal Rights Coalition, The Young Communists League and Progressives Unite!"

"I would have never guessed that sort of radical behavior would come out of such a shy young woman," said Rambler. "Engaging in that kind of activity seems the opposite of what I saw in her."

Echo had a different take. She understood Izdzán's behavior as a necessary and normal part of her growth as a Native American woman.

"What were they demanding?" asked Echo.

"According to Shelly their demands were all over the place without any sense of coherency. They held the building for a few days and the administration bent to some of their demands and that was that."

"Rambler have you talked to any of her old friends from her days on the Rez?" asked Zeb.

"She didn't have many friends from what I found out. I did find one woman who claimed she had a romantic fling with her back in the day. It sounded like the sort of thing where they were experimenting with their sexuality the summer after their freshman year of college. The woman told me it didn't last long and when it ended so did their friendship. She hasn't talked with her since."

"Dead end," said Zeb. "On that one."

"Check at the church?"

"The Evangelical Free and Baptist churches have nothing on them."

"Mormon church? Maybe she and her family were followers of Joseph Smith?"

"If anyone would have reasonably accurate records on them, it would the Saints. Unfortunately for us, they don't have a single thing," replied Zeb. "Therefore the one thing I can tell you is that they were not Latter-Day Saints."

"Her parents?" asked Echo.

"Shelly's research showed they moved away without leaving a forwarding address. They were older. Might be dead by now. Shelly said there's seemingly no records of any kind after they moved away. No utility bills. No change of address on their DLs at the MVD. No state or IRS tax statements in decades. No Social Security checks have ever been issued to either of her parents. No government IDs of any kind. The list goes on but it all adds up to nothing. It's almost unheard of for Shelly, but she found exactly nothing at all when she looked into the usual everyday stuff we all have to deal with."

"A clever Apache can disappear in the middle of a sunny day and never be seen or heard from again. That's a good thing," said Rambler. "And a bad thing."

"Right," replied Echo. "We used to say we could disappear like a drop of rain on a July desert."

"No one I talked to knew anything. The entire family was quiet, didn't engage in social activities or have any long-standing friends. One day they just packed up and moved off the Rez. That was the last of them as far as anyone can figure," added Zeb. "I'll have Shelly doublecheck on them. See if she can track anything new down."

"I heard my name mentioned. Were you talking about me?"

Shelly had a knack for popping up out of the blue when she and her special talents were required.

"We were wondering about Doctor Gouyen's parents. Did you by any chance find out anything new?"

"Not two minutes ago I caught a break. They were killed in a car accident up on the Hopi reservation about two months ago. A truck ran into them head on. They were killed instantly as was the other driver who happened to be a kid who stole the truck to take it out for a joy ride, at least according to his friends."

"Bummer," said Echo. "That's a tough way to go."

"It's quick," said Rambler.

"Do you think Doctor Gouyen extended her vacation because of that? The death of her parents, I mean. We all know that when something like that happens in our lives we understand just how short life can be," said Zeb.

"It's possible, even likely that a situation like that pushed Doctor Gouyen into a state of depression or an extremely anxious state of mind," suggested Echo.

"Or something else altogether," added Rambler. "Like a spiritual crisis."

"Makes perfect sense to me and seemingly to all of us," replied Zeb. "After I read through any and all reports that I'd like Shelly to download, I might have more ideas."

"Already downloaded, Sheriff. And a paper copy, since I know you're not particularly fond of computers."

She handed Zeb a file.

"If necessary one of us will go up to the Hopi Reservation and check out the car-truck crash that took their lives. You had a Hopi girlfriend at one time, didn't you, Rambler?"

"I still might."

"Okay. If someone needs to go up there, you can do the trip."

"No need to worry about motel money if you send me. I've a place to lay my head up there that will save the county on expenses."

"Shelly, what specifics did you find out about what Doctor Gouyen did for work at the Observatory?"

"In a general sense, most of what she did is what all the other scientists do up there. Or it was in conjunction with what the other scientists do. All kinds of collaboration happens on every project in the Observatory world. But Doctor Gouyen has special government top-secret clearances along with the regular ones."

"Do you by any chance know what they, the top-secret clearances, were for?" asked Zeb.

"Sort of. Not exactly. But based on the scientific research the telescope she works on is linked to, and from her input to recently published data on the specific telescope she was most closely associated with, I can make an intelligent guess."

"Yes? What did she do?" asked Zeb.

"For you to understand what she does you need to know that telescopes can signal satellites and keep in communication with them very easily."

"So?"

"The United States military has been more or less secretly funding some, actually quite a bit of communications research up there on the Mount."

"For what purpose?"

"Remember during the war in Afghanistan when our drones would accidentally blow up a wedding party or a school bus or a church or make some horrible error in which innocents were killed? You all must remember it from the news?"

"Yes," said Echo. "It happened way too often."

"The military got terrible publicity so they wanted to make sure it happened as infrequently as possible. They started using communication between America's most powerful telescopes, satellites that made regular pass-overs near battlefields and the drones linked to that battlefield. When they figured out how to do that, mostly through Doctor Gouyen's research, they got much better control over the active drones and what they did. Her work is likely responsible for saving more than a few lives," explained Shelly.

"And the effort was responsible for the deaths of quite a few high-level combatants," added Echo.

"You know that's how war works," said Zeb.

The words, which could cut either way in Echo's head, popped out of Zeb's mouth before he even thought. Echo's facial reaction made it clear he should have been more thoughtful.

"You're right, Zeb. That is how war sometimes does its business."

Rambler, sensing the potential tension spoke up.

"That's some serious science," said Rambler. "Seems like she knew what she was doing."

"The military and therefore the DIA and NSA, have been paranoid that the technology of the telescope-satellite-drone system might be stolen and/or duplicated. So they've spent a ton of money to make certain it won't be. If someone had the same information, they could use the knowledge to make their drones better. Or they could use it to block the links between the satellites and the drones, thereby rendering U.S./Ukrainian drones ineffective, just as an example. Perhaps even worse, they could use the technology to take control of our drones. That's what her latest publication was all about," said Shelly.

"That begs the question why did the NSA sweep up the body of the dead woman so quickly?" asked Zeb. "Could she possibly have been linked to the MGIO, the satellites or the drone technology or even possibly Doctor Gouyen?"

"Great questions," replied Shelly. "I really am short of information linking the dead woman to much of anything, much less what you've just mentioned. I just don't know enough about her and don't have enough knowledge to make a reasonably educated guess."

"Who the hell was she?" asked Zeb. "That's what we need to find out. If we know who she is the rest of the information should flow in right after she's been ID'd."

"We need to figure out if she was linked to Doctor Gouyen. No matter how peripherally."

The room echoed with a lack of answers to these most basic of questions.

Chapter 17

STRANGE BEDFELLOWS

HELEN PULLED INTO THE sheriff's office parking lot her usual half hour before anyone else arrived. She was more than a little surprised to find Rambler sitting on the bench just outside the main door, drinking a cup of coffee in the morning sun with a newspaper folded on his lap. Helen made an indirect jab at his chronic tardiness and his rumored behaviors.

"Rambler, my oh my, but aren't you up early. Or didn't you go to bed last night?"

"I'm always up by now. I just have other things to do before I come to work."

"You have an early meeting with Zeb?"

"No. But I hope he's coming in this morning."

"He'll be here in ten minutes unless Echo's having him drive the kids to school."

"Can't they walk? I walked to school every single day. Is Zeb raising lazy kids?"

"Rambler you told me you rode your bike, then got a ride from your mother and then drove your own car when you were fourteen. You're going to have to learn to keep your stories straight," chided Helen.

"I must have walked to school before I learned to ride a bike. Yeah, that's it."

Helen joined him on the bench allowing the beautiful morning sunshine to bathe her face. The sunbeams were evidently opening her spirit.

"God sent us days like this for a reason."

"The Creator wants us to be happy. The world is full of pleasures," replied Rambler.

"Are you happy, Rambler? I mean really happy?"

"Now that is a curious question, Helen."

"Not really. I was just wondering about you as a friend."

"I am happy. My life is good. Like all us men I'm not as virile as I once was, but that's okay. By my age, I think I know what love is."

"I take it you have a new girlfriend?"

"Let's say I'm working on it and it feels like it's headed in the right direction. I've also recently learned that good things happen to those who are grateful."

"You're quite the philosopher this morning, aren't you Deputy Braing?"

"And what about you, Helen. Would you consider yourself to be a happy woman?"

"I am blessed in more ways than I can count. Living in this aging, earthly body doesn't take away from my happiness. If the good Lord didn't call us all home at some point and I know He will, I guess that I would choose to live as long as I possibly could just for the joy of it all. That is, if I remained healthy."

The two sat back, enjoying a few minutes of contemplative silence. Rambler, newspaper now tucked under his leg, sipped his coffee. Helen sipped lightly on her tea as she warmed her face with the sun's rays. They both knew this was one of those mornings that are deeply felt but all too soon forgotten. Both closed their eyes and sat back, drifting off in their minds. So deep were they in contemplation that neither heard Zeb as he walked down the sidewalk and ended up right next to them.

"Fine bunch of county employees. Sleeping on the job. Do you realize what sort of example you're setting for others who work for the county? To say nothing of the citizens who pass by, see you and assume their tax dollars are being wasted."

Both lazily opened their eyes. Zeb's words were taken without offense.

"You need to slow down, Zeb," said Rambler. "Enjoy life a little."

"It wouldn't kill you, young man, to spend a little more time with your children," said Helen. "They'll be grown and gone before you can blink your eyes too many more times."

"I hate to break up the tea party but we're still trying to catch a killer, among our other work," said Zeb. "What say we start the day?"

Helen stretched her arms over her head and let the rays of
the sun flow onto her face for ten more seconds before leading
the way into the office. Zeb and Rambler followed close on her
heels. Once inside Rambler followed Zeb directly into his office.

"Something big must be up with you showing up early," said
Zeb.

"I'm not late every day, am I?"

"Four out of five," replied Zeb.

"When I have good news, I come early. I might have something that will change the course of the murder investigation."

Rambler followed Zeb around his desk and pulled his chair
out for him.

"What's going on?" asked Zeb.

"Sit. I've got something to show you and I'm not sure what
your response is going to be."

"What is it?"

Rambler pulled out a year-old copy of the *San Carlos Tribal
News* that he'd stuffed into his back pocket and opened it on
Zeb's desk.

"What do we have here?"

"This morning I was packaging up some of my grandmother's
chinaware for my daughter. I haven't used the stuff in years. It's
been gathering dust for over a decade."

"Tell me about it. We've got both my mother's and my grandmother's sets stuffed away somewhere. We use it once a year at
most. Thanksgiving, I think."

"Echo allows you to use the good china for that holiday? It's
not exactly our people's favorite. It's a day replete with gluttony
and awash with false history."

Zeb shrugged. He wanted to do the right thing by the tribes as
much as he could, but there was no changing history. There was
only what was, what is and what might be.

"What'd you find hidden among your grandmother's china?"

"I found a stack of old newspapers. Don't ask me why, but I've
got years of the *Tribal News* in boxes in the attic. I grabbed a
pile to wrap up the chinaware with and I found this."

Rambler pointed at a picture on the front page of the year-old
newspaper. The headline read 'Apache Women of Today.' The
article was about successful Apache women and other success-

ful women setting an example for young women and teenagers in today's world. The picture was taken at the San Carlos Community Center. The article spoke of four successful women who spoke to young Apache girls, women and others. The article also spoke of the senior tribal women who attended the meeting to support the younger Apache women and girls and to learn about the world as it is today as opposed to the one they grew up in.

"Okay," said Zeb. "I get what the article is about. I remember Echo was there. She lost a bracelet that day, a turquoise one that Song Bird had made for her."

"Look at that picture closely."

The image had faded with time but it was clear that one of the four women in the picture was Echo. Another woman Zeb instantly recognized was Gabriella Cocheta, San Carlos Chief of Police. Zeb put on his glasses for a closer look. The third woman was identified as Doctor Izdzán Gouyen from MGIO.

"The missing Doctor Izdzán Gouyen? This meeting where she and Echo must have interacted did come up when I talked with Echo earlier. Maybe Echo knows more than she realizes?"

"She might. Now take a look at the last of the women."

Zeb stared at the face in disbelief. His doubletake was followed closely by a triple take. Unless his eyes were deceiving him he was looking at the face of the dead woman and she was dressed in a nun's habit.

The yellowed newspaper was crumpled right through her photo. To top it off the crinkle in the paper also made it impossible to read her name. Zeb stretched the paper, making sure not to tear it, to get a better look. He still couldn't read it. Rambler turned on the magnifying glass on his phone and handed it to Zeb who read the name out loud.

"Sister Tavisha Karpenko, Order of Saint Eustace."

"That's the Priory out by Solomon," said Zeb.

"Yes, I'm certain of it. Hard to forget a name like Eustace. Who knew there was a Saint Eustace?"

Zeb grumbled a few choice curse words under his breath. Rambler assumed he knew what Zeb was cursing for, but in truth, he was only guessing until Echo's knife came to mind.

"I know," said Rambler. "And I don't like that there's a prior link between Echo and the dead woman any more than you do."

"Them being in the same picture doesn't prove anything," replied Zeb.

"Other than they had contact with each other a year ago," responded Rambler.

"Which once again could have happened to anyone. It doesn't mean shit."

"It does beget some interesting questions that the Feds might probe into, should they know about it. And if I found this picture, they'll find it."

Zeb's temper began to rise. Rambler's implications were obvious.

"They know nothing about Echo finding the body. Don't forget that."

"We don't know what they know. It's a guessing game. They seized the dead woman's body and all the physical evidence for some reason we can't figure out. They destroyed everyone's cellphone records and Doc's notes. God knows what else they have or what they've done. Somebody might put one and one together and come up with something. We're not exactly in the driver's seat on this one when it comes to Echo."

Zeb slammed his fist on the desk before grabbing the picture Rambler had found.

"There's nothing to come up with. I know Echo didn't kill that woman."

"Let's hope you're right for her sake and yours. Not to mention Elan and Onawa."

Zeb felt like a plum pit was stuck in his throat as his heart sped up.

Chapter 18

SYRUP AND PENGUINS

ECHO AND THE KIDS were fast asleep by the time Zeb arrived home. He laid the picture from the *San Carlos Tribal News* on the kitchen table, not that he needed a reminder to discuss it with Echo.

The next morning Zeb awoke before anyone else and began making chocolate chip pancakes, everyone's favorite. By the time Echo rousted the kids and hustled them down for breakfast he had made a large enough stack of pancakes to feed the proverbial army.

Elan and Onawa shouted out their enthusiasm and immediately began a bragging interchange about who could eat the most pancakes. Zeb allowed them to butter and syrup their own pancakes, which proved to be a messy mistake. As all that was happening in the background Echo picked up the year-old San Carlos tribal newspaper and took a look at her picture with the other women before laying it in front of Zeb.

"Why do you have this picture sitting out?" asked Echo.

"Do you remember it being taken?"

"Of course I do. It's at the San Carlos Community Center. Where'd you come across this? It must be from over a year ago."

"It's about that old. Rambler found it mixed among some junk he'd saved."

"I didn't imagine Rambler to be a hoarder. But I can see him as someone who never throws anything away."

Zeb smiled. There was much about Rambler that no one knew or even suspected.

"What can you tell me about the other women in the picture?"

"Can I ask why you're asking me about them?"

"You'll see. I'd tell you but it might prejudice your response."

"From the tone of your voice it sounds like you're interrogating me."

The defensive note in Echo's voice was more than a little out of character from her normal way of responding. The hint of instinctual doubt that Zeb called the little man in his gut reared its head. He suppressed the little man. Now was not the time to doubt Echo.

"I'm not interrogating you. I just want to know a few things about the picture and the day it was taken."

"Yeah. Right."

Zeb slid the picture directly in front of Echo.

What Zeb couldn't know was that Echo was defensive because it felt like he was speaking out, however subtly against the advancement of women in society. Echo was no radical but it was time Apache women, all women for that matter, spoke with stronger voices and that their voices were heard. Speaking to young women on how to become better at whatever they chose to become in life was becoming a mission of Echo's. She didn't care one bit for being called to task for something she was doing for the greater good of women. And for those of the next generation, like her own daughter.

Zeb pointed to the woman on the far left.

"You know Gabriella Cocheta, the chief of police."

"Yes, of course," replied Echo. "I've known her for quite a while. You probably know as much about her as I do. She's politically ambitious. She runs a tight ship on the Rez from what I hear. She's a woman working her way up the political ladder rung by rung and sometimes faster. A bit ambitious, but what political animal isn't?"

"What do you think of her? Other than her political ambitions, that is?"

"I like her for the most part. I'm not political because that game turns me off to be honest. But that's the path she's chosen. She's playing in a field that has always been dominated by men and not necessarily good men."

"Not all men are bad, even when it comes to politicians," interjected Zeb.

"Did I say they were? Regardless of what men are or aren't, Gabriella is starting at a deep deficit. She's a woman, a minority and an Apache to boot. That's not an easy starting spot. I guess I can pull for her because I almost always give the underdog a shot."

"Is she honest?"

Echo laughed so loudly, Elan and Onawa stopped eating their pancakes and began to listen in.

"She's a politician. Need I say more?"

"Well..."

"What's this all about anyway?"

"Be patient."

Zeb pointed to the next woman in the picture, Doctor Izdzán Gouyen. Echo examined the woman's face closely before speaking.

"This is the woman you asked me and Rambler about. The one who is away on vacation, right? She is an interesting woman. She is a direct descendant of the famous Chiricahua Chief Geronimo. Her clan got moved to the San Carlos when the Apache Wars ended in 1872. Listening to her speak you can tell she comes from long line of *nantan*. I listened closely to her speech. It was inspirational to everyone present. She works up on the Mount on the radio frequency telescope, which happens to be her area of expertise. In her speech she made a very complex scientific subject easily understood by everyone. I'd have to say she gave the best speech of the day. I was certainly impressed. In fact I met with her for coffee twice after that. Once up at the Observatory in the cafeteria and once at the Town Talk. I didn't mention any of this earlier because you only asked me about her early years on the Rez."

"What's she like away from her work?"

"Good question. She is so dedicated to what she does that I doubt she thinks about much else. To be honest I found her a bit socially awkward at first. After we talked a while she loosened up and talked a little bit about herself."

"Do you remember anything she told you?"

"Why are you asking?"

"This is all confidential."

"Of course."

"She might be missing. I'm looking into it. We don't yet know for certain if she is missing. It's just some things aren't adding up."

"What's going on?"

"She took a month off of work to travel the United States."

"Did she go with someone?"

"As far as we can tell we think she went by herself. But we don't know for certain."

Echo pulled out her cellphone.

"Who are you calling?"

"Doctor Gouyen."

"If she answers ask her where she is and when she's coming back."

"If you don't mind I think I'll say hello first."

Zeb realizing his aggressiveness in telling Echo how to handle an ordinary task, apologized. Echo let it ring until a computerized voice advised her that the number she was calling was no longer in service. Echo looked at her phone quizzically before explaining to Zeb what she'd just heard.

"Can I have her number, please? She's probably changed it, but I'd like it anyway."

"Certainly. I assume you're going to have Shelly backtrack and see what she can find out."

"Bingo," replied Zeb.

"Bingo," echoed Elan and Onawa.

Elan began singing.

"B-I-N-G-O."

And was immediately joined by Onawa.

"B-I-N-G-O."

After multiple verses of 'Bingo,' one of their favorite songs, Zeb interrupted their fun.

"Finish your breakfasts."

"Let them sing," said Echo. "It's good for their spirits."

With their mother's permission the kids singing became much louder. When they became raucous Echo put an end to it.

"If you want to go on the field trip to see the nuns at the Priory, you'd better finish your breakfast."

"Penguins," said Elan. "Nuns' clothes make them look like penguins."

"Be nice," said Echo. "That's the way religious women dress."

"Okay. But they still look like penguins."

"Elan, listen to your mother."

The precocious eight-year-old understood the seriousness of his father's voice.

"Yes, sir."

"Do you really believe she's missing?" asked Echo.

"She's two weeks overdue in returning to work and hasn't contacted anyone at the observatory. We've run her through the national data base of missing persons and nothing has come up."

"Strange," said Echo. "The few times I've interacted with her she seemed like one of the most responsible people I've ever met."

"That doesn't mean something might not have happened to her," replied Zeb. "Now, is there anything that you can remember about your conversations with her that might help us find her?"

"She said that someday she wanted to visit the Grand Canyon, Niagara Falls, drive through the heart of the country to see how big American actually is and visit the land Indians tribes from all across the country lost to the Whites. Nothing really out of the ordinary as far as I remember."

"If that's what she's doing, it sounds like she's on a pilgrimage," said Zeb.

"Yes. It's the kind of trip every Native should take."

Zeb had never considered looking at the whole of America through Indian eyes. The thought stopped him dead in his tracks whereas Echo seemed to take the statement for granted. And she was right. Every American native, be they Indian, White, Black, Hispanic or whatever should consider taking such a trip to better understand their homeland.

"You're right, Echo. Absolutely right."

"I know. We all end up living in our own small worlds. We all need to get out and see the land that now belongs to all of us, regardless of who conquered whom."

Zeb's mind lit up. He made a mental vow to show Elan and Onawa the United States.

"Well, if you do remember something unusual, please let me know."

"Got it. I'll root around in my memory and see if I come up with anything that might help you find Doctor Gouyen."

"Now look closely at the woman standing between you and Doctor Gouyen."

The newspaper was old and yellowed. Something had been spilled on the paper near the woman's face. Echo took out her cellphone and used her magnifying app.

"Her face is hardly clear. It's difficult to make out. About all I can see is that she is dressed in a nun's habit."

"Keep looking."

"Wait! What? Am I looking at who I think I'm looking at?"

Zeb waited as he let Echo study the image. Finally he spoke.

"You tell me who you think you're looking at."

"Do you have any other pictures from the event that would give me a better look at her?"

"Rambler has been trying to track some down. No luck yet. The paper didn't keep any pictures on file. The photographer deleted all of them from her camera and so far no one who was there has come forth with any cellphone or camera pictures."

"From what I can make out she looks an awful lot like the dead woman I found. But I can't make a positive ID from the picture, the story in the paper or my memory."

"My thoughts exactly," added Zeb. "The article refers to her as Sister Tavisha Karpenko of the Saint Eustace Priory in Solomon."

"I remember the name. As for identifying her as the dead woman, I'm truly sorry. I wish I could say for sure. But I honestly can't."

Echo's eyes seemed transfixed by the photograph.

"It's a hard image to see clearly. It took Rambler pointing her out in the picture for me to figure out that you might have met her. And then I wondered why you didn't recognize her the instant you saw her lying dead."

Echo bristled. "A woman dressed in hunting clothes lying dead in the desert looks a whole lot different than the same woman dressed in a nun's habit. The surprise to me is that you recognized her at all."

"Okay," Zeb said. "You're right. I think something just clicked when Rambler pointed her out to me."

"What's your next step?"

"I'll make some contacts with people who might have known both Sister Karpenko and Doctor Gouyen and see if they knew each another. I'll have Shelly dig around. I'll take a trip down to the Priory in Solomon..."

"Why don't you just come with us and see the penguins?"

"Elan. Enough," warned Echo.

"Yeah, come with us Daddy," said Onawa. "You can see the Sisters of Saint Eustace with us."

Zeb patted his children on the head.

"As much as I'd love to go with you three, I'll wait until tomorrow. I don't want to spoil your visit by making my presence official business. I have enough other stuff to do on the case right now. It can wait until tomorrow or the next day. My guess is that somebody down there probably knows something that we don't know."

"Okay."

Echo's reply was paired with two kids' frowning faces.

"I gotta run," said Zeb.

The kids, syrup all over their hands and faces threw their arms around their daddy and gave him kisses and hugs, after which Zeb grabbed a wet hand towel and cleaned himself up, smiling all the while. Echo walked him to the front door.

"What's the reason for your trip down to the Priory?" asked Zeb.

The look on Echo's face was that of a woman who had told her husband the answer to his question multiple times already and knew that he must've been listening with only half an ear.

"Class trip. Does that ring a bell?"

"Uh, er, uh, no?"

"The girls and women who heard Sister Karpenko speak, especially the grandmothers were interested in learning more about the Orthodox religion and what it is the nuns do. I guess they all thought she gave a very compelling speech last time she talked about girl power."

"Hmm."

"I believe we have as many chaperones going along as we do students. I would venture a guess some of the grandmothers are doing a bit of snooping as well."

"I'll keep that in mind," said Zeb. "Who knows what they might pick up and what I might be able to learn from it."

"Good idea. You know how sharp some of those older women are."

"Maybe some of them took pictures?" said Zeb.

"I'll check around. I'll also see if Sister Tavisha Karpenko is around and if she really does look like the dead woman I found."

Zeb checked himself to make sure he was syrup-free before holding Echo close and kissing her goodbye.

"Have a good trip and good luck checking out Sister Tavisha."

Echo kissed him one last time.

"No worries cowboy, I'm on it."

Chapter 19

TELESCOPES

WHEN CONSTRUCTION ON THE International Observatory began back in 1989 Zeb was a teenager and paid precious little attention to what was going on. As an adult he'd driven up the Mount on numerous occasions for picnics and fishing. Twice he'd visited the actual telescopes, mostly just to get a layout of the land in case he ever got called there on a professional basis.

Zeb had also heard some scientists speak publicly about what they did. Several of the meetings involved the town council regarding changes at MGIO. Those meetings were technical and boring. He also once attended a public meeting about the telescopes and the work they did but he found that information flew in one ear and promptly shot out the other. The science of it all was something he would never truly understand.

His only significant interactions regarding MGIO were his run-ins with the late Eskadi Black Robes when he was the Tribal Chairman. At that time Eskadi was working around the clock, getting anyone he could to join him in a lawsuit to return the land atop Mount Graham where the telescopes were situated back to the San Carlos Apache Tribe. Eskadi's claim was that *Dzil Nchaa Si'an*, the Athabaskan name for Mount Graham was eternally sacred ground to the tribe and therefore protected by treaties made with the U.S. government.

Zeb's awareness of the court battle between MGIO and the Apache Tribe was that it was decades old and no nearer to settlement than the day the first lawsuit had been filed.

After years of blissful ignorance he now needed to know what sort of scientific work was going on up on the Mount. Shelly would be his best bet on that. He knocked on her office door and walked right in.

"Shelly, you got a minute?"

"Of course, Zeb. What's up?"

"What do you know about the telescopes atop Mount Graham?"

"You want a one minute answer to that? Sorry. Can't help you. Google it."

"What? Why?"

"It's going to take more than a minute to give you even a rough outline. Maybe if you asked me what exactly you want to know, well, that might make it easier."

"I know there are three telescopes," replied Zeb. "One belongs to the Vatican..."

"That would be the Vatican Advanced Technology Telescope also known as VATT. It doesn't technically belong to just the Vatican, although they provided most of the funding."

"Why did the Vatican choose Mount Graham to locate a telescope?"

"Good question. The Vatican has been using the world's largest telescopes to study the universe since 1582. Back then I presume they were quite literally looking for God and in the name of the Church claimed all they could see as their own."

"They assumed ownership of the universe?"

"You could pretty much put it that way. Today they take a significantly more scientific approach to space and all that is out there."

"Decent of them."

"In one way, yes, but in another way, not so much."

"Meaning what?"

"The information they gather is shared with the international scientific community at large. But the land on which the telescopes sit is quite another matter."

"I presume you're referring to the ongoing court battle with the Apache tribe."

"Precisely. They, and the other groups that have put telescopes up on the Mount don't believe the Apache have any rights to the land on Mount Graham which was traditional Apache territory for ages. In court they've even gone so far as to denounce the religious beliefs of the Apache."

"That seems strange. Why bother to denounce the Apache religious beliefs?"

"Good question. It seems pointless to have done so, but they did. Maybe they did it because what they are looking for is the subject of much controversy and conspiracy."

"What are they looking for?"

"Life, the universe and everything, I guess."

"That's their goal?"

"It seems to be," replied Shelly.

"That seems absurd."

"Here's how ridiculous it gets. VATT, the telescope the Vatican does its research from on Mount Graham is situated right next to a large binocular telescope with a near-infrared spectroscope unit with camera and integral field for extragalactic research. Those who like acronyms dubbed it LUCIFER."

"Devil of a nickname."

"That would be funny if some of those who speak out against it didn't actually call it Satan's work."

"I imagine the Catholic Church doesn't much like that."

"They don't. And with the name LUCIFER comes all kinds of talk about extraterrestrials, one world government, Area 51 and all the usual weird stuff of conspiracy buffs."

"I can see it happening."

"In truth what is called LUCIFER isn't really a telescope at all but an imaging module for the large binocular telescope or LBT, that is up there too. Lastly there is the HHT which is a submillimeter radio telescope."

"I have a general idea of what telescopes do. Well, actually, no I don't. What is the primary purpose of these scopes?"

"Like I said earlier they're taking a long-distance peek into the universe to see what's out there."

"That's it?"

"That's not enough?"

"Do they have civilian uses, like say predicting global warming, that kind of thing?"

"They do have uses that are practical in everyday life. But none of those seem directly pertinent to our missing scientist," replied Shelly.

"You mentioned their military use a while back. Do you have anything to add to that?"

"I really don't have much else to add to what I've already said."

"From what Echo has told me the Department of Defense spends tens of billions of dollars on all sorts of things that could spy on you or me or anyone in any country at any time."

"Zeb, you're sounding a bit like a conspiracy nut."

"Just wondering. I'm not saying the scientists on Mount Graham are in collusion with the government militarily. However, it just doesn't seem to be out of the realm of possibility when I think about it."

"These telescopes, like you already know, do have the ability to connect with orbiting satellites, grab all kinds of data and beam that information back to earth. That most certainly could have other military implications or some other governmental espionage applications. But I highly doubt anything along those lines is their primary mission. They have bigger fish to fry."

"Look into it a little deeper, would you? I mean see what you can learn about the telescopes and the imaging module."

"I can put some time in on that. It would be helpful to know what you expect to learn. If I know what you're looking for I can maybe get there more quickly."

"That's just it, Shelly, I don't know what I want to learn. I want you to figure that out for me."

"You're the boss."

The minute Zeb had raised the specter of other military or espionage applications regarding the telescopes, Shelly's mind began to recall some of the odd conspiratorial articles she had briefed in the past. Most of them bordered on kookiness. Many of them were little more than deep craziness. However, a few had a touch of reality surrounding them, especially those that gave intelligent consideration to the military applications of telescope science.

Shelly allowed her mind to wander just to the periphery of possibility of there being something more going on with the telescopes. Would the government kill to stop certain information from being disseminated? She shook her head. Of course they would.

It was time to take a peek behind the curtain.

Chapter 20

PRIORY

ECHO WAS AMONG THE group of parental chaperones who rode the school bus to Solomon for the class outing at the Saint Eustace Priory. She sat in the back of the bus keeping an eye on how the kids, especially her children, interacted with the others. For the most part all of the boys and girls were well behaved and respectful. She found that general quality heartening.

Naline Pingjarji, the third grade teacher did an excellent job as she spoke to her class about the reasons for their visit to the Priory.

"Please be respectful of everyone and each other. The women of the Priory are called nuns but they have names just like all of us do. The head of the Priory is called the Prioress. Her name is Prioress Anna Nichinka. Any questions?"

"Will they talk to us?"

"Yes they will talk to you."

"Do they speak our language?"

"They do speak English. If they tell you their names, let's say one of them is named Mary, you will call her Sister Mary."

A boy in the back raised his hand.

"Yes?"

"Why do the sisters dress so funny?"

"Their dress is called a tunic. What they cover their heads with is called a coif. And their belt is called a cincture."

Another hand shot up.

"I don't think I can remember those new words."

"Don't worry. You can always ask the Sisters what something is called and they will be glad to tell you."

"Do we have to go to church today?"

"No. But I am sure they will show us their beautiful chapel."

The twenty children as well as fifteen chaperones were greeted by the Prioress as they departed the school bus. Her hands folded she smiled brightly at the children who lined up neatly in two rows. Behind them the chaperones stood at attention.

"Hello children. Welcome. My name is Prioress Anna, but you may call me Anna."

In unison the children responded, "Hello Anna."

"What should we show you first?" asked the Prioress.

The children were immediately put at ease by the very nice woman.

"Where do you eat? Can we have a snack?"

"Young man, I do believe after your long and bumpy ride out here..."

"It wasn't bad. We sang songs."

"Then you must be thirsty as well as hungry."

"Yes!"

"Follow me."

Anna turned and skipped down a stone pathway to the luncheon hall. Behind her the children mimicked her while managing to somehow stay in a single file. Near the end of the line Elan mimicked a penguin waddle until Echo flicked the back of his ear with her finger.

Inside the hall the children sat at two long tables as several of the sisters served them bread, honey and lemonade.

"Our bees make the honey. We bake the bread in our kitchen. The lemonade is squeezed fresh from lemons we grow in our orchard."

"My mom bakes bread," said one the children.

"We have honey bees," added another.

"It is lovely to hear such joyous children's voices," said Prioress Anna.

Her words were far more impressive to the chaperones than they were to the young students who downed the honeyed bread and lemonade like they hadn't eaten all day. When they finished eating one of the girls politely asked how many sisters lived at the Priory and did they have to share bedrooms like she did with her sister?

"Each of us has our own private room. There are twelve Sisters of Saint Eustace and myself, the Prioress. That makes a total of thirteen of us."

"Is thirteen an unlucky number for you?"

"No. I know that there is a belief that thirteen brings no blessing with it, but that is not our belief. All numbers come from God, so they are all lucky numbers."

"Have any of you children ever heard of Saint Eustace?" asked the Prioress.

Onawa's hand shot in the air.

No one was more surprised than Echo. Onawa had previously said nothing to her about learning anything of Saint Eustace.

"Yes, young lady. Can you tell the others what you know about our blessed saint?"

"Saint Eustace is the patron saint of hunters. My grandfather likes to hunt. My dad hunted when he was a boy. Now he's a sheriff."

"I see someone did their homework. What else do you know about Saint Eustace?"

"He lived in Rome a long time ago. I don't know where Rome is but I think it is in another country. Eustace loved to hunt. In fact, he was a great hunter."

"He used a bow and arrow and harvested enough animals to feed many, many people," added the Prioress.

"He's the patron saint of hunters because he had a vision of a Christian cross between a deer's antlers," added Onawa. "Before then he was a pagan."

As the Prioress explained what a pagan was, a flash of lightning shot through Echo's brain. The dead woman's amulet. She had to have been a follower of Saint Eustace or known someone who was. Was there indeed a connection to the nun, Sister Tavisha Karepenko, who spoke at last year's conference? Patience urged her to wait and ask Prioress Anna whether one of their nuns or friends who had been gifted a Saint Eustace amulet was missing.

"You're a smart young lady. Did you also know that this vision converted him to Christianity?"

Every one of the kids and chaperones shook their heads no.

"It did and his feast day is September the second."

"What's a feast day?"

"A feast day is like a festival or a holiday."

"Like Christmas?"

"In a way it is. But it's not as important as Christmas. In this case, on September second we celebrate the life of Saint Eustace. We have a meal in his honor and pray in his name."

"Cool."

"I hope they have a feast named after me someday."

"You never know young lady. Someday you just might have a feast day in your honor."

The Prioress gave a brief explanation of how such a thing might be possible before suggesting the children line up for a tour of the grounds, the chapel and various working buildings of the Priory.

As Anna showed them the grounds Echo lingered in the background. Periodically, when the option arose, she introduced herself to any of the Sisters who seemed available and appeared friendly. At the edge of the building that was used as a butcher shop she spotted the woman she believed to be Sister Tavisha. Echo looked around checking to see if Sister Tavisha would be approachable without interfering with anything that was going on. What was truly on her mind was the question of whether the woman was indeed Sister Tavisha. If it was her, then quite obviously the dead woman was not Sister Tavisha. Echo approached her with an open mind and a great deal of curiosity. When her eyes landed on the nun, she knew right away that this was indeed the woman she had met previously on the San Carlos Reservation.

"Sister Tavisha?"

The woman was standing near a large electric meat-cutting saw. Next to the machine were several tubs full of meat. The woman Echo assumed to be Sister Tavisha was wearing hearing protection. With the saw running she apparently didn't hear Echo, so Echo moved into a position where the Sister would see her. When she did, the nun cut power to the saw and removed her hearing protection. When Sister Tavisha turned to Echo, Echo saw no hint of recognition in her eyes. She didn't find it particularly odd since they had only met once previously.

"Sister Tavisha?"

The nun seemed to hesitate before responding.

"Yes?"

The Sister studied Echo carefully.

"I'm..."

Sister Tavisha held up her hand to stop Echo from speaking.

"No. Don't tell me. I like to think I'm good with names. You, you are the wife of the Sheriff of Graham County, Zeb Hanks. Your name is coming to me. Echo, Echo Skysong? Am I correct?"

"I didn't think you'd remember me. We've only met each other one time."

Tavisha's mind, from the look Echo observed in her eyes, was spinning through past acquaintances.

"Yes. Of course, I remember you. We met at the school, right?"

"Close. We met on the San Carlos Reservation Community Center when you and I along with Tribal Police Chief Gabriella Cocheta and Doctor Izdzán Gouyen from the Mount Graham International Observatory were speaking to young girls about future opportunities."

Echo watched Sister Tavisha as she seemed to be trying to retrieve a memory of the encounter.

"That was quite a day, wasn't it? The enthusiasm of children is priceless. Especially that of young girls."

Echo breathed a sigh of relief, grateful that the dead woman she had found that day had not been Sister Tavisha.

"It was a wonderful day. I remember your presentation very well and how the young women were moved by what you said."

"That is so very kind of you. Thank you, Echo Skysong."

"I take it that you handle the butchering?" asked Echo.

"I am the huntress and the butcher for the Priory. It may sound odd to an American, but it is an honor here at the Priory for me to hunt, kill, dress, cut up, prepare and wrap any game that I have hunted and harvested. I am blessed to be able to help feed all of us who live here as well as our guests. It is my mission."

"I fully understand your calling," replied Echo.

In the near distance the children, led by Prioress Anna, were heading toward the butchery. Sister Tavisha's head turned. Echo did a doubletake as the Sister's head moved to the exact angle the head of the dead woman had when Echo had come across it. In Echo's mind, the two women were identical. She tried to shake the thought from her head but continued seeing the dead woman in her hunting gear as she looked at Sister Tavisha's profile.

Echo couldn't help herself. She glanced down at Sister Tavisha's boots. They looked similar if not identical to the ones the dead woman was wearing. Instinct and training took over as she discreetly looked at the woman's wrist. Echo subtly searched for a birthmark but ran into an instant dead end as Tavisha's hands were gloved for the work she was doing. Boots covered her ankles where a Z could possibly be tattooed. While Tavisha looked at the cutting board Echo surveilled the room for anything that might tell her something more. Her eyes landed on the wall directly east of the meat-cutting machine where a rack of guns was displayed. Several Henry .30-.30s, as closely as she could discern, were similar if not identical to the one she found lying under the dead woman.

"Excuse me for a moment while I wash my hands. I want to clean up for our guests."

"Of course," replied Echo.

Leaning over the sink Sister Tavisha removed her gloves. In the dimly lit room Echo did not spy a birthmark. But when Sister Tavisha bent over, a necklace could be seen around her neck. Echo edged in closer. The solitary light over the wash sink provided just enough light for Echo to spot what seemed to be a close match to the stag deer and hunter amulet worn by the dead woman. She was unable to tell whether or not the Christian cross was woven in between the right and left antlers. Although Sister Tavisha was obviously not dead, was she somehow involved with the death of the woman?

After scrubbing away the blood and gristle from cutting meat Sister Tavisha wiped her hands. Reaching to the edge of the sink she grabbed a ring and slipped it on the fourth finger of her right hand. Noticing that Echo was watching her, Tavisha stopped and asked a question that seemingly came out of the blue.

"Do you like horses?"

"I've had one nearly all my life," replied Echo.

"Good. Come with me."

Leaving the visitors to Prioress Anna, Sister Tavisha led Echo to the horse barn where eight beautiful, well-groomed horses were kept. As Sister Tavisha explained the history of the Priory and their use of horses, Echo's eye fell on the saddles with their colorful saddle strings attached. Nearby, other saddle strings in various stages of preparation hung on a line. She walked over, grabbed a single colorful string and wet it with her mouth, keeping her back to Sister Tavisha.

"We make our own saddle strings. Not only are they functional but they are practically art."

Echo had been so focused on the saddle strings that she missed what Sister Tavisha said.

"Oh, I'm sorry. It's just that these caught my eye. They're so unique."

"Of course," said Tavisha. "You must have been lost in thought as I was just talking about them."

She immediately saw Echo's embarrassment and told her not to worry.

"People often lose themselves in beautiful objects."

Sister Tavisha ran some saddle strings through her hand. Echo held onto the one she had dampened. Tavisha, noting Echo's interest in the string, asked her if she had a question.

"I do have a question, as a matter of fact."

"Yes?"

"These little marks on the ends of the saddle strings. Do they have meaning?"

Tavisha tugged a little more than she needed to as she took the specific saddle string from Echo's hand and gave it a close look. She didn't miss the fact that Echo had moistened the end of the string.

"Oh, your hands are sweating. Are you warm?"

Echo was surprised how quickly she could produce a lie to a woman in a religious order.

"Just a touch. A bee stung me earlier. I put my hand in a bucket of water, that one near the sink, just a moment ago. Right before I grabbed the saddle strings."

"Yes, of course. Is the sting okay or would you like some bee sting ointment?"

"I'm good. You were saying about the saddle strings?"

"Yes. Each person who makes these puts their own little mark on the end of each string. It's our way of expressing individuality. Some find it curious. I find it artistic."

Trying to be nonchalant, Echo took a closer look at the ends of the leather strings that were still hanging up. She could clearly see what Zeb had described to her earlier, something he had seen when Clarissa and he had revisited the death site. Burnt into the tips of the saddle strings was a stag with a cross in the antlers.

"Who made these?" asked Echo.

Sister Tavisha pulled the saddle string Echo had been holding earlier close to her eye. By now it was almost dry.

"Let me see," said Tavisha. "Yes, these were made by..."

She stopped in mid-sentence. Echo observed as much as one possibly can, the nun's mind doing a flip-flop. Being the Knowledge Keeper, Echo's skills in this area were far beyond those who had been less fully trained in observation.

Sister Tavisha feigned getting something in her eye, pulled back and started anew.

"Why these are mine. How silly of me. I should have recognized them from across the room. Come let us join the others."

Echo ran her fingers across the saddle strings as she closely followed on Sister Tavisha's heels.

Chapter 21

DOPPLEGÄNGERS

ZEB'S CELLPHONE BUZZED. HE imagined it was Echo or one of the kids wanting to tell him about their trip to the Saint Eustace Priory. But instead of Echo or the kids' names popping up on the screen, it was Doc Yackley's.

"Zeb."

"Doc. What's up?"

"I suspect in about five minutes you're going to have a couple of federal visitors..."

"Any particular type of Fed?"

"Don't interrupt me Zeb. Let me finish what I was about to say."

"That I'm going to have a couple of Feds coming to the office to see me?"

"That's why you need to let me finish. I was going to say they're coming to see you if you're at home. But here's the deal. They ain't lookin' for you."

"Who are they looking for? Echo?"

"Damn straight."

"What kind of Feds are we talking about anyway?"

"Investigators of some sort. They flashed their badges so fast that I couldn't tell what branch of government they worked for. They talked even faster. Hot shots. Young bucks. One guy that looked like a right out of the book, cookie cutter Utah Mormon just graduated from college. The other one was an Apache. I'm certain of that."

"Probably FBI," replied Zeb. "They've always hired lots of Mormons, going all the way back to Hoover's days. I'd bet they're hiring Native Americans now to balance out quotas."

"That'd be my guess, too," replied Doc.

"What'd they want?"

"They were snooping about that dead woman you and Echo found in the mountains."

"The NSA already have the body. What'd the FBI, if that's who they were, want from you?"

"I can't rightly say that I can give you a straight answer on that one. They beat so far around the bush I have no idea what they wanted. That is, other than they were hoping I could tell them who killed that poor woman."

"How the hell do they expect you to know that?"

"Beats the tar and nicotine outta me. They seemed to think I know a whole lot more that I can possibly tell them."

"Did they try to trip you up on something specific?"

"Hell yes they tried. They didn't get anywhere 'cuz they were sniffin' around about the murder weapon."

Zeb didn't like the sound of that.

"The murder weapon? We all know it's a knife. With their advanced forensics they probably know what kind of knife it was or at least what metal the blade is made of."

"They know all that and more. Seems they've got a list of everyone in the county who ever purchased an Emerson CQC6. How the hell they figured it out that specifically from just the incisions made by the knife is beyond my expertise."

"How they got a list of CQC6 owners is more than a little weird, too," added Zeb.

"Your friendly government knows more about you than you know about yourself."

"Why'd they come to you, Doc?"

"I own two of them sons a bitches. Great knives if I must say so myself."

"I don't own one," said Zeb.

"But Echo does," replied Doc.

"How do you know that? The Feds say something to you about her knife?"

"They didn't need to."

"What?"

"I had one sitting on the passenger's seat of my old Caddy one day and Echo commented on it. Said she had one just like it. We both talked about how much we liked 'em. She also mentioned how easily it could cut through tactical clothing, even leather when it was properly sharpened. She told me the special forces guys love them. She said the elite commandos called them surgeon's scalpels. You at home? Echo there?"

"No. I'm at the office. Echo is on a field trip to the Saint Eustace Priory with the kids' school class."

"Nice women, those Sisters. Do a lot of good charitable work in the community. Don't cause fuss to anyone. Bunch of 'em are patients here at the clinic, even though they mostly like to do their own doctoring. Natural stuff for the most part. One of the Sisters is trained as a registered nurse. Sometimes she works a few overnight E.R. shifts on holidays when everybody wants time off. The other nurses say she's top notch at her job."

"As soon as I hang up I'll let Echo know she's got some federal boys coming her way. Thanks Doc. Appreciate the heads up."

"You and Echo be careful. Those fellas that stopped by here were full of bad juju."

Doc's final words cracked Zeb up. Doc was one hundred percent a country doctor but he loved to use twists of a phrase that sometimes caught his fellow conversationalists by surprise. Zeb's thought was simple. God bless you, Doc. You're a good man. One of a kind. I hope you live a long, long time. We all need you. With that he called Echo who answered after a few rings. In the background was the high-pitched racket of a bunch of excited kids making joyful noises.

"You still on the school bus?"

"You might say hi to your honey bunch before you start throwing questions at her," replied Echo.

"Hey, sunshine. I want to hear all about the trip to the Priory from you and the kids. How'd the day go?"

"Interesting," replied Echo. "I've got some strange things to share with you."

"Regarding anything or anyone in particular?"

"Precisely a someone. Now what's so urgent on your end?"

"What sort of strange things?" asked Zeb.

Echo lowered her voice, not that anyone could hear her over the din the children were making.

"Do you know what a doppelgänger is?"

"I've heard the word. Don't remember exactly what it means. Educate me."

"A doppelgänger is a biologically unrelated look-alike of a living person."

"Like an identical twin only not related?"

"Right."

"You saw one I take it?"

"I did."

"Was it the twin of anyone you know?"

"It was. And it was also someone you've seen."

"Now you've got my curiosity aroused. Who?"

"I swear to God I saw the doppelgänger of the dead woman we found."

"You saw this woman at the Priory? You saw a double of the dead woman we found at the Priory? Today?"

"I did. I'm sure of it."

"Did she have any of the identifying marks of the dead woman?"

"Therein lies the rub. I couldn't find any of the specific identifying marks, which makes sense if she's a doppelgänger and not the dead woman herself. But there were some strange coincidences. For one, she wore similar boots."

"I don't suppose you saw the bottoms of the boots?"

"I didn't have an opportunity or else I would have."

"I'm sure a lot of people wear boots like the ones on the dead woman," replied Zeb.

"The nun who I'm referring to as the doppelgänger is Sister Tavisha."

"Wait. You saw Sister Tavisha? Alive?"

"Yes. Alive and well. So she's not the dead woman."

Zeb sat back, stunned enough that he almost missed Echo's next statement.

"She's the hunter and butcher for the Priory..."

"Hold on a minute. She's alive and she knows how to handle knives and guns?"

"I would say so. Anyway, she has a rack of guns including several Henry .30-.30s that are nearly identical to the one I found under the dead woman."

"Lots of folks have that gun. It's hardly a rarity in Graham County."

"I know. She was also wearing a necklace with a stag deer on it. I saw it up closely enough to notice the stag deer but not close enough to see if there was a Christian cross in the stag's antlers. Let me just say it looked enough like the one on the dead woman's body to make me do a doubletake."

"Do the nuns have a gift shop?"

"Yes. Most of the products are honey-based as they have a lot of bees. They fed the kids homemade honey on homemade bread. They had a few other things that looked like they might be for sale. I saw larger handmade crosses but no necklaces, but that doesn't mean they weren't selling them."

"Anything else?"

"That ring on the dead woman."

"Yes."

"Sister Tavisha wore one on the same finger of the same hand as the dead woman. Orthodox nuns wear a specific ring on the fourth finger of their right hands. Maybe the dead woman was from the Order of Saint Eustace."

"That's interesting. Did you get a picture of the ring?"

"I had no chance to do that."

"Strange coincidences if you ask me," said Zeb.

"Here's one more thing. I also got a close look at a saddle string. The nuns make them there. The one I saw was identical to the one you and Clarissa found, right down the to the markings on the tips of the string."

"Did you see any of those for sale in the gift shop?"

"None were on display," replied Echo.

"Shelly told us that the stag deer is strongly related to Saint Eustace, so maybe it would make sense that their saddle strings would carry that marking. As for the necklace, I'd guess all the nuns wear one."

"That could be."

"I think you might be onto something. But everything you mention could be nothing more than coincidence."

"Zeb, you know when that thing you call the little man inside you speaks to you?"

"Yeah, I do."

"Well, this was like how you describe that. I sensed something. I mean it really seemed like there was much more to the picture than meets the eye. As a matter of fact when she was telling me about the saddle strings, which she had made, she did a weird thing."

"Yeah, what'd she do?"

"I think she stopped in the middle of saying her own name."

"That is odd. But it isn't much really. Maybe she stutters over certain words. There are a lot of things that could cause her to stop in the middle of what she was saying. We all find ourselves doing that at times."

"No. No! It was nothing like that. She was changing her story in mid-thought. I'd bet my life on it."

"Honey, you know I trust your instincts."

"I should hope so, that's how we ended up with each other and it's one of those things that keeps us close."

Zeb smiled as he thought back to the day their paths crossed and love was born between them.

"That being said, it's all good information that I will dig more deeply into. We'll talk more about the stutter step in Sister Tavisha's speech pattern. But there's something you've got to know right now."

"What?"

"You've possibly got some Feds coming to chat with you."

"How do you know that?"

Zeb explained his talk with Doc Yackley.

"You think they're on the way to the house?"

"From what Doc said I'd bet on it."

"How close to the school are you?"

"We just arrived. It'll take me about fifteen minutes to help get the kids unloaded and back to the classroom."

"Is your truck in the school parking lot?"

"West side, second row near the end."

"I'll meet you there and head home with you."

"I'll be waiting for you. I love you, Zeb."

"Love you, too, Echo."

Chapter 22

DIA

ZEB PARKED HIS SHERIFF'S vehicle next to Echo's truck and waited for about ten minutes before she appeared. He stepped out of his truck to greet her as she approached him with a smile on her face.

"You don't look at all worried about talking to a couple of Feds," noted Zeb.

"With you at my side, what is there to fear? Besides, I've got nothing to hide. But you do."

"What do you mean?" asked Zeb.

"What have you done with my CQC6?"

"Cleaned it thoroughly."

"Run the process by me."

"I cleaned the blade with rotor oil, washed it thoroughly with a deep cleansing solution, rotor oiled it a second time, washed it a second time. Detailed it clean with a soft rag. Put oil on the rag and cleaned both the blade and the handle along with one last go over of any nooks and crevices where blood might have collected. Then I rubbed it one last time with a dry rag. After that I used it for some routine things without getting any blood on it. It's as clean as a whistle when it comes to blood, DNA or any other possible markers that will lead them to the dead woman. It's now back in our safe where it belongs."

"I'm sure these guys are going to want to examine it with a fine-toothed comb," said Echo.

"If they're doing their job correctly, they'd better look it over closely. If not they'll be derelict in their duty," replied Zeb.

"Sounds good."

"Follow me home. We'll wait for them if they aren't already there."

Five minutes later when they turned the corner to their house Zeb and Echo saw a plain-looking late model Ford parked on the street in front of their home with two men sitting in dark suits that were much too hot for the day. Zeb pulled up behind them as Echo drove her truck into the garage and used the opener to close it behind her.

As the men got out of the car, Zeb got out of his truck and approached them.

"I'm Sheriff Hanks. May I help you?"

Doc had been dead on with his description of the pair. One was a pasty, white-skinned Mormonish-looking fellow. He was totally interchangeable with many guys Zeb had grown up with. The other was an Apache, more Eastern Apache than San Carlos Apache in appearance. Both men mechanically reached inside their suit coat pockets and pulled out identification badges.

"I'm Amon Beckette. This is my partner Ryne Hoazinne."

The men briefly showed Zeb their official IDs before quickly replacing them inside their jackets. Though Zeb couldn't place why, the name Hoazinne rang a bell.

"Not so fast, gentlemen. I'd like a closer look at those. That is, if you don't mind."

His request was met with an indignant glare. Zeb recognized the look from his younger days. He'd given it to many. On the inside, as pissed off as he was about the situation, Zeb was chuckling.

"Of course, Sheriff Hanks."

In unison they reached in their jackets a second time and handed them to Zeb.

"DIA?"

"Yes, sir," replied Agent Beckette.

Zeb admired the shiny newness of their badges before handing them back their IDs.

"What's the DIA doing in Safford?"

"We respectfully wish to speak with your wife, Echo Skysong Hanks."

Zeb kept the innocent act going.

"Regarding what exactly?"

"We'd like to discuss it with her before we say anything to you. You understand, right Sheriff Hanks? We're simply following the letter of the law."

"We're following orders, sir."

The Feds and their never-ending, never-bending protocols were once again proving themselves bees in Zeb's bonnet. Just once he'd like to stick his hat where the sun didn't shine. But, ever the professional, he held back and stepped into their world and for the moment played by their rules. It helped immensely that these two agents were not tarnished by experience.

"Fair enough. But since this obviously has to do with my wife I'm going to have to insist on sitting in on the conversation."

Before they had a chance to answer Zeb added one more sentence that carried the slightest hint of sarcasm.

"With your permission of course."

Agents Hoazinne and Beckette robotically twitched back and forth, each waiting for the other to make the final decision. Finally Hoazinne spoke up.

"It's uncommon since you're not an attorney. Given the fact that you're her husband and a sworn officer of the law I suppose we can allow that."

Zeb tipped his hat to the DIA agents.

"I suppose you can."

"But bear in mind we're the ones doing you a favor."

Zeb led the men to his house while holding back from calling the pair exactly what they were, wet behind the ears, impressed with their own authority, SOBs. Zeb tipped his head toward the front door.

"This way. My wife keeps a clean house, even with two kids running in and out. So check your shoes at the door."

It was not a case of Zeb's house, Zeb's rules. He just wanted to remind them that they were on his turf before they started debriefing Echo. His mentor, Jake Dablo had once said that if you take away a man's shoes he stands on less solid ground. Whether that applied here or not Zeb would see.

The men were good at following orders and did as instructed. Zeb held the door for them and directed the stocking-footed agents toward the living room. The agents surveyed the room and stumbled into each other when they turned toward the sofa where they eventually sat side by side. A few seconds after they were seated Echo entered from the other room with glasses of lemonade for the agents. She placed one in front of each of them with a smile on her face. As she turned to return to the kitchen to get glasses of lemonade for Zeb and herself, Zeb stopped her with an introduction.

"Echo, this is Agent Beckette and this is Agent Hoazinne. They're here to speak with you."

The men quickly stood and shook her hand while thanking her for the lemonade, which unbeknownst to them was flavored with chamomile and a few drops of lavender. Her intention was to relax the men. That way, they might be more likely to speak the truth or perhaps even let a little something slip.

The youthful agents, unskilled in small talk, got right down to business.

"Echo, we have a few questions about a missing woman we'd like to ask you," said Agent Hoazinne.

"Yes?" replied Echo. "Please allow me to get some lemonade for my husband and myself."

"Yes, ma'am."

Echo returned, took a seat and directed a question at the agents.

"You were saying something about a missing woman?"

"Yes."

"We believe the woman to have been a friend of yours."

"If not a friend, then at least an acquaintance."

Zeb and Echo shook their heads. What were these agents up to? Why didn't they just come out and say who they were talking about?

"I don't know that I exactly follow you. But, yes, go on, please."

"She may have been missing for several weeks now. We were hoping you could help us out."

Hoazinne was playing an Apache kids' game with her by trying to make her guess what he was talking about. Echo knew exactly what he was up to and wasn't about to bite. If he wanted something from her, he would have to ask it directly.

"I'd be glad to help you."

"Well?" said Agent Beckette.

"Well, what?" replied Echo.

"Are any of your friends or acquaintances missing?"

"None that I know of."

Agent Hoazinne stepped in to take over the questioning.

"Would you consider Doctor Izdzán Proteus Gouyen a friend or acquaintance?"

Now it was Echo's turn to be obtuse.

"I only met her a few times. I'd say we got along well."

"Good. Good."

"How close were you?"

Now Echo played the Apache children's guessing game.

"We were on a panel together. We spoke to young Apache girls about their futures and the opportunities that lay out there for them. We sat right next to each other, so I'd say we were close."

"I believe you know that's not what I meant," said Hoazinne.

"Then say what you mean, Agent," replied Echo. "Hoazinne."

Agent Hoazinne turned to Agent Beckette who set his brief-case on the coffee table. Opening it he pulled out the year-old copy of the San Carlos Tribal newspaper that showed a picture of Doctor Gouyen, Police Chief Gabriella Cocheta, Echo and Sister Tavisha Karpenko together at the San Carlos Community Center. When he laid it out on the table neither Zeb nor Echo bothered to give it as much as a passing glance. Their lack of a reaction was noted by the agents who both pointed directly at the picture. Fifteen seconds of silence and no movement on anyone's part produced a pointed clearing of the throat by Agent Hoazinne.

"Are you familiar with this picture?"

This time Echo casually glanced at it. She waited a second, took a second look and stared at it for a good ten seconds.

"Yes, I do believe I am."

"You're standing with Doctor Izdzán Proteus Gouyen, Sister Tavisha Karpenko and Police Chief Gabriella Cocheta."

"Yes."

"Did you talk with Doctor Gouyen that day?"

"Yes. All of the women chatted together and with each other as I recall."

"Have you talked with her since that day?"

"We had coffee at the Town Talk."

"Did you discuss anything in particular?" asked Hoazinne.

"No. We carried on our conversation about helping young women from the San Carlos in choosing careers."

Zeb was glad he wasn't the person in charge of debriefing Echo. She would give them nothing but headaches if things continued in this vein. She was their nightmare of an interviewee. Agent Hoazinne continued.

"Did she seem despondent that day at the San Carlos Community Center? Or any time after?"

"Anything but despondent. She was enthusiastic. Her speech was well responded to. She even cracked a few jokes, which seemed to be against her serious scientific nature."

"Did she mention anything unusual to you?"

"Such as?" asked Echo.

"Such as anything she had planned for the future, for example."

"She mentioned to the young and old women, it was mostly younger and older women in attendance, that they should plan their futures, no matter their age."

The game between the Apache agent and Echo was afoot. He knew it. She knew it. Agent Beckette sensing something, chose to speak next.

"That was the thrust of what she spoke about?"

"Yes. More or less."

"More or less, Ms. Skysong Hanks?"

"As I recall she spoke about opportunities in science, particularly physics and astronomy, which if I'm not mistaken she said were her chosen fields."

"Did she mention a desire to visit other telescope centers around the world?"

"She might have. When we had coffee I do remember she mentioned the projects she worked on were being done internationally. She mentioned wanting to see more of the country."

The questioning went back and forth and ultimately nowhere for the next half hour.

Hoazinne had one final question to pose. No one spoke as Zeb left the room, grabbed the lemonade pitcher and refilled everyone's glasses. When he finished with the refills Agent Hoazinne dropped a name that appeared to be directed at Zeb, even though he wasn't the one being questioned.

Chapter 23

ALMA LINK

"Alma Link."

Zeb's attention level immediately elevated. Alma was Helen's bridge partner, the one who had taken the place of his mother at the Saturday night bridge table after she died. He knew Alma much better than Echo did. What came immediately to mind was whether Agent Hoazinne knew something about the story Alma had shared with Helen, who later repeated it to Zeb.

"Alma Link?" repeated Zeb. "What about Alma Link?"

"Do you know her?"

"Yes. I know Alma," answered Zeb. "Very lovely woman. Has more than one or two tricks up her sleeve when it comes to playing cards. Sharp as a tack when it comes to the game of bridge."

The statement appeared to not light a candle of interest in either of the agents.

"Are you aware that she is on the cleaning crew at MGIO?"

"Yes, I am aware of that fact. But is the question for me or Echo?"

"Either. Both. Echo do you know Alma Link?"

"I know of her. I can't say we're friends, nor are we enemies."

"Then these questions are for the both of you. Did Alma have any particular connection with Doctor Gouyen, one of the scientists at MGIO?"

"Not that I'm aware of," replied Zeb. "Why?"

"One of the staff at MGIO said they thought they saw Alma going through some of Doctor Gouyen's private things."

"Alma going through someone else's personal items? For what purpose?"

"According to the witness, Alma may have taken something of Doctor Gouyen's."

"I doubt very much that Alma is a thief. The woman is as honest as the day is long. I've known her most of my life and I've never heard nor seen anything that would lead me to believe otherwise. Is something missing?"

"We're not saying she is a thief, Sheriff Hanks."

"Is something missing?" repeated Zeb.

Agent Hoazinne picked up the newspaper clipping of Echo, Doctor Gouyen, Sister Tavisha and Police Chief Cocheta and held it directly in Zeb and Echo's line of vision. This time Zeb had no clue.

"Yes, Sheriff Hanks. Something may be missing."

"What?"

"A professionally framed copy of this picture."

Echo and Zeb exchanged glances. The same thought buzzed through both their brains. Had the DIA really sent out two agents over a missing photograph?

Agent Hoazinne continued holding the newspaper at eye level in front of Zeb and Echo.

"Doctor Gouyen asked the photographer, the day this picture was taken, if she could obtain a copy of it."

"Did the photographer tell you why Doctor Gouyen wanted a copy?" asked Echo.

"A memento?" asked Zeb.

"Of a sort," replied Agent Hoazinne.

"What exactly are you talking about?" asked Echo.

"The photographer printed out, according to the people at her work who had seen it, a professional quality copy for her. She even had had it framed for Doctor Gouyen."

"Is that what's missing from Doctor Gouyen's desk?"

"Yes and no," replied Beckette.

"But not exactly to be exact," added Hoazinne.

"What on earth are you talking about?" asked Zeb. "Either the framed picture is missing or it isn't."

"It's not exactly this image that is missing. You see Doctor Gouyen had Echo and Police Chief Cocheta edited out of the original photograph. On her desk she had a framed copy of the picture that included only herself with Sister Tavisha. Just the two of them."

"You can't really be suggesting that Alma stole that picture?" asked Zeb. "Why would she? For the frame? That's just plain ridiculous."

"I think the more interesting question is why Doctor Gouyen would have had the photo altered in the first place," said Echo.

"When we interviewed Alma she told us that on more than one occasion she was cleaning the office when Doctor Gouyen was on the phone with Sister Tavisha."

"They're obviously friends of a close sort. The picture of the two of them on her desk would at the very least imply that," said Zeb. "What would any of that have to do with Alma Link?"

"Several employees at MGIO noted they were certain the picture was there for at least two weeks after Doctor Gouyen left for her vacation. The same employees noticed it missing after the monthly deep cleaning by the crew which Alma Link is a part of. In fact Doctor Gouyen's office is cleaned by Alma."

"Did you ask Alma if she took it?" asked Echo.

"We're doing some background information gathering before we consider suggesting a crime such as theft."

"You're kidding! Right? You're wasting our valuable time on some silly wild goose chase about a picture that may or may not be missing?"

Zeb was clearly annoyed that these two out of town Feds would consider Alma, a lifelong citizen of Safford and a longtime friend of both his mother's and Helen's to be little more than a common thief.

"Is pointing the finger at a hard-working older woman the latest methodology in crime-solving techniques used by the DIA?"

Echo could feel the rapidly rising tension in Zeb's body as she placed her hand in his. Her intent was to settle Zeb down and help him gather his wits about him before he went any further in his conversation with the federal lawmen. The effect of her touch was immediate.

"I apologize for my sarcasm," said Zeb. "I guess I don't understand your methods. I know how people in this county react. If anyone even has the slightest hint that a pair of federal agents were falsely accusing a Graham County local, I think you might dead end your investigation."

"We meant…well we meant no harm and mean to imply nothing about Ms. Link."

"It's Mrs. Link. She's been married for more than fifty years," said Zeb.

"I apologize if you misunderstood us," said Hoazinne. "Perhaps I spoke hastily."

"You did," replied Zeb. "And if you continue to do so, like I said, your investigation is going to go nowhere fast."

"Maybe you can help us out?" said Hoazinne.

The squeeze of Echo's hand on his own brought clever clarity to Zeb's mind.

"What I hear you asking is that we should work on the potentially missing person, Doctor Gouyen together? Is that correct?"

Echo observed Agents Beckette and Hoazinne as they separately and then jointly considered Zeb's proposal. Agent Hoazinne spoke for the three of them as a potential team.

"What do *you* mean by work together?" asked Hoazinne.

"Just that. One hand washes the other. If I find something of value, I share it with you two. If you find something of value, you share it with me. Good old-fashioned police work."

"How do we know we can trust you about information especially when it comes to possibly causing a local to be charged with a crime?"

Zeb's response was blunt and to the point.

"You don't have any idea if you can trust me or not."

"Then why should we enter into such an agreement?" asked Beckette.

"I am asking myself that same question," replied Zeb.

Echo chose this moment to interject her opinion. Mostly she was glad nothing about the murder weapon had been even vaguely talked about.

"Gentlemen, perhaps we should all take a deep breath and talk about this with clear heads. I am certain the three of you can come to a quick resolution."

"I am the eyes and ears of Graham County," said Zeb. "I know who will speak the truth versus those who will speak lies. If you are going to learn anything, I guaran-damn-tee you that you're going to also have to make this deal with Chief Cocheta on the Rez. Doctor Gouyen is a member of the San Carlos Apache tribe and without Chief Cocheta's cooperation, you're going to learn squat."

It was easy to see what the agents were thinking. There was no doubt they were going to have to deal with both Sheriff Hanks and Chief Cocheta if they wanted this case to move forward at anything other than glacial speed.

"Chief Cocheta and I may not be close but if one of us goes in on the deal, working with you two I mean, the other will most likely follow suit."

The agents walked to a far corner of the living room and huddled. Whispering lowly, not even Echo with her wolf-like hearing could make out a word. A few minutes later they returned to the couch.

"Your jacket at the DIA says you're an honest man and a good cop," said Beckette.

Zeb couldn't tell if Beckette was giving him a compliment or if he was letting Zeb know to watch his p's and q's. Either way he meant it Zeb was glad to know where Beckette stood. Hoazinne was another matter. At first glance he seemed to be an okay guy, but Zeb didn't have a good read on him. Thankfully, Echo had done his work for him. She whispered something in his ear and his decision was made.

Zeb reached out and shook their hands. A deal was made. Was that pact with the Devil? Time would be the teller of that tale.

Chapter 24

TWO BRAINS ONE MIND

ECHO AND ZEB LED the DIA agents to the door. Part of the agreement was the agents would contact Zeb immediately upon finding hard evidence, one hour on soft evidence linked directly to any previously found hard evidence and two hours on any other soft evidence. He would operate under the same rules. Now that he was technically working with the DIA, Zeb wished he knew exactly what they were thinking. Each time he neared that subject they led him down a rabbit hole and immediately changed the subject.

As Echo closed the door Zeb began to speak but was immediately hushed by his wife by the universal method of putting a solitary vertical finger in front of her lips. Zeb knitted his eyebrows together in response. Echo tipped her head to the side in classic follow-me form.

With Zeb on her heels Echo made haste to the flower table. No matter the time of year or the cost, Echo kept the house smelling of fresh flowers. To Zeb it was just one more reason to love her. She loved her flowers but this was the first time he'd seen her speak directly into the flower pot. Maybe this was one of her secrets to keep them healthy? What did he know anyway?

"Zeb, honey let's listen to some music. Your choice today."

This time Zeb furrowed his brows for a second before he caught onto the possible reasoning behind Echo's seemingly odd behavior and curious statement.

"Right," said Zeb. "You want to listen to something classical or the Grateful Dead?"

"I feel like dancing. The Dead. If you please."

Zeb grabbed one of Echo's hundreds of bootlegged CDs.

"Nothing like the Dead," said Echo.

Zeb couldn't tell if she was doing a double entendre using the music and the dead woman as the subjects. Or if it was just the way she was speaking. In fact he was now completely uncertain as to what she was up to at all.

"Turn it up. This is my favorite song."

As Echo began to sway her hips Zeb recognized the old Buddy Holly tune, 'Not Fade Away,' immediately. He used to prefer the Buddy Holly and the Crickets version but was coming around to the Dead version. He cranked up the music at Echo's silent suggestion. Echo walked over and turned it up even louder before dancing across the room in a magical way that Zeb wished he could mimic. When she reached the other side of the room, Echo beckoned him to her side with a finger curling in her direction. With that same finger she reached under the flower vase and pulled out what was apparently the latest in ultra-small bugging devices. It was flat, clear and half the size of a guitar pick. Not only was it tiny, it appeared to be attached to the vase by a glue-like substance that was likely activated for attachment or detachment by hand heat. Zeb immediately recognized what it was. He was certain these rookie Feds were trying out a device that was new to them.

Echo curled her finger twice more. Zeb followed her to a pair of additional, identical contrivances. The finger came up one more time as she dropped them down the toilet and led Zeb to the garage, a space the agents could not have entered without them knowing.

"How on earth did you spot those things?" asked Zeb.

"Agent Hoazinne has a hypnotic voice," replied Echo.

"Not surprised you noticed. He's a very handsome man to boot," said Zeb.

"What's your point in mentioning his good looks?"

"You think I'm jealous, don't you?"

"Zeb Hanks? You? The jealous guy? I don't think so."

"Aw right, aw right. I get the point. Yes, I was a touch jealous the way you looked at him," replied Zeb.

"Oh, good lord, grow up," said Echo.

"It's kind of a compliment," replied Zeb.

"Do men ever quit being boys?" pondered Echo.

"Er, well, yes. We grow up sooner or later. I think."

Echo pinched his cheeks together causing his lips to pucker and kissed him.

"That works for me," said Zeb.

"When Hoazinne was talking to you he was using a method of forensic voice hypnosis. You dropped into the tone of his voice hook, line and sinker. I allowed him to think I had done the same by acting with my eyes."

"Acting with your eyes?"

"Yes, by making them look just a hint glazed over."

"Where'd you learn to do that?"

"One of the Special Forces guys I was assigned with was a clinical psychologist. His specialty was using vocal tones for human mind control during the investigation process."

"Useful, I see. So you spotted him planting his gizmos by pretending to fall prey to his little trick that worked so easily on me?"

"Something like that. He had Agent Beckette distract you by asking you a question so that you turned your head. It took him about two seconds each time he did it. He's excellent at the sleight of hand it requires to get it done."

"Good observation. I guess they must have been concerned about me not toeing the line when it came to information."

"Would you have?" asked Echo.

"Are you kidding? Those bozos? They're still wet behind their ears and shittin' yellow," said Zeb. "Now that I think about it, I sort of feel undervalued that they sent rookies to spy on us."

"Rookies who fooled you."

"Well…"

"The lesson is to not let your ego get in your way. Listen up, I caught something else," said Echo.

"Do tell."

"They both are seriously concerned about Doctor Gouyen's situation. Which, if I were to make an intelligent guess, tells me she probably holds multiple top-security clearances."

"Yes?"

"Which means she's a federal employee, probably by contract, who the federal agents are worried may have given or been coerced into giving sensitive information to someone who shouldn't have it."

Zeb could practically see Echo's wheels spinning.

"So, that leaves you to find the missing Doctor Gouyen."

"Agreed," said Zeb. "I doubt Agents Amon Beckette and Ryne Hoazinne are going to find any evidence unless they trip over it."

In Zeb's excitement he elevated his voice but Echo's hand gestures had him quickly lower it. For the next thirty seconds neither Echo nor Zeb spoke above the lowest of whispers.

"They're still well trained. In fact they may have been playing dumb to lull you in," said Echo.

"You think so?"

"It hardly matters because you have someone who can dig deeper and faster than those two ever could. She will be the perfect person to help you find anything and everything about Doctor Gouyen."

"Shelly."

Zeb nodded. Echo was priceless.

Echo grabbed Zeb around the waist before gently softening her grip, leading him by sensually rubbing her free hand up and down his arm in time to the drifting Dead music. In two minutes they were out of the garage and in the bedroom. Taking his hand she grabbed him by the little finger and twisted it in such a way that his knees crumpled beneath him giving him no choice except to collapse onto the bed. He was totally under Echo's control. And that was just fine.

Chapter 25

POLICE CHIEF GABRIELLA COCHETA

ON HIS TRIP TO the Rez, Graham County Deputy Rambler Braing was divided of mind. He wanted to demand to hear what Chief Cocheta knew, if anything, about the missing Doctor Gouyen. At the same time he didn't want his attitude toward the woman who had been appointed to the job he coveted to interfere with helping him in finding the truth.

He'd known Cocheta when they were children. He'd even kept an eye on her career when she moved to Phoenix to further her ambitions. Now that she had returned he was certain her end game wasn't in line with the good of the community he desired to serve. Rather, he saw her as simply acting in her own self-interest. The rumor of her running for U.S. Senator was all the proof he needed. Still he urged himself to be fair and honest.

Pulling onto the Rez took some of the anger out of Rambler's heart but when he parked at the police station next to Chief Cocheta's vehicle his mind quickly dropped back into resentment mode.

Stepping out of his Graham County truck Rambler bent over and petted of pair of Rez dogs that everyone affectionately called dingoes. They were the abandoned, but communally raised Rez dogs. Since he was a kid there were always a dozen or more of these critters lazing in the sunshine on the wooden porch that fronted the building that held the Tribal Police office. He'd heard a rumor that Chief Cocheta was trying to clean up the area and one of her goals was to rid the area of the dogs. Of course, even when she had them moved to another part of the reservation they always returned. Treating dogs the way she did was just one more thing not to like about her.

Walking in the door he noticed the walls had been freshly painted and new carpet covered the floor. In his mind the money would have been better spent catching or at least slowing down crime. When he looked away from the upgraded interior, the person who Rambler assumed to be the office manager greeted him.

"Yes, how may I help you?"

First of all, the young man should have known by the uniform that Rambler was Graham County law enforcement and addressed him accordingly and secondly, he should have known who he was. A closer look at the office manager's face told Rambler this guy was definitely not San Carlos Apache. The name on the desk plate, a Mescalero Apache name, told him the man was an outlander and most likely one of Cocheta's political operatives. Rambler kept looking around, neglecting to answer.

"Do you have an appointment, sir?"

He pointed to his badge and the name on his uniform.

"Deputy Sheriff Rambler Braing."

The Mescalero ran a pencil along the appointment calendar.

"And no, no appointment for Deputy Braing."

"May I ask the purpose of your visit?"

"I'd like a few moments with Chief Cocheta?"

"But you have no appointment."

"That's right. Nothing's changed in the last ten seconds."

"What is this in regard to?"

"Official business."

"Yes? Regarding?"

"A dead woman and another woman that's possibly missing."

"Their names? Please."

"Your boss is familiar with both cases and she knows me. Just tell her I'm here to see her."

The man put down his notepad and went right back to work.

"Are you going to tell Chief Cocheta that Deputy Rambler Braing is here to see her or should I show myself in?"

"She's busy right now. Please have a seat."

The man flipped the pencil in his hand and pointed with the eraser end to a chair in the furthest corner, far away from his desk. Fifteen minutes passed before Rambler could take the nonsense no longer. He approached the office manager.

"Any idea when I'll be able to see the Chief?"

The manager looked at his watch and tapped it with his pencil.

"Soon, I suppose. Soon."

Rambler grabbed the pencil and broke it into three pieces and dropped them on the manager's desk.

"When? Exactly?"

"No need to get your panties in a bunch, Deputy. I'll check right now."

The office manager swiveled his chair, arose and stepped lightly to Chief Cocheta's office door with Rambler close on his heels. The man cleared his throat as he looked over his shoulder at the much taller Rambler.

"Just want to make sure you do your job right," said Rambler. "I used to work here once upon a time."

The man opened the door and stuck only his head through the partial opening. Rambler pushed it all the way open and walked right past him. When the man tried to stop Rambler, Deputy Braing pushed him away with a single finger just as Chief Cocheta spoke.

"Thank you, Nali. I can handle it from here."

The office manager nodded and headed back to his desk.

"Sorry to keep you waiting, Deputy Braing. May I call you Rambler?"

Rambler nodded. She knew him and he knew she was uppity.

"I was on a call that I thought might lead to a discovery of evidence that could help us both. I truly am sorry for keeping you waiting. Nali is new at the job, but he'll learn. Now what can I help you with, Rambler?"

"How well do you know Doctor Gouyen?"

"I know her. We met a few years back, then I met her again at the Community Center when we both were speaking to young women about their futures. At that time she asked me to help her find a piece of land where she could build a cabin. Actually she asked me if a non-tribal member could own property on the Rez. As you know, they can't."

"You bet they can't."

"She showed me a certificate of marriage. Gouyen is a member in good standing of the San Carlos tribe and can own property on her own. But when she found out she couldn't buy it jointly with Sister Tavisha Karpenko, she insisted they be allowed to lease it," said Chief Cocheta.

Rambler paused. He'd known of the relationship but not the marriage between the women.

"Do you think Doctor Gouyen believes that people other than Apaches should ever own Apache land?"

"No idea. I think she was hedging her bet by leasing in case something happened to her. Even if she's married to a White the lease remains good if she dies."

"You've got a point there. You think someone is out to get Doctor Gouyen?"

"She's missing, isn't she?"

"Late returning from vacation isn't exactly missing," replied Rambler.

"Then we are thinking differently about this. Anyway, I walked her through the process of obtaining a long-term land lease. She and her partner built a very lovely place to the east of Tanque near the Whitlock Mountains cliff dwelling. You know the spot?"

"I do. Nice spot for a cabin. What do you know about her late return that I don't?" asked Rambler.

"Nothing. Actually it's no cabin at all, it's more like a sprawling three-thousand-square-foot luxury home."

Chief Cocheta stopped for a fraction of a second to observe Rambler's reaction to the fact that two women had built a luxurious house together on the Rez. Rambler wasn't completely in the dark, though. He had previously gotten wind of the house building project by the pair and assumed that their relationship had been going on for a while. But he was enjoying their little back and forth and remained impassive while he waited for her next revelation.

"They can obviously afford it," he said.

"Rumor is that they paid for it in cash."

"Doctor Gouyen, I presume, has money. I can't image Sister Karpenko has much in the way of worldly goods."

"Not unless there is a buyout when you drop out of the Order of Saint Eustace."

"She must have quit very recently. I know for a fact just a few days ago she was at the Priory doing her routine daily activities," said Rambler, maintaining his poker face at this bit of news.

"I don't know when she quit the Solomon Priory to be honest with you. I'd only heard a rumor. Thanks for letting me know when it happened."

Rambler wasn't actually verifying the situation and didn't care one bit that Chief Cocheta would likely be using him as her source of information. He hissed through his teeth. She'd outwitted him. Damn it.

"Any idea when you last saw Doctor Gouyen?"

"It's been a while."

"Weeks or months?"

"I can't really say. Months, most likely."

Now it was Cocheta's time to be tight-lipped. Rambler could easily read that. His suspicion was that if she had seen Gouyen within the last six weeks she didn't care to share her information.

"She's been gone from work on vacation for a little over six weeks and was due back a little over two weeks ago," said Rambler.

"I've heard."

"How so?'

"Not long ago a couple of men flashing federal badges stopped by and asked where her home was. I directed them toward her house. I don't think they found who they were looking for because they stopped by here a few hours later..."

Chief Cocheta paused, opened her top middle desk drawer and pulled out two business cards.

"...and they left their cards."

She briefly glanced at them before handing them to Rambler who read the writing on the cards aloud.

"Agent Amon Beckette. Defense Intelligence Agency and Agent Ryne Hoazinne also of the Defense Intelligence Agency. Hmm."

"My thought exactly. What's the DIA doing around this part of the world?"

"Any ideas, theories?"

"Graham County doesn't know these guys are snooping around?" asked Chief Cocheta.

If he were the next police chief on the Rez this was the type of information that required sharing, regardless of what he thought of the current chief.

"They've made themselves known. They talked with Echo about her knowledge of Doctor Gouyen from the same meeting you all were at. The thing at the community center last year."

"Sure."

"They also talked with Doc Yackley."

"What about?" asked Cocheta.

"I think they were trying to find out if Doc knew anything more than he'd divulged about the death of the woman in the Pinaleño Mountains."

"Knowing Doc Yackley even the little bit that I do, I don't imagine he shot his mouth off for the agents."

"That is likely a correct assumption."

"But I also don't imagine he lied to them, either."

"He is thorough. I'm certain he gave them everything up front. That's the way he operates. On the other hand, I know he didn't care for them interfering with what he considered to be his job."

Chief Cocheta's intercom buzzed. Her man Friday at the front desk told her she had just received an expected incoming, important political call. Rambler couldn't tell from the tone of Friday's voice if he had been given instructions to chop his time off at the fifteen-minute mark, which was exactly how long he'd been talking to Cocheta. Or if she really did have an incoming call that was more important than their conversation. Since she was at heart a politician he had no way of telling.

Chief Cocheta picked the landline from its cradle and placed it near her ear while holding a finger over the incoming call button that was flashing.

"I want to thank you for being so candid, Rambler. Is there anything else I can help you with?"

Rambler shook his head, got up from the chair and headed for the exit.

"You owe me. I'll be in touch if I need something. Feel free to contact me as well," said Rambler.

Chief Cocheta was already on the phone call when Rambler closed the door behind him.

As Rambler passed by Nali's desk he grabbed his ponytail and gave it just enough of a tug to irritate him.

"You know the Aretha Franklin song, R-E-S-P-E-C-T?"

"'Respect?' Yes, I know it well."

"Next time listen to the words, young man."

Rambler didn't bother to shut the door as he left the police office building on his way to the house built for Doctor Gouyen and her not-so-secret partner, Sister Tavisha. Nali walked over to shut the door and gave Rambler the middle finger. Rambler tipped his cap and smiled.

Chapter 26

HACKED

THE EMAIL COMMUNICATION BETWEEN Doctor Izdzán Proteus Gouyen and Sister Tavisha Karpenko was riddled with missives of true love and compassion as well as odd inconsistences interwoven with an endless trail of what read like mysterious subplots.

In all Shelly had found over four hundred emails between the two women. All of them except the first five occurred during the last year, beginning on the same date as the picture of Sister Tavisha, Doctor Gouyen, Echo and Chief Cocheta at the San Carlos Community Center was taken.

Four of the first five earlier emails were prior to the date of the meeting at the San Carlos Community Center. All of them were requests for a private meeting to discuss scientific endeavors of mutual interest. The fifth email was a request from Doctor Gouyen for Sister Tavisha's curriculum vitae. Then, the email traffic died until after the meeting at the San Carlos Community Center.

After one additional reading of the entire set of email correspondence between Doctor Gouyen at planetmotion@proton. sra and Sister Tavisha at lovemother@yandex.ur, Shelly walked down the hall to Zeb's office.

"Knock, knock."

"Enter."

"You got a minute, Sheriff Zebulon Hanks?"

"Sheriff Zebulon Hanks? You sound like my mother...or Helen. Am I in some sort of trouble?"

"Nope. Just trying to be a little more professional at Helen's request," replied Shelly.

"Her heart is in the right place. But it's not necessary to call me Zebulon, ever."

A sneaky smile coming across Shelly's face told him she was yanking his chain.

"All right. All right. You got me. What do you really want, Shelly?"

"I want to let you in on what just may be a very strange love story."

"Have a seat. I'm all ears. Who are the main characters in this tale of passion."

"Love Mother and Planet Motion."

"Come again?"

"You heard me right. Love Mother and Planet Motion."

"Hippies?"

"Email names."

"Oh. Is this some sort of silly love fairytale/fantasy?"

"Maybe."

"Go on. Let's hear this tale of love."

"This story begins a year ago in earnest. But its seeds were sown before that."

"Hmm? Am I familiar with the characters in this play?"

"Vaguely. I'll read you a few of the love letters and you tell me if you know the people involved."

Zeb was generally not one for this sort of thing but he had some time, so he sat back, propped his boots on his desk, put his hands behind his head and listened as Shelly read a dozen or so progressively more come hither emails directed at Planet Motion by Love Mother. In one, Mount Graham was mentioned by its initials.

"MG has to stand for Mount Graham. Is Planet Motion our missing, or presumed missing Doctor Gouyen?"

"One for one," replied Shelly. "And she's using an email account that is designed to be difficult to track."

"Don't tell me who the party of the second part is," asked Zeb. "Read me a few more of the emails. Let me see if I can figure it out."

Twenty emails later Zeb was clueless as to the second party in what was becoming a progressively more provocative love story.

"I have no idea who the party of the second email is. Go ahead and tell me."

Shelly laid a copy of the picture of the four women at the San Carlos Community Center in front of Zeb.

"You're kidding me, right? Echo is having an affair with Doctor Gouyen?"

"Ha! Ha! Guess again."

"Police Chief Cocheta? I thought she was married. Hell, I know she's been married twice, at least."

"She was and is currently married to one of her male deputies."

"Sister Tavisha? I thought nuns had to be celibate."

"And the address uses a highly encrypted email server that is based in Russia."

"She is Russian, is she not?"

"As you like to say..."

Shelly pulled back, looked at the floor and did her absolute best impression of Zeb.

"...Yup."

"Pretty darn good imitation."

"Thank you."

"I just learned something that fits with what you are telling me. And truth be told I'm surprised you haven't heard this bit of gossip."

"Go on, tell me. This time I'm the one who's all ears."

"Do you know Alma Link?"

"Somewhat. Vaguely, I'd say. I've heard her family name. Friend of Helen's, right? She took your mother's seat at the ladies' Friday bridge table. That's about all I know of her."

Zeb pulled his boots off his desk and leaned over the photograph of the four women taken at the San Carlos Community Center.

"You're correct on all accounts. What you didn't know is that Alma is being indirectly accused by an employee at MGIO of removing a framed picture from Doctor Gouyen's desk after she went on vacation. In fact the photo was a copy taken from the photographer's original. Only the photo was edited to remove Echo and Chief Cocheta."

Shelly drummed her freshly painted fingernails rapidly on the newspaper photo a half-dozen times before tapping the faces of Gouyen and Karpenko.

"From this picture? Right here? The one those DIA guys are asking about?"

Zeb didn't need to think too hard about the number of ways Shelly might have scooped up that information.

"Yes. Er, I mean, yup."

They both smiled as Zeb imitated Shelly imitating him.

"Did you talk with the photographer?"

"Yuh—uh-er—yes."

"And?"

"Doctor Gouyen asked her for a copy of the original photograph. Only, like I explained, she wanted to make a copy without Echo and Chief Cocheta in it."

"Did the photographer have anything else to offer?"

"No, not really. She made an edited copy for Doctor Gouyen in her private developing room, had it framed and gave it to her a few days later. Her involvement ended there."

"What do you make of the picture and the emails?"

"The picture is self-explanatory. I'm talking about their emails. It seems not much in this world is private anymore."

"Trust me on this one, Zeb. Nothing is private in this world anymore."

Zeb sat back in his chair and put his boots back on the desk. Shelly did the same.

There was much to talk about. Shelly began the conversation.

"We know that Gouyen and Karpenko...or would you prefer Izdzán and Tavisha or Doctor Gouyen and Sister Karpenko?"

"For simplicity's sake let's leave it at Gouyen and Karpenko."

"Gouyen and Karpenko it is then. Like I mentioned, Karpenko made first contact under the guise of science and when she couldn't produce a proper CV was dissed until they met in person. I suppose we should ask Echo and Chief Cocheta if they noticed any fireworks going off between the two women."

"Echo doesn't remember noticing anything at the time of the speeches. I already asked her. Rambler is out talking to Chief Cocheta as we speak."

"This, then might interest you."

Shelly pulled up a picture on Google Maps of a fancy-looking house that appeared to be in the middle of nowhere.

"She, Doctor Gouyen, built a lovely home deep in the woods on the easternmost part of the Rez. It's near some ancient cliff dwellings. Has anyone checked out there?"

"I'm certain the Feds have. They must know about it."

"Maybe not. She used a pseudonym when she leased the land it's on and built a rather lavish house. There are actually two people on the lease. The other is not a pseudonym, unless someone is using the name of Tavisha Karpenko illegally," said Shelly.

"Interesting twist," said Zeb.

"Doctor Gouyen probably used a pseudonym because there are some radical groups on the Rez that don't want any Whites building there at all. They might come after Karpenko, but she's only a temporary leaseholder. A radical group would likely look at land ownership for obvious reasons and they'd be more likely to turn their attention to the Native leaseholder."

"I get that. No one wants to lose their land twice."

"Or maybe she really wanted to go off the radar and never be bothered," suggested Shelly.

"Also a good possibility. But whatever reason she did it for, she clearly wants to remain unnoticed."

"Maybe the anonymity was Karpenko's idea because she's White?"

"That would make sense. Plus I doubt she's a naturalized citizen..."

"She's here on a permanent work visa. I checked."

"You could hide out for a long time deep in the Rez and keep the Feds at bay. Hell, Echo's told me of people who ended up hiding from the Feds for decades on the Rez."

"We don't know exactly why Gouyen did what she did. However, she is a tribal member and she does have the right to build on the Rez."

"If she did it to disappear, it wouldn't be very effective. Someone on the Rez is aware of the house she built. She would have needed Rez construction permits."

"I imagine a few bucks could make the right person look the other way on that one," said Shelly.

"Maybe she's up to something illegal?"

"Like what?"

"Gouyen seems like anything but a troublemaker. I checked her out. She's a highly educated and pedigreed woman with a pile of money. Sometimes that is the perfect profile to hide behind. The truth is, all we really know is that she is two weeks late in coming back from a vacation."

"Which is totally out of character, based on my digging into her background. Her profile speaks of a woman who goes by the book and never varies from that way of doing business. She's never drawn outside the lines. Always perfect in everything she does. In fact, she's practically infallible," said Shelly.

"Sometimes it's the perfect person who has a deep yearning to do the wrong thing just to see what it feels like," said Zeb.

"I know the type. But I just can't see her doing that. That's more of a macho type thing. In my opinion, women who live the straight and narrow lifestyle are far less likely to change as part of something like a mid-life crisis than a man would."

Zeb heated some water and made tea for the two of them. Shelly stared at the picture of Karpenko, Gouyen, Cocheta and Skysong. What was she missing?

Chapter 27

SOCIETY PAGE

"SUNS WIN LAST NIGHT?" asked Zeb.

Rambler's head was buried so deeply in the pages of the *Scottsdale Bee* that Zeb's words either went right over his head or in one ear and out the other without stopping to register. Zeb coughed to grab Rambler's attention.

"Morning, Zeb. How goes it?"

"Suns win last night?"

"You serious? They suck. The Rockets kicked their butts right out of town. They play the Heat next. Maybe they'll win one out of three. Can't count on them this year. I'm thinking of becoming a Celtics fan."

Zeb glanced over Rambler's shoulder and saw that it was the social media page that had captured his fancy.

"Going to a swanky wedding in Phoenix or just planning on hanging out with some movie stars?"

"Music is more my thing. If I could hang, I'd be down with some singers."

"Anyone in particular?"

"Given my druthers I'd go with some OG rappers."

"That's right. You had a band back in the day, didn't you?"

"Almost had a record contract with a medium-sized label, but you know...didn't happen. No regrets."

"Any rapper news on the social media page?"

"Nope. There oughta be. But there is something I just spotted that I think might interest you. Actually, if my eyes and my brain are working as a functioning unit it might give us a break in our murder case."

"What have you got?"

Rambler pointed to an article about a society woman, an international woman of note who had wriggled herself in a very short time span deeply into Scottsdale society.

"Her name caught me. Then when I looked at her picture I did a doubletake."

"What's the woman's name? As if it would mean anything to me," asked Zeb.

"This one might ring a bell or two for you. The name is Karpenko."

"Don't tell me there's another Tavisha Karpenko."

"No. Not a Tavisha. This one's name is Bronya Karpenko."

Zeb's neck swiveled back toward Rambler, his best ear leading the way.

"What's the story about?"

"The very wealthy elite of Arizona, mostly from Scottsdale along with every politician of note in the entire state, gave Sister Bronya Karpenko, a religious socialite, a going-away party sometime in the last few weeks."

"What's a religious socialite?"

"In this case a nun from the Order of Saint Eustace known for her good works."

"I suppose that's a thing. But a religious socialite? That strikes me as a bit odd. Doesn't it seem strange to you?"

"I'm just telling you what the story says," replied Rambler. "Can you really believe everything you read in the paper? I think we both know the answer to that one."

"Where is she going?"

"Back to an area of Ukraine that borders Russia. It's called the Donbas region."

"I've heard about it lately on the news. Russia wants to annex it as I recall."

"You recall correctly," said Rambler. "Says here its people are Ukrainians who speak Russian and are generally loyal to Russia."

"Hmm."

"Sister Bronya feels that she should be there to support both the Russian and Ukrainian troops fighting in Ukraine. Specifically she has been raising a boatload of money to help wounded soldiers with obtaining prosthetics and the rehabilitation that goes with it. She says in the story she has many relatives fighting on both sides of the war and that her father is retired from the Russian Army. He was a Major General who fought in many campaigns and lost his right lower leg. In the story it claims he then became a pacifist because of his combat experience. She followed suit."

"That's noble of her," said Zeb.

"Wait a second," interjected Zeb "Two Saint Eustace nuns named Karpenko? What are the odds?"

"Maybe Karpenko is a common name over there. You know like Smith is in middle America. Or like Tessay is in the Apache culture or Chee to the Navajos."

"Could be. I suppose Doctor Google could figure that one out for us. I can't imagine all Karpenkos are related."

Zeb put on his glasses and slid the newspaper under brighter light. His previous statement notwithstanding, Bronya Karpenko was so similar in appearance to Tavisha Karpenko that they had to be related. That meant that either could be easily mistaken for the dead woman Echo came upon.

"Well, well, well. I think I'd better put Shelly on this. It's a hell of a long shot but maybe, maybe. Shit. I don't know. It's a long shot, that's all I know."

"Long shots, they do come in," said Rambler.

Zeb picked up his cellphone and called Shelly. It turned out she also read the social media page of the *Bee*.

"What the heck are you and Rambler doing reading the social page of the *Scottsdale Bee*?" asked Zeb.

"It's a thing we have."

"Wait. What?"

"We try to out-gossip each other when it comes to the Arizona upper crust," replied Shelly.

"Why?"

"I do it for the humor. You'd have to ask Rambler what's in it for him."

"I don't think I care to know. Find out what you can about Bronya Karpenko, gossip included."

"Okay big boss man. I'm on it."

"I'm interested in any links to her, her background, her..."

"Sheriff, uh, Zeb, I know what I'm doing. I thought you had that figured years ago. Well, maybe I thought you'd figured out that women know what they're doing since marriage enhanced your experience."

Zeb kicked himself. Echo had been teaching him for years on how to interact with women, especially highly competent women. Once again, he'd stumbled over his own tongue.

"Right. Sorry. Get back to me when you've got something. I know you know what you're doing."

Shelly winced as she could tell by his tone that Zeb was unnecessarily beating himself up. Feeling bad she used an old trick to snap him back to himself. She did something she never did. She barked at him.

"Zeb!"

The sheriff's brain jumped from self-pity back to normal as Shelly's voice popped in his ears.

"Yes?"

"Nothing. Just a passing thought. Adios."

Chapter 28

CLARISSA AND RAMBLER

"I'M HEADED OUT TO the Rez to poke around," said Rambler. "Interested in making the run with me?"

It was Clarissa's day for rural patrol and a poke around the Rez would definitely lead to a longer day.

"Zeb's idea?"

Rambler grinned with his entire face.

"Mine first."

"Really?"

"Well, maybe only a fraction of a second between us, but definitely I thought of it first."

"Yeah?"

"Or maybe my thinking was spiritual in the sense it might lead us to an answer."

"What are you looking for?"

"I'm going to take a trip out by the cliff dwellings, east of Tanque in the Whitlock Mountains. You know that area don't you?"

"Just another of my old haunts. My brothers and I used to ride our horses back when we were kids. I know every nook and cranny out that way. I'd be willing to bet I know it better than you do."

"How much would you care to wager?" asked Rambler.

Clarissa had been investing heavily in the stock market lately and her cash flow was not what it usually was. She also knew when Rambler wanted to bet, he liked to gamble real money. In no time she was having second thoughts.

"Well, maybe not this time," replied Clarissa. "But maybe next."

Rambler hadn't paid close attention to Clarissa or her gambling skills. Now he knew that he should. She might be a real comer.

"Then you know the house built by Doctor Gouyen with her partner, Sister Tavisha Karpenko?"

"I've heard stories about it being a fancy place. It's news to me that Sister Karpenko was the White that built it with her. I generally know the area where it's located but I haven't been out that way in five or more years, so I haven't seen the house. I doubt the landscape has changed much. It's remote. But you know that."

"I could use a second set of eyes. There's a lot of turf to cover."

"What do you have in mind? What are we looking for?" asked Clarissa.

"To be honest, I'd like to figure out anything that might give us a better understanding of how come Doctor Gouyen is missing. I'm betting on finding something out that way that will clue us in or at least lead us to something else."

Clarissa had all day to do the rural patrol of Graham County and to the best of her knowledge nothing was pressing. Therefore there was no real need for her to cover the entire county today. She looked at her watch. It was early. Rambler's idea seemed like a good one. She figured she could help him.

"Sure. Why not?"

"Let's go. I've already got an order for food and coffee from the Town Talk. I've got a cooler full of water, soda and a couple of light beers."

"Sounds like you knew I was going to say yes."

"I was betting on it. You like chimichangas?"

"From the Town Talk? Heck, yeah."

"Can you eat two of them?"

Clarissa patted her flat stomach. She'd been working out a lot lately. A couple of chimis weren't going to do her any lasting damage.

"You know I can."

"Good, 'cuz that's what I ordered for you. Let's roll, Deputy Clarissa."

Between picking up the food, gossiping for a few minutes at the Town Talk Café and driving directly to the Rez a good hour had elapsed. Rambler had asked Clarissa to drive, claiming tired eyes, but she knew his pot habit was the cause of their redness and fatigue. Pulling into town Rambler pointed to the Cochise Café.

"Pull in there."

"You have to use the bathroom or something?" asked Clarissa.

"Nope. Let's get a thermos of coffee."

"We've already got enough hot java for the day," replied Clarissa.

"I want to see what we can pick up in terms of gossip. This time of day the chatterbugs are still drinking their coffees and are likely pretty wound up. When they get like that they want to share the latest news, whatever the news is. Let's see what we can find out."

Rambler was roundly greeted as he entered the Cochise Café. A few of the locals greeted Clarissa but for the most part she was ignored. Rambler placed his thermos on the counter and asked the waitress to fill it up. Once she walked away he spoke loudly enough for all to hear.

"What's new around here?"

The people who were doing the loudest chitchatting focused on him and somewhat suspiciously on Clarissa. When Rambler bought a round of donuts for the house, everyone opened up. The subject of conversation quickly led to the latest rumors concerning Doctor Gouyen and Sister Karpenko. Clarissa, knowing few of the people present, listened closely making note of who said what. The topic seemed to be stirring everyone's interest and just about everyone was willing to offer up an opinion.

"They came in here a few times."

"Both of them seemed kind of stand-offish if you ask me."

"I heard the council allowed them to buy land."

"That's against the law, isn't it?"

"I heard they got a one-hundred-year lease. Rich people know how to figure that kind of thing out."

"Rambler, you work for the sheriff's office and so does your gal partner, right?"

"That's what the uniforms say," replied Rambler.

"You still want to be Rez police chief some day?"

The room hushed as everyone waited for an answer to a question they already knew.

"I think I might be good at the job," replied Rambler.

The best-looking woman in the group, who everyone knew had her eye on Rambler, answered for them all.

"We know you'd be good at the job."

Rambler tipped his hat and smiled broadly. He knew he'd be good at the job. The customers suddenly seemed more at ease, even in the presence of Clarissa, an outsider.

"I hear that Doctor Gouyen is missing. Is that true, Rambler?"

Rambler carried on with a lengthy tale that ended with the most likely situation being that she was simply taking more vacation time than originally anticipated and that she was expected to be home soon. The questions and speculations were in no short supply.

"Maybe she and her lover are on vacation?"

"Where do lesbians go when they need to get away? That's where I'd look."

"How long have they been together?"

"Were they planning on having kids and staying on the Rez?"

"Maybe they went to one of those liberal states where they could get married?"

"How can a nun get married? Aren't they celibate and considered married to the church?"

"That's what I've always heard."

"Maybe it's different because they were Orthodox, not Catholic."

It was all followed by a conversation on how many Apache women preferred women to men. Of course every unmarried woman over the age of 25 was suspected of being gay. In the end no one seemed to really care all that much whether or not they were a couple, other than it made for new and unusual gossip. Eventually when Rambler had heard all he wanted, he and Clarissa headed toward the cliff dwellings and the home of Gouyen and Karpenko.

"What do you make of all that?" asked Clarissa.

"Not much. Small town gossip. No one who was there seemed to really know much about them."

"There didn't seem to be all that much prejudice against them."

"You mean because they are a gay couple or because Karpenko is White and living on the Rez?"

"Both, I guess."

"Sexuality, unless it's something illegal is pretty much left alone," said Rambler. "But, when you start seeing Whites building homes and settling on Apache land, well that's another story."

"They didn't seem to have any trouble getting all the permits for everything they needed. How does that happen?" asked Clarissa.

"Money don't sing, dance or walk, but it talks on the Rez, just like everywhere else. It didn't hurt that they hired all locals to do the work. That's a big deal because good paying jobs are always hard to come by. Besides, the land is leased not owned. Big difference."

On the road to the women's home and eventually the cliff dwellings, Clarissa thought about her own feelings of being immersed in Native culture. She'd been around it her entire life, but the stop at the Cochise Café was the first time everyone seemed to let their guards down around her and speak as though she weren't an outsider. She found it refreshing and saw herself and the local Apache with a new perspective. When it came right down to it the real differences between Whites and Natives were little to nothing, except for traditional cultural beliefs. Then again cultural beliefs gripped mightily on the thinking of each of the separate societies.

The last few miles of the ride were smooth sailing. Clarissa knocked on the door of the missing Doctor Gouyen and Tavisha Karpenko's beautiful home. The security cameras were in plain sight so if someone was home they would know the sheriff's deputies were at the door. After a long minute, a woman's voice came through the security speaker.

"Yes. How may I help you?"

"I'm Deputy Clarissa Kerkhoff and this is Deputy Rambler Braing."

Rambler politely tipped his hat.

"To whom am I speaking?" asked Clarissa.

"Tavisha Karpenko. May I ask what you want?"

"Sister Karpenko…"

Clarissa was abruptly interrupted by a harsh response.

"I have recanted my vows. I am no long a member of the Order of Saint Eustace."

"I'm sorry. My mistake."

"It was very recent. What is it that you want?"

"Would you mind coming to the door?"

"I just got out of the shower. Yes, I mind coming to the door. Come back in one hour."

"Is Doctor Gouyen with you?"

"No. She's traveling."

"Have you talked with her recently?"

"She's been doing some wilderness hiking for the last two weeks in the Smoky Mountains. She's out of human contact for another week, maybe two."

The look in Rambler's eyes said he wasn't believing a single word he was hearing. Clarissa wasn't buying it either. Rambler nodded his head toward some nearby hills.

"We'll go for a walk up in the hills to the north. We'll be back in an hour so we can talk to you face to face," said Clarissa.

Suddenly the fact that she just got out of the shower didn't seem to bother Tavisha.

"Wait, I'll be right down. Stay right there."

Two minutes later Tavisha opened the door. Her hair wasn't wet and she was fully dressed, with makeup on. She'd been lying about the shower. She cordially invited them in.

"Tea? Coffee?"

Neither accepted the offer but Tavisha poured herself a tea.

"Now, how may I help you?"

"We have a few routine questions about Doctor Gouyen."

"I told you, she's away from civilization in the Smokies. You can find her near or in Great Smoky Mountain National Park somewhere between Tennessee and North Carolina. At least according to the schedule she told me she was following."

Both Rambler and Clarissa knew of the endurance required to complete the famed hike that drew many to the Great Smokies, but neither of them had personally hiked the trail.

"When you last talked with her, how did she sound?"

"Normal. Happy. Happy mostly because I had made the decision to leave the Priory."

"Is there any reason you didn't go with her on the trek to the Smoky Mountains?"

"Yes, of course. I was praying as to whether or not I should leave the Priory. I needed to be alone. If she were around me it would have been too great of an influence on my decision-making process."

"I understand," replied Clarissa.

"Has Doctor Gouyen had any recent bouts of depression?"

"No. Absolutely not. Why do you ask?"

"It's a routine question in a possible missing persons case," explained Clarissa.

"I've told you already. She's not missing. She's hiking."

"Yes, of course. Just a few more questions. Strictly routine."

"Did she possibly have a secret life that you didn't know about?"

"Impossible. I know everything about her. We keep no secrets from each other."

"When do you expect to hear from her?"

"Tomorrow, maybe the next day. It all depends on how the hike is going."

"Is she a skilled outdoorswoman?"

"None better. She's done survivalist training as a hobby for years."

Rambler made a mental note about the survivalist training. Song Bird had mentioned to him years earlier in passing that Gouyen owned a significant amount of camping gear. That bit of information had not popped up on any of her background information nor was it among the notes Shelly had given him. He was certain Tavisha was lying. It was a stupid thing to lie about as it could be so easily checked.

"Would you mind if we looked through her extra hiking gear?" asked Rambler.

Tavisha hesitated one second too long. Her answer was another indication that the words coming out of her mouth were not the truth.

"She took everything with her. All of her hiking gear that is, I mean."

Song Bird had stated to him that Doctor Gouyen, who was also his cousin, had a garage full of camping gear. She certainly wouldn't have taken all of it with her. Rambler also flashed on something else Song Bird had noted; Doctor Gouyen had studied old maps of forgotten places on the Rez. Some of the charts were hundreds of years old.

"Is that everything?" asked Tavisha. "I have an appointment to be at soon."

"That's all for now," replied Clarissa. "Here's my card. Call me if you think of anything else."

"I'm certain there is nothing to worry about and that Doctor Gouyen will contact me soon."

Back in the truck on their way back Rambler spoke first.

"She's a bloody liar."

"You don't think?" said Clarissa.

"What's she hiding?"

"My first guess is a dead body. But I've got no proof of that. Yet."

"Pull over behind those rock formations," said Rambler.

"What for?"

"Let's see how urgent her appointment was that she had no more time for us."

Two hours passed and Tavisha did not pass down the only road out of her home.

"I gotta run the county roads," said Clarissa. "Give me a lift back to my truck. You can come back and wait by yourself."

"What if she makes a move? We might miss something," said Rambler.

"You might miss something. Let's roll outta here."

Rambler knew the rules. He had no choice except to comply. Clarissa took the county rounds seriously. Today she was scheduled to make a few stops visiting old people living by themselves in the middle of nowhere and check on the county garbage dump. It was important that rural folks who had little contact with the outside world notice the law worked for them too.

Chapter 29

ADOPT A HIGHWAY

LIKE MANY OF THE good citizens of Graham County, the Kiers family did their civic duty. The kids had chosen the Adopt-A-Highway program and the parents saw to it that it got done. The family volunteered to take care of miles four and five off Arizona Highway 366. Mile markers 118 and 119 were four and five miles up the paved section of the only road to the top of Mount Graham.

On this excursion, only half an hour into cleaning up discarded trash, it was all seven of the Kiers family who saw the turned over and burnt vehicle. Dutch, the father of five told the others to stay back as he moved forward and spied inside the vehicle. His eyes landed on the partially burned body that was clinging upside down to a seat belt that was somehow intact.

"Move back and keep away. I need to call the sheriff's office."

His wife and children slowly stepped away from the burnt vehicle as Dutch made the call. He wasted no time in explaining what he'd seen.

"Thank you," said Helen.

"Yes, ma'am," said Dutch.

"And Dutch?"

"Yes, ma'am?"

"Please stay where you are so you can show Sheriff Hanks exactly what you've found and explain how you found it."

"We were doing our civic duty, but..."

"Yes, you were," said Helen. "Don't think for one moment it isn't appreciated by many who talk the talk but don't walk the walk. I'll say it for them. Keeping the road to the top of the Mount pristine is a blessing to all the people of Graham County. We humbly thank you for volunteering. We're sorry you had to discover such a tragic accident."

"Thank you ma'am. It's just that..."

He was quickly drowned out by the fast-speaking Helen. He had no chance to explain they'd given up half the morning already and that they had a full day's worth of work ahead of them with cattle and in the cotton fields.

"We'd like all of you to wait until Sheriff Hanks gets there. This could be very important."

"What do you mean?" asked Dutch.

"I'm not at liberty to say," replied Helen. "Just wait there or you'll be stopped by one of the deputies following Sheriff Hanks up 366."

Dutch clicked off his phone and looked at his family.

"We wait here."

One of the kids, the seven-year-old piped up.

"What are we waiting for?"

"The sheriff."

"Why?"

"In this case it's the right thing to do."

The kids spread out and began investigating everything they could see. Dutch and his wife, Corey, stayed in the van and waited. It wasn't long before Zeb came blazing up SR366.

"You Dutch?"

"Yes, sir."

"And this is your family?"

"Yes, sir."

"All of them?"

"Every one of them," replied Dutch.

Corey pointed to the damaged car as the kids wandered back one by one.

"We can't really tell you much."

"No," echoed the kids. "We didn't even get to look at it."

Zeb turned to the five kids who were circled nearby.

"You didn't sneak over and have a look?"

The oldest child answered for the others.

"Our father told us to stay away."

"Dutch, you're the only one who looked inside the wreck?"

"I was the only one. Thank God the children didn't see what I saw."

Zeb and the Kiers clan all looked over their shoulders as a train of three county vehicles, all of them bearing deputy sheriffs came racing up the hill, tires screeching as they rounded each switchback.

Zeb waited for Dutch to look away from the oncoming vehicles and asked the same question a second time.

"Yes, sir, Sheriff. I was the only one who looked inside."

"Come with me," ordered Zeb.

The youngest, a three-year-old boy, raced after Zeb and Dutch. Dutch stopped, picked up the youngster and walked halfway back to meet Corey where he handed her the child. He double-timed it to get back to Zeb who by now had stuck his head inside the overturned vehicle. Thankfully, the face of the dead woman had not been terribly damaged. Someone should be able to identify her. As soon as his deputies arrived he'd have them take statements from the Kiers family.

"No need to rush, Dutch. I had a look. She's not going anywhere."

Dutch proceeded to hurriedly tell Zeb about the Adopt-A-Highway program and explain how they'd come across the wreck and he looked inside and saw what he described as a little slice of hell. Zeb took everybody's names and the number of the single cellphone they shared between them. He looked at those five kids and thought of his own. Dutch and Corey were teaching good citizenship.

Zeb phoned in the license plate while Kate and Rambler quickly took statements from the children and Corey before sending them on their way. The kids waved and smiled widely at Zeb and his deputies as they headed down 366.

Zeb took a call, spun and went into action. He moved at a clip that none of his deputies had ever witnessed before.

"Clarissa call Doc. Tell him to get up here right away. This car belongs to Doctor Gouyen. I'm as sure as I can be that that's her in there."

If this was who they thought it was, the DIA and NSA would soon be fighting each other for control of the body. None of the deputies knew precisely why the high-powered agencies were so deeply involved. None of them, not even Zeb, had seen anything like it before. They had no doubt that the NSA was

catching every cellphone call that used the tower atop Mount
Graham. Dutch Kiers' call had been one of them. As a consequence, they all knew that time was of the essence.

"Doc said to meet him on the top of the Mount in seventeen
minutes," said Clarissa.

Deputy Kate jumped in her truck and headed up to the sum-
mit. When she got there Doc was just hopping out of a helicopter. He ran on old legs over to Kate's truck. Kate pointed to
the chopper as Doc got in her vehicle.

"Never been in one."

Doc looked exhilarated and a touch wild-eyed.

"Been in a few hundred of 'em myself," said Doc. "We had
some great pilots in Nam. What's up?"

Kate explained about the turned-over vehicle and the partially burned body who Zeb believed was Doctor Gouyen.

"Thank you, Kate. I know what Zeb wants."

"Cause of death?" asked Kate.

"And absolute certainty the dead woman is Doctor Gouyen,"
added Doc.

Kate's truck flew back down the gravel road. Doc compli-
mented her on her fine driving. Zeb opened the truck door for
Doc at the scene.

"Please get on it as fast as you can," asked Zeb.

"Roger dodger," replied Doc.

"Do it right, "said Zeb. "But don't make it obvious."

Doc grabbed his pocketknife to cut the seat belt away. Together he and Zeb lowered the partially burned remains to the
ground where Doc went right to work. He checked the dead
woman's eyes, drew blood, quickly obtained skin, hair and nail
samples, did a cursory examination of the head, checked for
bullet holes and made an imprint of the teeth.

Zeb and his deputies stood back a few steps and watched
as Doc removed a syringe with a long needle from his ancient
medical bag. He jammed it into the dead woman's lungs and
filled a tube with fluid. Then Doc spoke, out loud but to himself.

"I only got one chance at this one."

The wily old medical expert pulled out a second syringe
which had an unusual looking pincher on the end, slid it under
her left breast and pushed it directly into her heart. Upon ex-

traction he examined it with a keen eye. He spoke once again to
himself.

"Yes. Got it."

From Zeb's point of view Doc had managed to get everything
he needed in less than ten minutes. Doc quickly gathered his
things, did one final check on the body, hopped in Kate's truck
and they headed back up to the top of the Mount and the waiting
chopper.

"You're good at what you do, Doc," said Kate.

"As are you," replied Doc. "Just doing my job. A little duress
keeps an old man's ticker free from lipid build up."

At the top of the Mount Doc hopped out of the truck and
into the chopper where he gave the command to fly over the
hills to Tucson. He'd already called his old pal Doctor Zata, head
pathologist at the state medical school. On the trip he dictated
a note to Shelly on a phone that she told him was the only way
to temporarily keep information from being tracked by the NSA
or DIA.

Five minutes after Doc's helicopter departed, DIA agents
Beckette and Hoazinne arrived closely followed by a single NSA
agent who identified herself as Claire Densk. They brought with
them an ambulance and a tow truck. The helicopter pilot wisely
disappeared with Doc over the other side of the mountain. In
the hubbub the DIA and NSA agents were none the wiser.

The NSA agent and the DIA agents, unaware that Doc Yackley
had come and gone, marched directly to Zeb.

"We'll take it from here," said Densk.

"Under what authority?" asked Zeb.

Beckette handed over a blanket warrant giving the Feds authority over the scene. Zeb read it thoroughly before comment-
ing.

"How many of these do you guys carry with you?" asked Zeb.

The agents found no humor in his remark.

"Like I said, we'll take it from here. We would like you and
your deputies to cordon off the area," said Densk.

Zeb nodded to his team to set up the perimeter just as his
cellphone rang. When he eyeballed the number he saw it was
Doc. He held up and pointed at the cellphone the agents had
heard ring before walking far enough away so he couldn't be

overheard. He explained the situation to Doc. In return Doc mentioned to Zeb a few things he suspected after what he saw. Zeb ended the call, walked over the Feds and lied easily and with a straight face.

"My apologies to the DIA and the NSA but we've got urgent county business to attend to. It can't wait. We'll mark the scene and then be out of your hair. The scene is officially and completely yours."

Zeb called his troops over with a brisk wave of the hand. Clarissa tied off the last piece of yellow crime scene tape and joined the others.

"Let's get the hell out of here. We're only going to get aggravated if we stick around. Let's meet at the office when we're off the Mount."

Chapter 30

STAFF MEETING

ZEB HAD PHONED AHEAD. Helen would have the meeting room stocked with coffee, tea and snacks. Everyone was a bit edgy when they gathered. Shelly walked into the room just as the meeting began.

"Can you believe those guys?" asked Kate.

"Who the hell do they think they are?" added Clarissa.

"The government does exactly what it wants to. You can't fight them," replied Rambler.

"Well, we're going to try," said Zeb.

Zeb let his tea steep as the others drank coffee and ate some healthy, homemade Helen snacks.

"After I talked with Doc, he sent me a text and copied Shelly in on it."

"What'd it say?" asked Kate.

"Doc, you know Doc, he's got a theory."

Warm chuckles helped drop the level of tension from the interaction with the Feds. Doc always had theories and though they often seemed far-fetched at first, they were usually spot on.

"Here's what he found at the site. No bullet wounds, no knife wounds, no residue on the body, which he says would likely have been burned off anyway."

"Yeah, so what?" asked Rambler. "No findings do us no good."

"Hang on. Here's the interesting part, at least according to Doc. Severely constricted pupils in both eyes. Fluid in the lungs. Cardiac tissue that once he looks at it under a microscope he thinks will show cardiac arrest."

"What's all that add up to in Doc's mind?" asked Kate.

"Potentially, and he emphasized this is a working theory only, we are likely dealing with a poisoning. In fact at this point he's seventy-five percent certain of it. He ordered the chopper to

fly to Tucson so his pal Doc Zata, the pathologist, can look at
it more closely. He'll contact us the second he has any idea at
all what the poison was, if indeed it was poisoning. He thought
he'd know in the next few hours but some of the tests may take
a few days in order to have absolute confirmation."

"What's our plan in the meantime?"

"First I'd like to ferret out why the NSA and DIA are sniffing
around like dogs in heat. I'm referring to their extraordinary
interest in the deaths of Doctor Gouyen and the as-yet unnamed
woman Echo came across."

Shelly spoke up.

"I have a pretty good explanation for Doctor Gouyen and the
NSA. I've been digging deeper and deeper into her scientific
bio. I've checked her other background data including her ed-
ucational contacts, fellow scholars, published papers, personal
stuff, etcetera. Because she's a signal processing expert for the
telescopes up on the Mount she is definitely a candidate to
be on federal radar. No pun intended. The NSA is responsible for global monitoring, collection and processing of data
for foreign and domestic intelligence. They specialize in signal
intelligence."

"Which is what, exactly?" asked Zeb.

"Intelligence gathered by interception of signals such as communications between people, between machines, basically any
manner in which people or machines communicate. Let's call
those communications systems and signals. They also keep an
eye on all radar and weapon systems communications. They
have the capability to have us all bugged right now. In fact
I have no doubt, based on how quickly they made it up the
Mount, that is exactly what they are doing. I'm doing everything
in my power to disrupt them from hearing us. I've put signal
interrupters on all of your phones so expect even local calls to be
a bit jumpy, maybe even difficult to complete for a while. They'll
figure out exactly what I'm up to pretty quickly but I've also
set the interruptions to cycle through frequently on an irregular
basis."

"No wonder they've known what we're up to," said Clarissa.
"It's their job."

"From the sounds of it, tracking spies, civilians and just about anyone they want to is how they justify their incredibly huge budget."

"Right," said Shelly. "Like I said I've done whatever I can to protect us from their snooping ways, but they're always going to be able to catch on to what I am doing and possibly be at least one step ahead of me."

"Fuck," said Rambler. "We're screwed."

"Wait, there's more. They also gather electronic signals not directly used in communication."

"Hot damn," added Rambler. "Who stands a chance against those guys?"

"We do," replied Zeb. "Right? Shelly?"

"I certainly hope so."

"So? What does all of that tell us?" asked Zeb.

"And what does it have to do with our two dead bodies?" asked Rambler.

"Based on Doctor Gouyen's areas of expertise, which fall into the cutting edge of signal communications, the NSA would naturally know her and be constantly surveilling her work as a matter of national security."

"Any way we can figure out what she was currently working on?" asked Zeb.

"She's most recently published several papers on signaling between telescopes and satellites with a primary focus on signal intercepts from satellites to drones. In particular, and I'm reading a bit into this, those with military proficiencies."

"What does that mean?"

"The first thing that popped into my mind, probably because I read about it online today and like everyone I suffer from confirmation bias, is that several Russian generals were killed and Russian tanks are being blown up routinely by Ukrainian drone attacks."

"That's a Ukrainian issue then, isn't it?" asked Rambler.

"Yes and no. The drones and their signaling capabilities are likely supplied and almost certainly controlled by United States intelligence agencies. Of course, I can't prove that, but it's logical."

"And it is an American proxy war," added Rambler. "Isn't it?"

"Makes sense," replied Zeb. "Echo calls it a proxy war, too."

"This sort of thing falls into an area known as dark intelligence. The level of intelligence is known and accessed by only a very limited number of people," explained Shelly.

"I've got a pretty good guess as to what is going on."

"Let's hear it," said Rambler.

"Based on what Echo has explained to me about how combat is actually fought, I have no doubt we have a fair number of spooks behind Russian lines in Ukraine," added Zeb.

"Spooks that are gathering Russian military intelligence and sending it to us?" asked Rambler.

"Yup. Spooks that are trained in drone and satellite signaling. Echo tells me this kind of thing can only be done by people who train for years. The Ukrainians don't have the experience so it's the U.S. military that's ordering the attacks and killing Russian leadership," replied Zeb. "At least in theory."

"You're probably spot on," added Shelly. "That is how it can work in theory."

"According to Echo that's how it actually works in the field of combat."

"And the DIA?" asked Clarissa. "Why are they so deeply entrenched in all of this?"

"As you know the DIA is a branch of the Department of Defense. It's an intelligence agency and combat support agency of the DOD, specializing in defense and military intelligence. Doctor Gouyen was probably a high-level contractor for them. My guess is that this is somehow all tangled together and she did something that got her killed."

"Her partner is Russian," said Rambler.

Shelly interjected with a nuanced point that seemed to be linked to little but yet might be of value.

"The Abbey of Saint Eustace, the parent organization of Sister Karpenko's Priory..."

Zeb abruptly stepped into the middle of Shelly's explanation.

"It's ex-Sister Tavisha Karpenko. She's dropped out of the Order of Saint Eustace."

Rambler had shared this information with Clarissa and eventually everyone had heard. It now officially became part of the investigation because it came from the top.

"Okay, now that information is on the record. Let me start over. The Abbey of Saint Eustace, the parent organization of Sister Karpenko's Priory, is located in territory that is claimed by both Russia and Ukraine. Technically she may be a Ukrainian. I don't know for certain. Many Russian-speaking Ukrainians live in that area. Loyalties are known to bounce back and forth. It's a bit like living in the old wild west."

"Right. Rambler why don't you and Clarissa go back out to the Rez where Sister Tavisha and Doctor Gouyen built their getaway home," said Zeb. "Even if we can't get into their house, have a look around the nearby area."

"We are all aware Tavisha is formally no longer a nun," said Clarissa. "I think you should know that she said she secularized by personal choice."

"Speaking of Tavisha. Echo picked up what might be valuable information when she went on a class outing with the kids to the Priory," said Zeb.

"Yes? What'd she find out?" asked Rambler.

"She said it was weird interacting with Tavisha. She said Tavisha acted almost like she didn't recognize her."

"So? They only met once before, right?"

"True," replied Zeb. "She also said Tavisha looked surprising like the dead woman, wore identical boots and what she believed to be an identical stag deer/hunter necklace," added Zeb.

"It almost sounds like you think the dead woman was Tavisha," said Kate.

"Clearly she can't be," said Zeb.

"Did Tavisha have the Z tattoo or the birthmark on her hand?" asked Rambler.

"No, not that Echo could see. But Tavisha did have a rack of Henry .30-.30s like the dead woman had."

"Zeb, there have to be several hundred of those in the county," said Kate. "Josh sells them wholesale."

"I know. But she also saw saddle strings identical to the ones Clarissa and I found on the trail near the scene of the crime in the Pinaleño Mountains."

"They were handmade," said Clarissa. "Very unique. If they were the same it's a link we can't ignore."

Zeb could see that everyone was spinning through the possibilities. There was only one thing to do. Get to work and prove that what they knew were facts not coincidences.

"Shelly, please dig up what you can."

Shelly saluted Zeb.

"And the dead woman that Echo found? Do we know how she plays into all this yet?" asked Kate. "Anything that ties her into Doctor Gouyen at all?"

"We don't know yet."

"Kate, you and I will head back out to the death scene. I have a suspicion that we probably missed something."

"Does everybody know and understand their assignments?"

Heads nodded around the table. Rambler had one final question.

"Anything specific you have on your list that you want us to be on the lookout for?"

"Anything that links Doctor Gouyen or the other dead woman to anything at all. If we can find some physical evidence that links the two dead women we'll be in business. You're all great deputies, use your imaginations. Now, let's move."

Kate, Rambler and Clarissa grabbed everything they considered essential and were out the door in nothing flat. Zeb stopped at Helen's desk before departing.

"Helen, I'm not telling you what's up or where we're going because I think the DIA and the NSA are going to show up here while we're gone. I don't want you to have to lie to them."

Helen harumphed.

"I can handle those whelps. Roast 'em on a fire spit if I have to."

Zeb high-fived his Auntie.

Chapter 31

CAVES AND CLIFF DWELLINGS

THIS TIME RAMBLER TOOK the wheel of the county vehicle. On the way to the home of the late Doctor Gouyen and the caves in the area around the ancient Apache cliff dwellings Clarissa used her cellphone to read up on the different types of things that were being done every day right under their noses at the Observatory. Specifically she dug into Gouyen's work.

"Did you know the three telescopes on the Mount have been operating jointly for almost the last fifteen years?"

"I did not," replied Rambler. "Other than what I've recently learned I've mostly just heard a lot about the nickname LU-CIFER."

"It's truly interesting stuff."

"Go on. Tell me more about LUCIFER."

"LUCIFER or LUCI as it is now called is actually two powerful add-ons to the LBT, which is the large binocular telescope on the Mount."

"Don't you find a touch of irony in all of that given the Vatican telescope shares space with LUCIFER?"

"Actually, I don't find it ironic at all. The devil has always played a huge role in Catholicism. All western religions for that matter have the devil as one of the main characters in their moral tales," said Clarissa.

"Are you suggesting the entirety of the telescopes are the work of the devil?"

Clarissa's eyes lit up.

"Listen to this. Collectively around the world the Vatican astronomical observatories are looking for something very specific. According to the Right Hemispheric Remote Viewing researchers what they are looking for is in deep space and should it come near the earth it would cause three days of darkness, create an environment characterized by fire and sulfur, and would be a source of great fear for those who are aware of the search."

"Sounds like a cross between a baloney sandwich and the devil herself."

"So the devil is real and is a woman, huh, Rambler?"

Rambler was half kidding but was beginning to enjoy the banter with Clarissa more and more. He guessed Clarissa had a wilder imagination than he had previously surmised. Sometimes it was difficult to tell if her analogies were brilliant or ridiculous. At this moment he stood on the cusp of believing either one. He couldn't fault her enthusiasm.

"You'll dig this, Rambler. The Large Binocular Telescope was originally named the Columbus Project."

"Now there's a conspiracy I can get behind."

"And rightly so," replied Clarissa. "But that's a topic for another day."

"We will discuss it later," replied Rambler. "You can count on that."

Knowing how Rambler's mind could wander, Clarissa immediately drew him back into her explanation.

"Every great astronomical community in the world had their fingers in the making of that specific telescope, the LBT. The LBT, which I mentioned earlier uses the LUCIs, recently discovered a galaxy seven billion light years from earth."

"New galaxies for the White man to conquer."

Clarissa purposely ignored Rambler.

"Aha."

"Aha? What?"

"This is what we're interested in."

"What this are you talking about?" asked Rambler. "And tell me why."

"One of the telescopes is a radio wave telescope. It has a tracking accuracy of one inch over very great distances, millions of miles in fact. Since Doctor Gouyen was working with drone-satellite intercepts she was likely working on that telescope. It's a link to something we're dealing with. I can just feel it."

"And what connection might that be since it involves the NSA and the DIA?"

"That part I don't have figured out just yet. But I will. You can count on it."

The pair rode in silence for the better part of the next half hour until Rambler finally announced they were coming up to the driveway of Doctor Gouyen and Tavisha Karpenko's remote love nest.

"Want to knock on the door and see if anybody's home?" asked Rambler.

"We should. Just in case she has booby traps around."

"What made you think of that?" asked Rambler.

"Well, you know, Echo's folks do that kind of thing."

"So you think everyone on the Rez has their property boo-by-trapped?"

"Touchy, touchy. No, I don't," said Clarissa. "I just don't want to be surprised if and when someone sees us trespassing on their property. I may be a deputy for Zeb Hanks, but I follow the letter of the law anyway."

"You know what Zeb says. There's the letter of the law and then there is the intent of the law," responded Rambler.

Clarissa studied Rambler's facial expression as he made his statement about Zeb and getting the intent of the law to work in his favor. It was impossible to tell if he shared Zeb's views or was yanking her chain. She let it go and got back on the subject at hand.

"Right," replied Clarissa.

"Remember, it was never Karpenko's land and never will be. It's leased from the San Carlos Reservation."

"Gotcha."

Repeated raps on the door and multiple rings of the bell proved that either no one was home or no one was answering. The most likely person who might be at home had to be Tavisha Karpenko. But neither Rambler nor Clarissa ruled out a visitor, even though no vehicles were in sight. Rambler pointed to the north.

"Nobody home. Let's head up toward the ruins and the caves. We'll just have to watch our step."

An hour later they were deep inside their third cavern of the day. Outside the cavern Clarissa spotted a tiny owl's nest quite unlike any she had ever seen.

"That is a rarely found nest in these parts," explained Rambler. "It belongs to a family of ferruginous pygmy owls. I have personally known such a nest to be a harbinger of death and destruction."

Inside the cavern the acrid odor of recent smoke clung to the floor and walls. Flashlights illuminated the interior as their noses led them to what had been an unusually large bonfire for such an enclosed space. On the perimeter of the fire pit were remnants of women's clothing, jewelry and half-burned notebooks. A brief look showed them to be full of scientific data. Also amongst the mostly burned items was a fair amount of what once had been camping gear.

"What do you think?" asked Rambler.

"I think someone was going out of their way to get rid of a whole lot of things."

"From the looks of it I'd say they were trying to only partially get rid of stuff."

"As in making certain some things were left intact so we'd find them?" asked Clarissa. "Is that what you're thinking?"

"Women's clothing? Scientific data entries in multiple notebooks? Camping gear? Kind of looks like Doctor Gouyen had a fire sale or Tavisha burned it all up for some unknown reason."

"Lovers can have difficult quarrels that can lead to fiery destruction. Destroying someone's personal stuff is an aggressive way to get back at someone in a most heinous manner."

"Like this?" asked Rambler.

Rambler stuck his knife into the still-warm ashes and lifted an object out for closer inspection.

"What's that? A bracelet?"

"Not just any bracelet," replied Rambler. "This is one made by Song Bird specifically for Echo."

"How do you know that for certain?"

Rambler held the barely burned bracelet directly in Clarissa's line of vision. He shined a small flashlight on it. Inside were Song Bird's mark and Echo's name written in Apache.

"Where did you learn to read Apache?" asked Clarissa.

"It was my first language. My grandmother taught me. It was one of the greatest gifts she gave me and she gave me many."

"You're lucky."

"I'm blessed," replied Rambler.

"Let's bag as much as we can of what seems important and get it back to the office."

Among the many items that hadn't been completely destroyed were two glass vials that had partially burned labels indicating the bottles at one time contained poison.

As their flashlights led them out of the dark cavern Rambler spotted something out of place.

"Clarissa. Wait. One second."

Instinctively she flashed her light in the direction Rambler was headed. There sitting on a rock near the low entrance was a United States military boonie hat. Rambler flashed his light on the hat and saw the insignia of the Black Shadows. Turning it over he saw Echo's name on the inside rim.

"Clarissa?"

"Yeah?"

"You're going to want to have a look at this."

He held the boonie hat up so Clarissa could see the insignia.

"The Black Shadows. What are the odds? That was Echo's unit."

"I know."

Rambler flipped the hat over and shined his light on Echo's name.

"Shit. You don't..."

"I don't know what to think. First her knife at the first dead body and now her bracelet and hat in the same place as belongings from the missing Doctor Gouyen. I'm not saying it's direct proof of anything, but Echo seems to be involved. And if we are going to do our jobs correctly, we can't rule out the possibility that she knows more than she's telling us."

"Remember Rambler, the knife was stolen. The boonie hat may have been taken at the same time. Echo misplaced her turquoise bracelet the day Doctor Gouyen, Echo, Chief Cocheta and Tavisha Karpenko spoke at the San Carlos Community Center."

"That's her story, isn't it?"

Chapter 32

PINALEÑO MOUNTAINS

"KATE, WHAT SAY WE pick up Echo and take her with us to the Pinaleños. She knows the lay of the land better than either of us and..."

"Say no more. She'll be a good addition to the hunt."

An hour later Echo had directed them via a concealed pathway neither of them knew existed to the exact spot where she had found the dead woman.

Echo lay down on the ground where she'd found the dead body and re-created how the body was situated. When she had Zeb roll her over a knife was revealed where she had secretly placed it. She had replicated the position of the original knife to make things as realistic as possible.

"From the way you described the wounds someone had to have sneaked up behind her at this very spot. It's so open that it seems almost impossible to believe someone could do that here," said Kate.

"Turn your back," said Echo.

"What? Why?" asked Zeb.

"Just do as I ask. Turn around, half close your eyes like it's dusk and count to three."

Not understanding what Echo was up to, Zeb turned before he even got to the count of two. Echo was nowhere to be seen. Kate was better at following instructions.

"Echo knows how to disappear?" asked Kate. "Neat trick. Where is she?"

Together Kate and Zeb walked directly at the rocks and only when they were mere inches from Echo could they see that the rock wall had a vertical crack that was well hidden. With time and erosion a large enough space to hide a single person had formed and was nearly impossible to see even at an intimate distance. Echo popped her head out just as they reached her.

"Crazy. Right? A hiding place that could have been used to jump the dead woman and slice a couple of her arteries before she even had a chance to know what hit her."

"Why didn't you tell me about this earlier?" asked Zeb.

"I just saw it for the first time myself. Talk about a perfect hiding place. I've been by this exact spot many times and I've never noticed it."

"Now we know how the killer was able to hide himself. It would be nice if we could find some physical evidence."

"I did notice one thing when I was hiding. It might be nothing," said Echo.

"Let's have a look."

Kate walked into the hiding spot and knelt on the ground. Running her fingers across a small shelf of rocks at ground level she found something. After digging around for a moment she held up a carabiner. Echo seemed to stare right past it to the interior wall of the small space. She extended her arm and tapped it against the soft rock where there appeared to be an unnatural gouged out scratch. The marking was roughly five feet off the ground.

"Just the right height for a carabiner on a backpack."

"It's just like the ones I have," added Clarissa.

"Now we just have to find a backpack with a missing carabiner," said Zeb.

Kate handed it to Zeb but not before saying one more thing.

"It's from a SwissGear pack."

"How can you tell?"

Kate pointed to the red Swiss flag insignia.

"I recognize the mark."

Zeb squinted as Echo chimed in with an all too familiar refrain.

"Zeb, you need to wear your glasses all the time."

Sheriff Hanks dutifully slipped on his cheaters and the trio hunted the surrounding area for another two hours, finding nothing of value.

Chapter 33

POISON

"Doc, everybody, including Echo is gathered in my office. I'm going to put you on speaker. You okay with that?"

"Hell, yes. You ready?"

"You own the floor, Doc."

"Here is what I found at the scene. Bilateral miosis..."

"What's that, Doc?"

"Constriction of the pupils in both eyes. I also found fluid in the lung. The amount of fluid was greater than what is found with severe pneumonia. I also grabbed some cardiac tissue. Doc Zata has given me a preliminary report that states there is damaged heart muscle tissue indicative of cardiac arrest. The lab report, which is not yet complete, strongly hints at the presence of a Novichok nerve agent."

"What the hell is a Novichok nerve agent?" asked Zeb.

"It's a nerve agent developed and used almost exclusively by the Russians. It's...wait a second...here let me have Doctor Zata explain. I'll let him do the talking."

"Greetings Graham County."

"Hello, Doctor Zata."

"What I am sharing with you is to be considered a preliminary report and nothing more. I do believe the victim, Doctor Gouyen was killed by a Novichok agent which is a binary compound. That's just a fancy way of saying the poison is formed by combing two compounds. The most current literature regarding this type of poison states that no one knows exactly what the compounds are. It is only known how they react on humans and animals."

"Obviously, they kill people," said Rambler.

"As little as ten milligrams is deadly."

"How large is ten milligrams?"

"Tip over a salt shaker in the restaurant and about ten milligrams of salt will fall out."

"That's not a lot."

"It's a highly concentrated deadly poison."

"How would the poison have been administered to the late Doctor Gouyen?" asked Kate.

"Easiest way would have been for someone to rub it on her skin. If someone were very sneaky and knew how to handle the poison, they could have dropped it on her without even touching her," explained Doctor Zata.

"Doctor, just to make certain that we understand, could you please run down how the nerve agent would work on a human once they have direct contact with it on their skin?"

"Great question, Sheriff Hanks. It's a sneaky varmint of a poison if you ask me. At first the person might get a runny nose or sweat a little, feel like they were coming down with a cold or exposed to an allergen."

"How long do they feel that way?" asked Kate.

"Depends on the amount of exposure. That unfortunately, at least in this case, is something we do not have the ability to determine. I know from Doc Yackley the Feds took the body. Am I correct in assuming you have not been able to retrieve it?"

"That's correct, Doctor Zata. Though if you work with the DIA or the NSA the body just might end up in your lab," said Zeb.

"Mmm-hmm. That would be remarkable wouldn't it?"

"To the point of being truly ironic," added Doc Yackley.

"That being said, when the poison kicks in and starts to kill someone, what happens?" asked Zeb.

"Let's say you wouldn't want to have it happen to you."

"Got that."

"Pupils constrict, eyesight changes, salivation becomes excessive, chest constricts, breathing gets difficult, nausea followed by vomiting. Then it gets real bad."

"Shit," whispered Rambler.

"Yes," replied Doctor Zata. "Loss of bowel function is next, followed by almost instant liver failure, kidney failure, spleen dysfunction and then the stomach shuts down, etcetera, etcetera. All of this leads to full body muscular spasms, convulsions and perhaps coma."

"And everyone who is exposed dies?"

"It's believed that most die from respiratory failure. A very torturous death to say the least. But to be exact, not all of those exposed die. Some have survived."

"Thank you, Doctor Zata. This information is all very helpful."

"My pleasure to aid the good people of Graham County. Doc says you owe him a beer and the price of a roundtrip helicopter ride."

"Done and done," said Zeb.

Zeb hung up the phone and looked up at his deputies.

"Kind of points the finger directly at Tavisha Karpenko, doesn't it?"

"Just because she's Russian?" asked Rambler. "Remember she was a Sister in the Order of Saint Eustace. Where in hell would she have gotten a nerve agent?"

"She had access," replied Zeb.

"What's the motive for killing her lover?" asked Kate.

"I've got a few ideas," said Clarissa.

"Go on. Let's hear them."

"Spurned lover syndrome is one theory. Let's assume for one moment that their relationship is going sour. Doctor Gouyen goes on vacation and when she comes back tells Tavisha she wants to break up. In a fit of anger Tavisha poisons Doctor Gouyen."

"Makes sense. Except for one thing."

"Yes?"

"Where does she get access to this sort of poison? Especially when you take into consideration that she's not a scientist, nor does she work in a lab and she's been in a convent most of her adult life as far as we know," said Zeb.

"Maybe she's a Russian spy?" suggested Clarissa.

"What exactly do you base that theory on?" asked Zeb.

"Well for one thing..."

Clarissa stopped in mid-sentence, grabbed Rambler by the arm and led him to the adjoining room. Seconds later they rolled in two large carts of bagged evidence."

"You found all of this by the cliff dwellings?"

"This and more," said Rambler. "It was among a lot of stuff that had been burned. Fortunately for us whoever built the fire left before it turned everything to ashes. Big mistake."

"What'd you find?" asked Zeb.

"There's enough here to prove there was burned clothing, camping gear, scientific notebooks, and much more that belonged to Doctor Gouyen," explained Clarissa.

"From looking at it, do you believe everything you found was the property of Doctor Gouyen?" asked Zeb.

Rambler spoke adamantly. "No! There is property of both women amongst all that we found."

"Do you think Karpenko or Gouyen burned their past as part of letting go of their old life and starting a new one?" asked Zeb.

"It could be just that," said Clarissa. "But several things lead us to believe otherwise. Rambler, you go first."

Rambler reached into a bag and pulled out a necklace. There was not a single person in the room who did not recognize Song Bird's beadwork.

"What's this?" asked Zeb.

"It's a protective necklace given as a sacred gift from one family member to another. We can all see it was made by Song Bird. To an Apache, this is a holy object. And we must never forget that Doctor Gouyen was an Apache above all else. If Song Bird, a holy man and a relative of Doctor Gouyen, gave it to her it had to have very deep meaning. It is something she would never discard, much less destroy," said Rambler.

Two thoughts filled the room. Either Doctor Gouyen symbolically destroyed her personal/professional life by burning up her possessions or Tavisha Karpenko was hell-bent on destroying it.

"There's more."

Clarissa put on two pairs of latex gloves and grabbed two bags from the top of one of the carts. She laid it on Zeb's desk. Zeb's hands instinctively reached for the bagged evidence. Rambler grabbed his arms and stopped him.

"If what Doctor Zata said is true, you're going to want to glove up. It's also why I made the suggestion about Karpenko being a Russia spy."

Zeb gloved up after putting his glasses on. He gingerly pulled the baggie forward. Inside were two small vials that carried the universal symbol for dangerous poisons, a skull with crossbones. Kate, eyeing the situation, also double-gloved her hands.

"Doctor Zata said that Novichok is made by mixing together two compounds. I'll bet these are those two compounds," said Zeb. "So I'd say we have our killer."

One look into the eyes and faces of the gathered deputies revealed that not everyone agreed with this simple conclusion. Kate and Zeb were certain of the evidence in front of them. The expressions on the faces of Rambler and Clarissa spoke to a different view. Rambler grabbed a small evidence bag that held one object. With a gloved hand he pulled it out and held it up for all to see. Echo gasped at the sight of it.

"That's my bracelet. It's been missing for a year," said Echo.

"Yes, it was among the evidence in the burn pile," said Rambler.

Clarissa who had stepped away returned with a boonie hat in her hand.

"What on earth was my missing turquoise bracelet doing there?" posed Echo. "And my boonie hat?"

"We were hoping you could tell us," said Rambler.

Chapter 34

TO PROVE NO GUILT

ECHO GLOVED UP AND took a closer look at the bracelet that had been found in the cliff caverns. There was nothing to say about the boonie hat except that it was hers. She struggled trying to put it all together. It was more than obvious that between being the first on the scene of the body, the knife that killed the first victim being hers, her skills at close-up combat and now her bracelet and military hat being found near the burn pile, that even she had to consider herself a murder suspect.

"This is unquestionably my bracelet. And that is definitely my hat."

"Echo, you haven't been read your rights. I'd advise you not to say anything else at this time," said Zeb.

"I've got nothing to hide. Nothing! I'll speak my piece and that's that."

"The bracelet?" asked Rambler. "I assume you're not guilty, Echo. But all the evidence points in that direction."

"I misplaced the bracelet over a year ago. I've told all of you that before. You all know it's missing."

"That's what you told us," said Clarissa.

"Do you have any reason not to believe me?"

"I don't," said Kate. "I know you're not guilty."

"Me neither," added Clarissa. "But we had better be able to explain all these coincidences."

"I want to believe you," said Rambler.

Rambler unfolded the picture of the four women taken at the San Carlos Community Center just over a year ago. Opening the magnifying glass on his phone, he shined the light on the picture and specifically on Echo's left wrist. There in plain sight was Echo's lost bracelet.

"That's the weekend I lost it," explained Echo. "I know I've specifically mentioned that to all of you. Haven't I?"

On the surface there appeared to be universal agreement that she had lost it. However, Rambler played devil's advocate. Someone had to.

"Let's say I'm a lawyer asking you a question in front of a jury," said Rambler.

"Go on," replied Echo.

"Echo Skysong, you say you lost this bracelet on the same weekend you were with the late Doctor Gouyen, Chief Cocheta and Tavisha Karpenko?"

"I did."

"Yet in this picture it's on your left wrist, is it not?"

"It is."

"So you must have lost it after you left the San Carlos Community Center?"

"I think so. I lost it. I don't remember exactly when, but it was that weekend. I only remember that I couldn't find it that night when I took my jewelry off."

"And the turquoise bracelet in question, the one you freely admitted was your own, was found in a pile of burned belongings some of which definitely belonged to the late Doctor Gouyen and her Tavisha Karpenko?"

"Yes."

"And your boonie hat from your military deployment in Afghanistan where you worked with Special Forces soldiers, was that not also found in the cave with the pile of items belonging to Doctor Gouyen and Tavisha Karpenko?"

"Yes. But..."

"And was it your knife that was found under the body of a dead woman?"

"Yes."

"A body that you discovered after two days spent alone in the desert?"

"Yes."

"And is it true that the dead woman looks like Tavisha Karpenko?"

"Yes, but she's alive. She may be the key to all of this."

"Is she alive? No one has seen her in the last few days."

"Then let's find her," said Echo.

"Do you suffer from PTSD related to your war experiences in Afghanistan?"

Zeb had about reached his limit.

"Enough Rambler. God damn it all to hell."

"I'm only playing role of devil's advocate, which is precisely what a prosecutor would do. Do you want me to stop? Are you afraid of what might come out?"

Zeb inhaled deeply to keep from exploding and wisely took the temperature of the room. It was evident that everyone, including Echo, wanted to see where Rambler was going with this.

"Go on, Rambler. But watch yourself."

"Would you agree that the fact that many of Doctor Gouyen's and Tavisha Karpenko's belonging were destroyed by fire indicates an act of hatred or revenge?

Steam rising in her heart made its way to her brain and reddened Echo's face.

"And in this act of hatred against Doctor Gouyen and the missing Tavisha Karpenko you let a bracelet that was in reality never missing at all, slip off your wrist?"

"Why would I have said a year ago that I lost my bracelet if I never truly did?" asked Echo.

"Crimes that come close to being perfect are always set up in advance and well planned right down to the smallest details. You could have hidden the turquoise bracelet and your boonie hat for the last year knowing that you were going to plant them later and that's exactly what you did."

Echo eyed Zeb and barked a warning at him.

"Stay out of this. I can handle the truth."

"A well-laid plan, Echo?"

"Why would I leave anything of mine at a crime scene? It would only make me look guilty."

"Even the best laid plans often go astray," suggested Rambler.

"No!"

"Maybe you lied all along about losing the bracelet and hat so you could say someone else found them and planted them to make you look guilty. You were covering your own butt, weren't you Echo? But your plan went south on you, didn't it?"

"STOP!"

Zeb could tolerate Rambler's damning inferences no longer.

"Zeb, it's okay," said Echo. "He's right. A prosecuting attorney could make it look just like that. But we all know I didn't do it. So what do we do?"

"Find Tavisha Karpenko," said Zeb. "That's our next move and I have the feeling it's going to be a big one."

"How are we doing to work that plan, Zeb?" asked Kate.

"Kate, you go to the Priory and see what more you can find out about Karpenko, especially where anyone thinks she might be. Even though she has formally left the Priory, it seems she was still working there as their hunter and butcher. Someone may know where to find her."

"Got it."

"Clarissa and Rambler I want you to go through every single bit of collected evidence as well as go back to the cliff dwelling caverns and bring back anything else you might find. How did that fire start? Can you find evidence of who might have been there? Anything related to Echo or Gouyen or Karpenko or something not related to any of them."

"On it," said Clarissa.

"Shelly."

"I'll find everything I haven't found on Tavisha. Including where she might hide out."

"Good."

"I'm going up to the Mount Graham Observatory. My plan is to talk with everyone who works there and see what they know but haven't told us about Doctor Gouyen and her relationship with Tavisha Karpenko. But first, everyone get a good night's rest so you're sharp tomorrow."

Chapter 35

RAMBLER AND BAISHAN

RAMBLER HAD A COUPLE of beers and a few tokes before crashing hard. He was deep in a dream of the other side and interacting with his ancient ancestors when his cellphone jolted him to the present moment. He checked the name on his phone and glanced at the alarm clock.

"Fuck."

It was Baishan and it was three o'clock in the morning. He was about to let it ring through when some unknown thing told him to pick up.

"Rambler? Rambler? Dude?"

"You called me, Baishan. Are you stoned?"

Baishan chuckled.

"Yeah. Why?"

"Never mind. What do you want? It's three o'clock in the morning."

"Wow. It's three a.m. here too. And I thought time was relative."

Rambler was irritated.

"What the hell do you want, Baishan?"

"We need to talk about a couple of things."

The timing of the call was all wrong. Rambler needed to be razor-sharp in the morning. He had important things on his plate that required one hundred percent of his attention. Keeping Echo out of prison being not the least of them. He sighed.

"What's the first?"

Rambler became irritated when Baishan, who was stoned out of his gourd, took a long time to answer a simple question.

"It's about the band."

"Can it wait? Is it really that important?"

"Yeah, man. Dude, it's really important."

"What is it, then?" asked Rambler.

"I talked with Song Bird. He said it was Sawni's choice whether or not to join the band. But if she asked him, he'd tell her to think wisely about her choices, which of course means she shouldn't join us. She must have been sitting right next to him because not two minutes later she calls me and says she's made her choice and it wasn't Hip Hop."

"Yeah, I know. I got the same message when I talked with them," said Rambler.

"Cool."

"What else do you want, Baishan? Out with it."

Once again the long hesitation irked the tired Rambler who not only had serious business on his mind but a dream waiting for him to reenter it.

"Could you come over here? To my pad."

"When?"

"Like now?"

"Can't it wait?"

"Okay, it can wait. But you're going to want to hear what I've got to say ASAP."

"Can you give me a hint?"

"Do you want to become the reservation police chief or not?"

Rambler glanced at his watch.

"How long will this take?"

"Ten, maybe twenty minutes, tops," replied Baishan.

Even though he knew the exact time, Rambler glanced at his watch a second time.

"Okay. I'll be right there. But it better not take all that long and it better be good."

"Mellow my good man, mellow. I'll be waiting."

Twenty minutes later Rambler lifted his hand to knock on Baishan's trailer door. When it opened, smoke rolled out as a hand with a joint in it appeared from behind the door.

"This better be good," said Rambler.

"It's killer weed dude," replied Baishan.

Rambler took a couple of deep hits just to placate his friend who he knew wouldn't move forward until he flowered up.

"Come on in Ram man," said Baishan. "*Mi casa* you *casa*."

Rambler found his way through the mess of Baishan's life to a chair that was covered with a traditional Apache blanket.

"Now what is up that you're having me come all the way out here in the middle of the damn night. It better be for real."

"Like I said, do you want to be police chief or not?"

"I sure as hell do. You know that better than anyone."

"What makes someone a police chief on the San Carlos?"

"Usually a big case and a majority vote from the Tribal Council."

"Right on brother. If you can get the votes I got the big case you need."

"Okay. I'll play along. What've you got?"

"Shit. I thought it was right here. I had it just before you got here. Just a second. I must have put it down somewhere. Hang on. Hang on."

Rambler shook his head and rolled his eyes as Baishan threw things every which way in search of God knew what. Finally, at long last he pulled something from a pile on top of the refrigerator.

"Yes. Here we go. I got the munchies and put them down by the fridge. My bad."

Baishan handed Rambler three pieces of paper carrying a DIA letterhead. Rambler began to glance through them. Halfway through the first page he read what Baishan was so excited to show him.

"Where'd you get this? Wait, wait don't tell me. You stole it from your brother Ryne, the government agent?"

"I'm no thief. I'm a lot of things, but not that."

"Then how did this highly confidential report end up in your hands?"

"My little bro owed me one and I owe you a bunch. I figure this evens things out, until you're police chief, that is. Then, you owe me big time."

Rambler held each of the papers up to the dim light to check the ink mark of the letterhead. If this report wasn't real, it was one hell of a fake.

Chapter 36

REVEAL

ZEB WALKED INTO THE room late and a little bit peeved that Rambler had given no one a clue as to why he called a special, non-scheduled meeting right when everyone should be out on their assignments. By the time Zeb arrived everyone else was already sitting around the table. Zeb barked at Rambler, who he was still pissed off at for his accusations against Echo.

"Rambler, you've got the floor. This better be damn good."

"It is. You won't be sorry, I promise."

"What've you got?"

Rambler reached to the floor and pulled up a briefcase his mother had made for him before she died. He placed it gently on the table. It was made of deep brown leather and was engraved with a hopeful mother's dying wish.

POLICE CHIEF RAMBLER BRAING

Zeb pointed at the inscription.

"Good luck on that."

"Thanks, Zeb. My mother who is with her ancestors thanks you for your support of her only son."

"What's in the briefcase, Rambler? Let's not waste any time here."

"An original report and five copies. One for each of us."

"Mind if we have a little look-see?" asked Zeb.

"These are not stolen and they are official. If we use them as evidence it could end a career and maybe put some or all of us in jail."

"Discretion it is, then," said Zeb. "Everyone, I believe Rambler is asking us that this information not leave this room."

"At least for the time being," added Rambler.

Heads nodded in agreement as Rambler handed the three-page report to each of his cohorts and the original plus a copy to Zeb. Not one of them could get past the first half page without dropping their jaws.

"The body that Echo found was Tavisha Karpenko? How the hell can that even be?" asked Zeb.

"Finish the report," suggested Rambler. "She has a twin sister, Bronya Karpenko, who lives in a different Saint Eustace Priory up in Scottsdale that's associated with the Priory near Solomon."

The story of the socialite nun in the *Scottsdale Bee* with all of its potential implications came front and center to everyone's mind.

"That opens this case up real wide," said Kate. "I'm headed to the Priory."

Kate picked up her things and exited without another word. The trip to Solomon and the Priory of Saint Eustace could not go quickly enough.

"I'm outta here," said Clarissa. "The caves at the cliff dwellings await."

"Wait for me," said Rambler.

"I'm all set to switch it into high gear," said Shelly. "I'll have something on Bronya Karpenko when we next meet, I promise."

"I'm headed up the Mount to the telescopes. Someone up there knows something. I'd stake my office on it."

Chapter 37

KATE AT THE PRIORY

"CAN I GIVE YOU a lift, Prioress?"

Prioress Anna Nichinka was removing the hat from her protective bee suit as Kate drove down the road to the Priory.

"Bless you, my dear. I am so overheated. The bees were a bit testy today and it took longer than usual to get my work done."

"Glad to be of assistance."

When Kate reached over to turn down the music the Prioress stopped her.

"I like this music. Who is it?"

"Jason Isbell. It's called 'Mother, Son and Holy Ghost.'"

"I don't know his music, but then again I don't have as much time as I once did to listen to music."

"I take it you're busy."

"Two of our Sisters have recently renounced their vows."

"I've heard that Sister Tavisha left the Priory. Who else is no longer with you?"

Prioress Nichinka's voice became wistful.

"Sister Monesha. She fell in love with a real live Arizona cowboy. I think she'll be back. She's young and I do believe lust got the better of her. It happens from time to time. In one way I am happy for her."

"What about Sister Tavisha? Do you think she'll return?"

Kate pulled her vehicle up to the communal hall. The Prioress invited her in for cold lemonade before saying anything more about Sister Tavisha.

"Come in. Let's talk."

One of the Sisters immediately waited on the Prioress and Kate bringing them lemonade and cookies.

"Actually, I am here to ask you about Sister Tavisha," said Kate. "Are you okay with that?"

"Is this official Sheriff's Department business?"

Kate handed the Prioress her official identification which the Prioress looked over thoroughly.

"Deputy Kate Steele Diamond. I believe we work with your husband on gun safety classes. Does he own Diamond Gun and Ammo?"

"He does and he has mentioned working with you."

"Somehow that makes me trust you."

"Thank you. My husband speaks highly of your program."

"If we can prevent just one injury, we've done our job."

The women exchanged small talk while the Prioress cooled down from the day's heat and Kate familiarized herself with the surroundings.

"Perhaps we should talk about Tavisha Karpenko. That is the real reason I'm here today," said Kate.

It was clear as she spoke that the Prioress wanted to talk.

"I have great concerns about Tavisha. She had been acting strangely for some weeks, maybe even months before she moved in with the telescope scientist from Mount Graham and gave up her vows. I understand love. I myself have been in love. But Tavisha's relationship made no sense. I don't know what got into her. I even saw her on several occasions smoking a cigarette. It was totally the antithesis of her character. Something happened. Something changed in her."

"You say the relationship made no sense. What do you mean?"

"They had nothing in common. It's almost like a spell was cast upon her. No, that's too strong a way to describe it. I'd say it's more like Tavisha just wasn't herself."

"What did you notice? How did Tavisha's behavior change?"

"She was the huntress for the Priory. She carried out her duties with excellence. She prayed with great regularity and interacted with the others, especially the younger Sisters."

"None of that sounds strange, Prioress. In fact it seems rather normal."

Before speaking the Prioress looked around to see if who might be listening.

"We discuss our sexuality quite openly here at the Priory. Even though we cannot marry or engage in sexual contact as part of our vows, we all have human feelings that we must deal with."

"Of course."

"Sister Tavisha was always quite open about her feelings regarding such matters. She felt her mission came first and that was that. She claimed to not be tempted by the ways of the world when it came to her sexual desires."

"I take it you were surprised when she left the Priory for the love of a woman?"

"I was surprised that she left for anyone, woman or man. But in truth that is hardly the thing that surprised me."

Kate and the Prioress both bit into their cookies after sipping on some lemonade. Kate's eyes detailed the sparse room. The white walls had niches holding religious icons. Religious images of Saint Eustace were the only pictures on the walls. Although Kate knew only part of his story she could easily see that the art depicted an in-depth look at his life. More than once she saw the stag deer with the Christian cross in its antlers and Eustace nearby. The tragic tale of his death at the hands of Holy Roman Emperor Hadrian was seen repeatedly as well.

"Like I mentioned earlier, Tavisha was our huntress and provided meat for all of us. Believe me, we never went hungry for lack of her skill."

"Is it true you are almost totally self-sufficient here at the Priory?"

"We are and every day we are grateful for what has been provided by the good Lord for us."

"Of course, as we all should be," added Kate. "You were saying that something other than Sister Tavisha giving up her vows for love surprised you. Can you possibly share with me what you mean?"

"Although Tavisha had not been with us here at the Priory since its inception, she has been with us for more than a year. If you talked with most of the other nuns they would tell you they knew her very well. Her actions have been consistent and her love of God Almighty was unfailing. Recently however she seemed to change."

"What about her changed?" asked Kate.

"It's almost impossible to describe. Her transformations were so subtle that unless you didn't pay very close attention you might notice nothing at all. For instance, the first thing I noted was the way she held her hands in prayer. It's nothing a lay person would even think to notice, but as Prioress it is my job to be aware of such things.

The Prioress made a prayer gesture with her hands, followed by a second one. The difference was slight, Had the Prioress not specifically shown Kate the subtle change she might not have noticed it.

"As I watched her hands, I realized I could not see the birthmark Tavisha had on her right wrist. It struck me as quite vain that she should cover it up."

She pointed to her own right wrist. "The birthmark was right here. Now that I think about there is another thing I noticed."

"Yes?" asked Kate.

"Although her hand gestures seemed to change slightly her devotion seemed to be a bit exaggerated. She was always a prayerful woman but her devotions carried an increased fervor in the short time prior to her departure."

"What did you make of that?"

"Sisters of a Holy Order periodically go through periods of increased passion. It is usually related to something that has made them feel closer to their maker. Even though Tavisha had given up her vows, I believe she was going through something similar. In this case, however, I sensed that Tavisha's faith was flagging. Most everyone goes through periods when their faith is put to the test. Probably due to my own travails I was sensing that in Tavisha."

"Is there anything in particular that you'd like to share that would clarify things?" asked Kate.

"Most likely this is going to seem trivial to you."

"Everything is important."

"Tavisha seemed to allow her mind to go elsewhere. It's almost like she wasn't present with us here at the Priory. In fact only a short time ago she disappeared completely for several days. When she returned she said she was wandering the desert and praying. Yes. I hadn't thought of it until right this moment but that's when I first noticed the biggest changes."

"Maybe her mind was on her love affair?"

"That is what I thought at first. But upon further prayer and examination it didn't seem like Doctor Gouyen was the issue at hand. It was more like Tavisha could no longer share with us what she was thinking. Her personality changed. She became withdrawn."

"Was she depressed?"

"No. Nothing like that. It's like she was absent or not present in the moment. Her mind was elsewhere. I would say it was in another place she did not care to share it with anyone else."

"Go on. Please tell me more about her behavior."

"I suspect she was hiding a sin of guilt that she could not overcome. I thought it was related to her twin sister leaving the Scottsdale Priory for home in order to help with the returning injured soldiers from the war."

"Thank you Prioress Nichinka. I think you are more insightful that you know."

Chapter 38

CLARISSA/RAMBLER AT CLIFF DWELLING CAVE

ON THEIR WAY TO the cave near the cliff dwellings Clarissa and Rambler stopped at the Cochise Café in San Carlos to get her thermos filled with iced tea.

"Rambler, please let me go in by myself. I want to test a theory."

"What theory?"

"I'll tell you when I come back to the car."

"Get going then. We've got work to do."

Without Rambler at her side the locals treated her completely differently. Not a single person gave her a second glance. When she left with her thermos filled she glanced through the café window to see if anyone had watched her leave. They hadn't.

"Well?"

"I just proved my own invisibility," replied Clarissa.

Rambler was beginning to believe more than ever that Clarissa was a bit touched in the head.

On the road to the cave where they'd previously found so much evidence Clarissa noticed they were met by no oncoming cars. Rambler appeared to have read her mind.

"One in twenty times you'll meet someone on this road. The rest of the time, nobody."

As Clarissa parked near the home of Doctor Gouyen and Tavisha Karpenko it appeared as expected, vacant. Still, before making the hike up to the caves near the Apache cliff dwellings she knocked on their door and rang the bell.

"Nobody's here are they?" asked Rambler.

"No, but it was worth a shot," replied Clarissa.

"Let's see what we can find."

Entering the cave they were more prepared than when they'd looked around the first time. They had increased their total illumination by a factor of ten. Fifteen minutes later they'd done little more than bag four half-smoked cigarettes. They all had been flattened by a boot but the brand appeared to be similar to the one Clarissa had found on the riding trail earlier. If this was the case it could turn out to be solid evidence.

"Someone sat her and smoked four cigarettes," said Rambler. "They must have wanted to watch things burn."

"We need to be at least as diligent as the criminal," replied Clarissa.

One hour later after sifting through piles of cold ashes Clarissa and Rambler sat back to look at the items they had missed in their original search.

Clarissa held a metal cigarette case that was charred on one side. The heat from the fire had partially melted the contents together. Still, when she pried it open she could count roughly twenty-six photographs. All of them were of the two same girls. Melted together on one edge they weren't completely clear pictures. However, they could tell that when the photos were taken the girls were possibly as young as twelve and in others perhaps twenty years old. The color photos were faded. In some of the earlier photos the girls were dressed identically. Others showed the girls studying or kneeling in church, praying. Two showed them practicing firing assault rifles, the style of which was foreign to Rambler and Clarissa.

As they examined the first of the final two photographs more closely it was clear the girls were pointing at something on their right wrists. The shot was a close-up. One of the girls had a mark on her right wrist and the other did not. Clarissa turned over the small photograph. On the back something unrecognizable was written...**Разница между нами**.

The final photograph was quite different from the others. The women were older, thirtyish perhaps and displaying their ankles. Clarissa examined the final photograph. One woman had a Z tattooed on her right ankle while the other did not. Turning over this photograph she found a smiley face. Next to it was a large Z followed by the words...**бить Зеленского**.

Chapter 39

OBSERVATORY DIRECTOR

DOCTOR MICHAELA LEE, OBSERVATORY Director met with Zeb in her private office. She immediately offered him a seat.

"Doctor Lee, thank you for meeting with me on such short notice."

"My pleasure, Sheriff Hanks."

Zeb tipped his hat. Realizing it was on his head, he took it off and set it on the chair next to him, apologizing to the Director for his poor manners.

"It's been over a year since I've seen you. Thank you and your staff for periodically stopping by to check on us."

"Yes, Doctor," replied Zeb. "One of my deputies covers the area of the Observatory grounds twice a month. So we're here even if you don't see us."

"Sheriff Hanks, I can only assume you are here to discuss Doctor Gouyen. Am I correct?"

Zeb appreciated her getting right to the point. In the past he had found Lee to be a dawdler who extended her conversations to the point of excess, hence his lack of interest in stopping at her office when he traveled up the Mount. From the traffic moving past Lee's office window it was apparent that others were as curious as Lee was regarding the unexpected death of their colleague, Doctor Gouyen. Doctor Lee nodded toward inquisitive scientists.

"As you can see from the interest of my fellow scientists your presence in my office has caused quite a stir. We have all been postulating about what happened."

"To answer your question, yes, this is in regard to Doctor Gouyen."

"Is it true she was poisoned?"

The cause of her death had not been publicly released. Zeb was surprised that Doctor Lee was aware of it.

"What makes you think she was poisoned?"

"Was she not? Poisoned, that is?"

"Doctor Lee do you have some information you would like to share with me?"

"What information might I have?" asked Lee.

"Perhaps why you are so certain she was poisoned."

"It might be fantasy, but I doubt it. You see I read spy novels at the rate of two per week. The scientist in fiction novels is almost always killed by poison or drugs Then when you consider her level of security clearances..."

"What level of security clearances did she have?" asked Zeb.

Zeb continued his statement with a lie that he felt would make Lee more likely to speak freely.

"I'm waiting for her personnel folders from the DOD, NSA and DIA," added Zeb. "I only know she had Top Secret clearances. The other clearance levels and what they were related to should be hand-delivered to my office today or tomorrow. It would be helpful if you could save me some time."

"Of course. You were so good to us when we had the mountaintop fires the last two years, it's the least I could do to help you out."

Zeb's mind flashed back to the horrific fires and how one of his rescue team members, Josh Diamond, had risked life and limb in order save the doctor's Pekingese Chow Chow, Sagittarius A*, from certain death. He distinctly remembered how Doctor Lee had wept nearly to the point of having a nervous breakdown when she feared the one thing she was closest to on this planet had possibly suffered the terrible tragedy of death by fire.

"We were just doing our job," replied Zeb.

Tears welled in Lee's eyes as she recalled the incident. Zeb glanced away to save her embarrassment. As Lee reached into a file cabinet Sagittarius A* came promenading into her office like he owned the place. A silly, almost human, grin covered the dog's face. He licked Zeb's hand before curling himself under the doctor's desk. Lee grabbed a file, handed it to Zeb and reached down to pet her baby.

"There's my little man. Ooh. Ooh. And how's the best dog in the entire known universe doing today?"

Sagittarius A* blinked a few times as Lee gave him a treat, quickly followed by a second treat and a third.

"Regarding the current status of Doctor Gouyen's clearances, please look at Section B," said Lee.

Zeb opened the manila folder at tab B. The first page of Section B carried a table of contents titled "United States of America: Governmental Clearances."

Cosmic Top Secret (CTS)
Top Secret
Secret
Confidential

The section marked CTS was followed by five pages of single-spaced lines detailing exactly what CTS was about as it related specifically to the work Doctor Gouyen had been assigned. Zeb was starting with paragraph one when Doctor Lee interjected.

"No need to read all the details. I'll go through the material with you."

"I have never heard of CTS."

"It's a most interesting moniker, a double entendre of sorts, when you consider how it is related to the cosmic research work we do."

"Of course," replied Zeb.

"Cosmic Top Secret is essentially the same as U.S. Top Secret. The only difference is that CTS information includes an agreement to share knowledge with all NATO nations. Since the work we do is international, universal actually, CTS is first on the list. As you can see her CTS clearances are directly related to her work. The secret information, if in the wrong hands, could cause serious damage to NATO nations," explained Lee.

"Of course you cannot divulge what any of her work is?"

"No. I think you know that Sheriff Hanks."

Dr. Lee's comment was followed by a sly wink.

"And number two, Top Secret is United States Top Secret?"

"Correct."

Zeb's eyes dropped to the third heading. Secret Clearance.

"And Secret clearance? What's that?"

Sagittarius A* jumped into Doctor Lee's lap. Immediately she began softly caressing her dog.

"Secret clearance provides access to data that if released without authorization would cause serious damage to national security. In this case I believe I can tell you it is most likely related to Doctor Gouyen's technical writing."

"Technical writing on a specific subject?"

"Yes, but I can only share with you what has been published."

"Which is?" asked Zeb.

"She writes about telescopes and their capacity to signal satellites which then transmit that signal on to drones."

"Drones? What kinds of drones?"

"Drones are not my area of expertise. Maybe weather, photography, mapping or maybe even military usage. I can't say for certain. I do know she has published numerous papers on the subject. Most are in the public domain. I would check them out if you desire greater details."

Zeb allowed himself a private smile of satisfaction at receiving this confirmation of the data that Shelly had dug up.

"Thank you," replied Zeb. "Number four is listed as Confidential clearance."

"Yes. She also has confidential clearances, numerous ones. That level of security also involves national security concerns should it be leaked. In Doctor Gouyen's case this likely has to do with her interaction with others on both national and international levels."

"Can you tell me what it's about?"

"Sorry. I don't know and I couldn't tell you if I did. Once again if you take the time to read her published papers you could start to imagine what areas she is an expert in and that might lead you to your answer."

Zeb immediately thought of what Shelly had earlier said. Perhaps this situation had to do directly with military drones and possibly even somehow with the Russian invasion of Ukraine.

"May I take this with me?"

"I'm sorry, you can't. But I have to powder my nose. If you accidentally look through them while I'm gone consider it a favor for saving Sagittarius A* from the flames of hell."

Doctor Lee slid a small notebook and a pen across the table towards Zeb before leaving the room. By the time she returned he had transcribed what he felt was the pertinent data.

Zeb's shook the Director's hand and petted Sagittarius A* one last time much to the Director's delight.

He headed down Mount Graham trying to piece it all together.

Chapter 40

SHELLY DEEP IN THE ETHER

SHELLY DID SOMETHING SHE had never done. She outlined a plan on paper. If there was one way to get to the bottom of who killed who and why, she needed a roadmap. This case had so many crisscrossing and overlapping threads that they made no sense until she laid it all out and could visualize them.

First, she manipulated the image of Bronya Karpenko from the *Scottsdale Bee* and rotated it in such a way that it overlapped almost perfectly with the picture Echo had taken of the dead woman killed by her knife. The images were close enough but proved nothing of value when it came to identifications. Next, Shelly ran the images through facial recognition scanning. The result was a near enough match to predict a possible genetic relationship based on bone structure. It also ruled out the possibility that these were the same woman. That was helpful because it eliminated an insane theory that had been running through Shelly's head, that the two were actually the same person. The information at her fingertips told her without a doubt they were not. She breathed a sigh of relief knowing that one of them had not come back from the dead.

A quick review of the *Bee* article told Shelly the approximate date of Bronya's departure. In the article she was quoted as saying that her flight was headed directly to Moscow before going on to the heavily disputed Donbas region. Digging into all direct flights to Moscow within the following three days showed no one by the name of Bronya Karpenko on the passenger manifest. Shelly expanded her search to one week, then two. Still nothing. Unless she was flying under false documents, which was possible but unlikely, she was still in the United States. Shelly concluded the most likely scenario was indeed that Bronya had never left. It was a theory, but not a one hundred percent-provable hypothesis, just currently the most likely one.

Additionally she researched all local newspapers from Luhansk and the Donbas region for any stories regarding her return, as certainly she would have been welcomed home as a heroine. Again nothing.

Shelly also contacted the office of Metropolitan Epifaniy, head of the Orthodox Church of Ukraine, for any information regarding the intended good works of Sister Bronya Karpenko and the fundraising she had done. The only response came in a brief note stating that she was on a mission in the United States of America seeking assistance to help injured soldiers and civilians.

Using the latest in enhanced facial recognition she pulled up video from the gala thrown in her honor and compared it with the photos from Echo's phone. Similar but not the same was what she found again.

But she got a huge break when she matched a photo taken during Elan and Onawa's school visit to the Priory. Before they left, all the children and all the nuns posed together. Although a streak of sunlight crossed Sister Tavisha's face, when she fine-tuned both using the Kairos and Animetrics facial recognition software to its maximum functional capacity there was a greater than 99% chance that the images of Bronya at the gala and Tavisha at the Priory were identical. Shelly double and triple checked her work. In the end there was no doubt the woman posing as Tavisha the day of the school children's visit to the Priory was really Bronya.

Shelly grinned as she thought of how easily almost anyone could be deceived. It brought to mine the famous line from Edgar Allen Poe.

All that we see or seem is but a dream within a dream.

Chapter 41

GOODBYE

"Zeb?"

"Yes, Helen?"

Helen held an overnight parcel in her hand. She handed it to Zeb as though it were something rare and precious.

"What have we got here?"

"It's from some professor at the California Institute of Technology."

Kate and Shelly popped their heads around the corner from Kate's office.

"That's where Doctor Gouyen got her PhD," said Shelly. "What's the professor's name who sent it?"

"Doctor Erin Malvala," replied Helen. "I signed for it. Her name was on the register as the person who sent it."

"I know for a fact she was Doctor Gouyen's advisor," said Shelly.

Zeb slipped the parcel under his arm, walked to his office and closed the door tightly behind him without saying so much as a single word. Once inside he put his boots up on his desk, grabbed an old-fashioned letter opener with a bull carved into the handle and slowly ran the sharp edge along the seal. As he pulled out the document a ferruginous owl landed in the ancient cactus that was the only natural interruption to his view of the telescopes atop the Mount. Song Bird had taught him the dark omen associated with the pygmy owl. That knowledge touched him with queasiness.

Inside the larger envelope was an opened, undated and un-postmarked letter addressed to Doctor Erin Malvala. The return address was that of Doctor Izdzán Proteus.

Zeb opened the one-page neatly handwritten, undated letter and began reading.

Erin,

As my dear friend, advisor and colleague I am writing this confidential letter to you. Please read it with all seriousness. Should I lose my life in the near future please hand it over to the local authorities here in Safford, Arizona. The sheriff, Zeb Hanks, is a true and trustworthy man. He will know what to do. If he can do nothing or if he does not contact you within two days of receiving this from you, please contact LaDonna Spring at the NSA in Washington, D.C. She is my direct contact at the administration. Her card is enclosed.

More to the point. I am either going mad, which I believe to be highly unlikely, or the world has changed around me in an incomprehensible manner. At first I was certain that the illogicality of love was guiding my thinking. Upon further thought, I concluded otherwise.

Then I made a presumption that my life partner, Tavisha Karpenko, a former Sister of Saint Eustace was having a mental breakdown. Why, you are likely asking yourself, would I go out on such an awkward limb as mental illness in my thought process in describing my partner?
Tavisha's and my relationship, while not terribly longstanding, was replete with shared private thoughts and other intimacies that are held dear in one's life. Yes, I shared with her my most heartfelt secrets. Then, one day, prior to the time that I felt a change in her ways, she simply transformed into someone I no longer knew. An affair of the heart turned sour? If so, I missed every sign.

Tavisha changed in unimaginable ways. The small personal things we shared, as well as the secret treasures of my heart seemed to have fallen from

*her mind as if they were autumn leaves. At first I
blamed fatigue and stress but I quickly came to see
that this woman who I had chosen to spend my life
with was not the same person she was only days
prior.*

*Then everything collapsed. She became abusive
and threatening when it came to my work. I caught
her going through my computer. I chose not to directly confront her. However, I logged into my computer and followed her digital footprints. As you
know I have been working on some Cosmic Top
Secret data related to my contract with the NSA. It
was these files that held her interest. I moved them
to a place that she could never access. The next day
I left on an extended vacation. It is from the Grand
Canyon that I am writing you this letter.*

*Erin, at this time I fear for my life and well-being.
I do not know whether I can ever return home
or to my job. I am going to wander the Americas
for a month to find myself and perhaps a better
understanding of what is going on with Tavisha.*

I remain your colleague, mentee and friend,
Izdzán

*Doctor Izdzán Gouyen, PhD
Mount Graham International Observatory
Division of Steward Observatory*

Chapter 42

MEETING

ZEB SAT AT THE head of the round meeting table. Kate, Rambler, Clarissa and Echo. Shelly was held up and would be joining as soon as she could. Helen's left ear parked itself near the door that was slightly ajar.

"It's time for us to share our findings and discuss our individual conclusions. Leave nothing off the table. Let's figure out who the dead woman Echo found really was and who killed her. It is imperative that we also figure out who poisoned Doctor Gouyen. I feel like we have all the information we need but simply have not put it together in such a fashion that will allow us to close these two murder cases."

"Echo, do you have any theory why someone apparently wants you to be the one who falls on the knife for these murders? It appears as though someone or some ones have gone out of their way to make you look like a killer."

"I've thought about that in every rational and non-rational way that I could come up with. My intuition tells me I'm simply being used to get at Zeb. With all the information you all have, I can sure as hell look like a cold-blooded killer. I suspect I'm being set up because my guilt can make Zeb look dishonest and inept. It may begin and end with that. I don't know of anyone who has a personal vendetta against me that would lead them to all of this."

"Okay. Anyone want to add anything?" asked Zeb. "Anyone think she's guilty?"

"If I didn't personally know her, I'd conclude she was guilty based on the evidence," said Rambler.

Zeb shot Rambler a hard glance.

"So would I," added Echo.

The room settled into an uncomfortable silence until Rambler spoke in a comical rapper voice.

"But if you're going down, I'm going down with you. Down, down, down. Down with you. Down with you. Sister if it's true, I'll go down with you. But that ain't what we're gonna do."

"I can see why your career with Tribu de Deux didn't make it," said Clarissa.

The mood shifted from foreboding to humor and eventually hopefulness. Zeb stood and walked around the table handing each of them a copy of Doctor Gouyen's letter to her mentor, Doctor Erin Malvala.

"As you will note, the letter is not dated. In reading it, I am certain you will all find it self-explanatory."

The team took a few minutes to study the letter.

"Thoughts? Anyone?"

"It sure as hell makes Tavisha appear involved in the murder of Doctor Gouyen," said Kate.

"But the information given to Baishan from Agent Hoazinne clearly states that the dead body Echo found was Tavisha Karpenko," said Rambler.

"Why would they give up that information to us?" asked Zeb.

"Your agreement with them," said Echo. "Using Rambler as a go-between."

"I don't think so," replied Rambler. "Doesn't feel right to me."

"Maybe they played us all along," said Zeb. I have to believe they gave us disinformation. Can anyone give me a good reason to convince me they didn't?"

The general consensus with very little dispute was that they'd been duped.

"Bastards. We owe them one," said Zeb. "For now let's get back to what we have. Kate, you were about to say something?"

"Doctor Gouyen's letter to her mentor could be a letter written by the hand of a spurned lover," said Kate. "We only see Doctor Gouyen's side of the story in the letter."

"Agreed. By itself, it is not enough."

"The premonition of her own death is telling," added Rambler.

"Her mention of Tavisha transforming into someone she no longer knew...," said Clarissa.

"The Prioress all but said exactly the same thing to me," said Kate.

"Go on, Kate," urged Zeb. "What else did the Prioress have to offer?"

"When I returned to the Priory and chatted with Prioress Nichinka she noted that Sister Tavisha had become withdrawn. especially after her sister, Bronya, departed from a Priory in Scottsdale for home."

"That seems natural," said Rambler.

"True. But, and once again these may be small things or nothing at all, the Prioress said that near the end of her time at the Priory, Sister Tavisha changed the way in which she held her hands during prayer," said Kate. "She even took up smoking, which she had never done."

"So?" asked Rambler.

"According to the Prioress, Sister Tavisha found smoking repulsive."

"Do you know if they were NPIMA brand?" asked Zeb. "Clarissa and I found one in the vicinity of the person who looked like Tavisha."

"They were. But I also saw other nuns smoking that same brand."

Shelly popped into the room and answered the question as she took her seat.

"It's the most popular brand in Ukraine," added Shelly.

"The Prioress thought Tavisha was hiding her guilt about something."

"That could be a lot of things," suggested Rambler.

"When we put it all together it's more than enough to make Tavisha a leading suspect in Gouyen's murder. But how would a nun know anything about how to poison someone?" asked Zeb.

"A learned skill for a specific purpose?" said Clarissa.

"Okay, Tavisha is a top suspect in Doctor Gouyen's murder and the cigarette butt and saddle strings found nearby link her at least peripherally to the other dead woman. But remember if the DIA is telling us the truth, Tavisha died before Gouyen was poisoned."

"*If* they're telling the truth," added Rambler.

"They might be telling the truth," offered Shelly.

"Go on," said Zeb. "Sounds like you have something."

"I used the latest in facial recognition software and looked at all the images of Tavisha I could find. I cross-referenced them with all available pictures of Bronya Karpenko. Although the software is not infallible, I found that there is a 99% chance that the images of Bronya Karpenko at the gala in Scottsdale and the photos of Tavisha at the Priory on the day of the school outing are one and the same person."

The evidence was damning but confusing, unless, as everyone was thinking, Bronya had somehow taken Tavisha's place. If that was the case, it was no stretch to believe that Bronya had either killed Tavisha herself or had her done away with.

Zeb moved the meeting along.

"Clarissa, what have you got?"

"Two items. The first might be trivial."

Clarissa placed an evidence bag on the table.

"These are from the cave."

With a gloved hand she pulled out four partially smoked cigarettes.

"These are NPIMA cigarettes. When Zeb and I were searching near the site of the dead body in the Pinaleños we found one cigarette butt that is similar to these."

"Similar?" asked Rambler.

"We found one near a popular horse-riding tourist trail. It was dirty and not all the letters on the brand were present, but it's similar enough to be the same brand."

"Once again, by itself that tells us nothing. The Sisters of Saint Eustace are horse riders and I witnessed more than one of them smoking when I visited the Priory," said Zeb.

"You've got one other thing, Clarissa?" asked Kate.

"Yes. Rambler and I found this." With great caution she placed a partially burned cigarette case on the table.

Clarissa opened the case and took out the pictures.

"The case they were in was charred and these pictures partially melted together on one edge."

Everyone stood and moved behind Clarissa so they could get a better look at the pictures.

"What've you got?" asked Zeb.

"A couple dozen faded photographs that were damaged by the heat of fire. They appear to be photos of the same two girls from ages say twelve to twenty, plus one more when they are in their thirties. I haven't gotten all the information from the pictures since they are partially melted together. I didn't try to take them apart."

"Smart," said Shelly. "I know a method for doing that. In order not to destroy them, that will take some time."

Heads nodded.

"You looked through the pictures as best you could?" asked Zeb.

"Yes. My impression is that the two girls are twins, like I said roughly twelve or thirteen years old to their early twenties."

"What are the pictures of?" asked Rambler.

"Two girls, dressed identically in every picture doing everything from studying to kneeling in church to practicing shooting assault rifles."

"Can I have a look at the one with the assault rifles?" asked Echo.

With great caution Clarissa partially pulled back the pictures one by one until she came to the assault rifle photo.

"That's a SHAK-12S," said Echo.

"Right," added Kate. "Josh showed me one once."

Shelly pulled a picture up on her computer and shared it with everyone. Heads moved back and forth between the old, small photograph and the computer screen. There was no doubt about it, the gun was a SHAK-12S.

"It's primarily used for close-up urban combat. It's considered to be a hard-core killing weapon with the ability to limit collateral damage," said Shelly.

"A target-specific weapon," added Echo. "I wonder who they were practicing to kill?"

"Probably someone specific."

"Which would make them trained assassins, wouldn't it?"

"It would appear that way," replied Zeb.

"It's the final two photos that are telling," said Clarissa. "I think."

"In one picture the young women are standing next to each other and pointing to each other's right wrists. One young woman has a mark on her wrist and the other young woman does not. There is something written on the back in what looks like Russian. I haven't translated it yet."

Clarissa carefully turned it over and showed everyone what it said...**Разница между нами**.

"It's Russian," said Shelly. "I recognize that much."

Shelly pulled up a language translation program on her phone.

"Translated into English it means, the difference between us."

"Makes it almost a certainty they're twins," said Zeb.

Everyone gave the photos a second look. Everyone agreed with Clarissa that the women must be twins.

"What about the second photo?"

"One woman is pointing at the other's ankle. This picture looks more recent. More shockingly, both women look like Tavisha Karpenko."

Shelly enlarged the image on her laptop. The blur on the right ankle of one of the women was clearly a Z.

"Is anything printed on the back of that one?"

Once again Clarissa flipped the picture over and showed them what was written...**бить Зеленского**.

It took no time at all for Shelly to translate.

"It means Kill Zelenskyy."

Zeb pulled out copies of the images Echo had taken when she found the dead woman. One of them showed a Z on the right ankle and another a birthmark on the right wrist.

"Echo, the dead woman you found..."

"I know. Since it was Bronya I saw at the Priory, the dead woman must have been Tavisha Karpenko."

"Have we been chasing a ghost?" asked Kate.

In Helen's office the sound of a phone could be heard ringing. Five seconds later she was knocking on the meeting room door. She let herself in without waiting for a response.

"Zeb, line one. Now!"

"Sheriff Hanks?"

"Speaking."

"This is Prioress Nichinka of the Saint Eustace Priory."

"Yes, Prioress?"

"I know you're looking for Tavisha Karpenko. She's here and she's taken her hunting weapons and loads of ammunition. In the process she shot and injured one of our Sisters."

"I'll send an ambulance. One of my team will be there right away. Are you and the other Sisters safe?"

"Yes. I believe so. We are in God's good hands."

Do you have any idea where she might be headed?"

"She took off toward the Pinaleño Mountains."

"How do you know that?" asked Zeb.

"There are two roads out of the Priory. One goes to town and the other is a back road that is almost never used. It leads directly to the Pinaleño Mountains. Tavisha used it all the time when she'd go deer, elk or bear hunting out there. She always went to a place she called the U-Loop at Skinny Pass."

"Thank you, Prioress. Deputy Kate is headed your way. She'll keep you safe. The ambulance team will be right behind her. But there is one thing you should know."

"Yes?"

"The woman who came to get the guns is Bronya Karpenko, not Tavisha."

"Her hands when she prayed...the missing birthmark."

"Yes, Prioress. You were correct when you noticed how Tavisha had changed. She changed because it wasn't Tavisha at all, it was Bronya."

"Tavisha is with the Lord?"

"I'm afraid she is, Prioress. My condolences."

"God bless you and your deputies, Sheriff Hanks. Please catch Tavisha's killer."

"We will."

Zeb ended the call and turned to his staff.

"Everyone. That was the Prioress Nichinka. Bronya Karpenko returned to the Priory and has armed herself to the teeth. She's headed on the back road from there to the Pinaleños. She knows the U-Loop at Skinny Creek from hunting there after taking Tavisha's place. I'd bet that's where she's headed. Bronya also shot one of the nuns. Kate, I want you to call the ambulance service and ask for Sahara and Porky to meet you there. They are best suited for a situation like this one. Everyone, arm yourselves

selves with your rifles. Bronya has taken a cache of weapons and ammo with her."

"Is she carrying the SHAK-12S with her?" asked Rambler.

"Unknown."

"It's made for killing up close," said Shelly. "If she pulls it out protect yourselves maximally."

"Everyone, Kate, you too, full body armor."

"I'm going with you," said Echo. "I know that road she is on better than all of you put together, well except maybe Clarissa."

"Echo my best bet is that she set you up from the beginning. She must want you dead," said Zeb. "I'd prefer you wait here and handle communications with Helen."

Echo didn't say a word, but if looks could kill, Zeb would have been sucking down his final breath.

"Okay. You can come with us. But follow procedure. I want to take her alive."

"And if that's not a possibility, especially if she's got the SHAK?" asked Rambler.

"Do your best. First and foremost I don't want anyone on our team to get hurt."

In a flash they were out the door and on their way. Kate headed to the Priory. Rambler and Clarissa were in one vehicle. Zeb and Echo in another. The road to the U-Loop and Skinny Creek was their destination.

Chapter 43

SEEKING BRONYA

WHEN THE ROAD FORKED into two separate paths that would re-join in five miles Zeb pulled over. Clarissa pulled behind him. He laid the area map on his hood. The others leaned in.

"Rambler, Clarissa you take the north fork from here. We'll meet in roughly five miles down the road near the U-Loop intersection just east of Skinny Creek."

Echo and Clarissa knew the spot well. The road was a figure eight and the roads intersected there.

"We have to be on high alert at all times. Bronya is a dangerous woman who is very likely responsible for her sister's death. We know for certain she has at least one and maybe more Henry .30-.30s and a truckload of ammo. We know from the pictures she apparently has trained on a SHAK-12S. We know how dead-ly that weapon is, especially up close. I doubt we'll meet her on the road. I suspect she will drive to a specific spot that she has already predetermined and take off from there."

At the same instant Echo and Clarissa put their fingers on the same spot of the area map.

"Here, is the best spot to stay hidden, protect yourself and see everything coming your way," said Clarissa.

"I'm in one hundred percent agreement with that," added Echo.

The four of them studied the map intently.

"Clarissa, Echo, what's the best way to approach that loca-tion?" asked Zeb.

The women pointed out four spots that could possibly give them an edge over Bronya.

"Is any one or any two of these better than the others?" asked Zeb.

"If we don't cover all four of these points she could easily escape," said Clarissa.

Echo looked overhead at the sun, then fidgeted with her Special Forces watch.

"The sun sets at 6:42. That give us four hours and nineteen minutes as of right now."

"It's going to take us roughly an hour to get in position, give or take," added Clarissa.

"That is if she doesn't backtrack on us," said Rambler.

"We can have no way of knowing if she does that," said Zeb. "But if that happens, is the only other way out through the Priory and Kate?"

Echo and Clarissa answered in a single voice.

"Yes."

"Unless she wants to hike for two, maybe three days," added Echo.

"I don't think she wants to do that. There's no running water out that way this time of year. Even if she knows every inch of the territory, which seems highly unlikely, she would go at least two days without water," said Clarissa.

"More likely she'd be without water for a week if she got lost. The weather is going to be unseasonably hot for the next five days. She'd have some trouble surviving depending on how much water she could carry if she tries to hike out that way," added Echo.

"Let's assume she's carrying three days' worth of water," said Echo. "That's what I'd plan for and it appears Bronya has survival training."

"Just out of curiosity, in case Bronya gets lost out there, what happens after three days without water?" asked Rambler. "I assume dehydration, mental confusion and chills all set in."

"Organs begin to shut down," replied Echo. "Especially the brain. Besides what you mentioned a person would become faint, possibly even have a stroke and die. But more often than not a person lives for greater than three days."

"Most people can live about ten days before dying," interjected Clarissa. "If they can keep their wits about them."

"We're wasting time on this. Let's get rolling," demanded Rambler.

"Communication by cellphones is sketchy out here. Bu you all know that already. We'll be better off using our two-ways. They're VHF and digital. The higher the ground you're on the better the signal. Let's all use channel three in case she's got her own two-way. Got that?"

Zeb put the map on the ground and gave each person their assigned location.

"We've got a little over four hours. I'll make contact with you on the half hour and on the hour. When we're all in position, we'll decide on next steps. If anything and I mean anything comes up, make contact with everyone ASAP."

"If we get nothing are we here for the night?" asked Rambler.

"No. I want everyone back at their vehicles fifteen minutes before sunset. It's a bad day to die."

His words sent shivers up everyone's spine. Such talk, although none of them was truly superstitious, was considered bad luck.

"Questions?"

"You said you wanted her taken alive," said Rambler. "Shoot to wound?"

"Your call. She's armed and dangerous. She's killed more than once. Take no chances," replied Zeb.

Chapter 44

FINDING BRONYA

AT THE HALF-HOUR MARK Zeb checked in with the others. No one had seen or heard a thing. The going was rough and only Rambler had spotted the road Bronya had most likely travelled on. He reported it as a non-maintained road with deep ruts and multiple places to turn around. He had altered his route slightly in order to keep an eye on the road.

At the one-hour mark Echo had found footprints from a woman-sized pair of boots. Zeb signaled the others and all four were listening on channel three simultaneously.

"I don't believe they belong to Bronya," said Echo.

"Why not?" asked Rambler.

"The brand name from the bottom of the boot is easy to see. I am operating under the assumption that Bronya's behavior is consistent with her prior behavior."

"You're assuming she cut the brand name off the soles of all her footwear, I presume?" asked Zeb.

"Roger that."

"Reasonable thinking. Stay alert. The best criminals know how to break patterns that they assume we might have become aware of," replied Zeb.

The sun arcing across the sky had warmed the day to its highest temperature when Zeb checked in with the others at the ninety-minute mark. Everyone was at their intended destination. No one had anything suspicious to report.

"If we all move toward the center of the area we have surrounded we might have a better chance at finding her, especially if she knows we're on her trail," said Zeb.

"That increases our risk," said Echo.

"It does, but not significantly. Anyone else have thoughts on tightening the noose on her?" asked Zeb.

"Let's get this killer," said Rambler.

"Let's remain alert but yes, let's tighten things up," added Clarissa.

"I'm in," said Echo.

Twenty-eight minutes later a shot rang out. The others waited for Zeb's call. Nothing. Echo weighed her options and called him. No answer. She contacted Rambler and Clarissa on her two-way to reformulate their plan. They'd all heard the shot. None had been able to reach him.

"Let's move toward Zeb's location," said Echo.

"What's your plan?" asked Rambler.

"My phone is working intermittently. I tried to call Zeb first. No answer. Then the call dropped. It didn't reconnect after two more tries."

"You worried?" asked Clarissa.

"Not yet."

Echo continued, "While my phone was connected I pulled up MAPFINDER. I had it up long enough to download a local terrain map."

"Zeb's about fifteen minutes from me and Clarissa and about twenty minutes from Rambler. I want to approach his location with the sun behind us. Here's what to do."

Echo proceeded to give them directions to a spot where they could meet. The way she had it figured it was close enough to Zeb that they might see him and well enough hidden from Bronya that she wouldn't see them approaching.

"Do you think she's at Dead Gulch?" asked Clarissa.

"I do. I think we both know it's the best place to hide."

"Any guess at which end of the outcroppings Bronya's hiding at?"

"Can you two give me a lay of the land?" asked Rambler.

"Dead Gulch runs east and west. It's been dry for at least a hundred years. To the north and south of the dry gulch the land is rough, rocky and heads steeply uphill in both directions. If she's moved either way she'll own the high ground. Zeb was approaching from the southwest so he's between Clarissa and me. If you head straight south we can all meet in the middle and look for Zeb. Got it?"

"I'll circle around to the west a bit and head south. See you in twenty," replied Rambler.

Five hundred yards away from the bottom of the gulch Clarissa met Echo. In the distance to the north they could see Rambler creeping closer.

"See Zeb yet?" asked Clarissa.

Echo handed a pair of binoculars to Clarissa and pointed to the east. Zeb was flat on the ground sheltering beside a rock. The land was otherwise open between him and Dead Gulch. His two-way radio was lying out of reach in the open where he must have dropped it.

"Think he's hit?"

"I saw him move his head. His gun is by his right shoulder. I don't think he's hit. I think Bronya's got him pinned down."

Another shot fired. This one cracked off a rock to their north. They turned just in time to see Rambler dive behind a long wall of rocks. He was a few hundred yards away but safe. Looking up he gave Clarissa, who still had her binoculars trained on him, a thumbs-up before secreting himself behind the line of rocks that would lead him directly to his partners.

"Bronya took that shot from right over the ridge at forty-five degrees north-northeast."

Clarissa swiveled her head as another shot rang out. This time she witnessed the fire from Bronya's barrel. Echo had turned toward Rambler and saw the shot hit fifty feet behind him. Bronya was shooting wildly. Her guess as to Rambler's position was calculated and close, but wrong. She'd lost track of him. Staying low and behind the wall of rocks he joined Echo and Clarissa.

"That bitch," said Rambler. "She tried to kill me."

"Language Rambler, language," said Clarissa.

Gallow's humor out of the way, the trio concentrated on how best to help Zeb, who from their vantage point seemed hopelessly trapped, literally between a hard and some much harder places.

"We've got to use the landscape to our advantage," said Clarissa.

Rambler nodded toward the setting sun.

"It's going to be dark behind those rocks where she's hiding before the sun goes completely down," said Rambler. "That's to her advantage. We've got maybe fifteen to thirty minutes at best."

Echo looked at her watch.

"You're right. I'd say we've got fifteen, twenty minutes at most and she'll not only have the high ground but dusk on her side. Any ideas? Anyone?"

"I think she took both shots from the same spot. She must feel safe and protected there for now," said Clarissa.

"Zeb is the only one with a chance at a decent shot at her in that timeframe," said Rambler.

"Right," replied Echo. "We've got to somehow give him fifteen seconds to cross that open ground and he might have a shot at her."

"Or get himself killed in the process," replied Clarissa.

"We need a diversionary tactic of some sort and we need it now," said Rambler.

"It would help if we had some way to communicate with Zeb," said Clarissa.

Echo checked her cellphone. Nothing.

"If I could only get a hundred feet closer to him I could slip behind that rock and communicate with him if he's got binoculars," said Echo.

"He has them. They're at his left side near his hand," said Clarissa.

"How are you going to communicate with him?" asked Rambler. "And what the hell are you going to say?"

"We both have deaf relatives. We've shown off to each other what we remember of our sign language skills a number of times over the years. Clarissa, keep an eye on him and see if he uses his binoculars to look our way."

"He looks up here, but he does it randomly."

"Next time he looks our way point a finger at me. Hopefully, he'll get the message I want to communicate with him."

"I'm on it."

"Rambler, if I can get closer can you throw a rock in his direction to get his attention? I mean in case he's not looking toward me and I feel like a target for Bronya?"

"The old soup bone ain't what it used to be, but I think I can get close enough to him to get his attention. I mean he's downhill from us so the rock will roll pretty good if I bounce it off that angled stone wall to the south."

"Clarissa, show Rambler where Bronya is firing from. I need to move now. On the count of three fire three or four times in her direction a few seconds apart. Don't give her time to get a shot off."

"Shoot to kill if she aims at anyone of us?" asked Rambler.

"Don't miss," replied Echo. "Ready?"

Both Clarissa and Rambler were ready to fire.

"One, two, three."

Echo took off for the protected area. Zeb spun around to see what was going on once the firing commenced. Bronya showed her rifle barrel then quickly backed off. Rambler and Clarissa each fired five rounds. Echo made it to the safe zone.

"You good?" shouted Clarissa.

Echo stuck her arm out from her hiding place and gave them a thumb's up. Zeb turned his binoculars on Echo who began speaking to him in sign language. He responded accordingly. Echo spoke to Clarissa through her two-way.

"Time to create diversion number two so I can get back to you."

At the count of three Rambler and Clarissa fired away at the presumed location of Bronya Karpenko as Echo raced back to them.

"Have a nice trip?" asked Rambler.

Echo gave him a beauty pageant smile.

"Piece of cake."

"What were you two talking about?" asked Clarissa.

"I told him we'd each fire two clips in rapid succession. That should give him time to slip away through the lowest part of the gulch and come up the far side at a point where Bronya can't see him. If we keep her busy and he gets through he should have a good shot at her."

"Do you know what the other side of the hill even looks like?" asked Rambler.

"I don't."

"Jesus H. Kee-rist," said Rambler. "Don't ever do that to me."

"I will if I have to."

"I know," replied Rambler.

"I'm hoping he gets a clean shot. If he doesn't he'll signal us from the far side of the gulch and we'll try to bring him back the same way we sent him there. That is, unless he has a better idea once he sees what's over there."

"No sense wasting time," said Rambler. "What's the go signal for us to create diversion number three?"

"He's going to rub his hand across his chest. We spread out a little then fire one at a time in this order, Clarissa, Rambler, me. We each unload two clips with one second between each other's shots. You set? We go on three."

Rambler and Clarissa were immediately in place, rifles aimed and at the ready.

"One. Two. Three."

Each clip held eight bullets. Clarissa fired first. One second elapsed then Rambler shot. One more second elapsed. Then Echo fired. That was repeated with clips being changed after their eighth shots. That many high-powered rifle shots would hopefully keep Bronya from seeing what was going on.

The bullets cracked loudly from the rifles, blasted into the rocks and ricocheted in all directions. Forty-eight shots later there had been no return fire. When they ducked to safety Bronya began firing, two barrages in twenty-round bursts.

"I guess that answers the question about whether or not she brought the SHAK-12S with her," said Rambler. "Stupid choice. It's only accurate to one hundred yards."

"Next time she blasts at us you want to stand up and check that out?" asked Clarissa.

"Not a cool idea," replied Rambler. "Not a cool idea at all."

"Did Zeb make it?" asked Rambler.

Echo had kept the binoculars on him through the barrage of bullets.

"He's safe and he set a piece of cloth just on the other side of the gulch about three feet off the ground."

"Is that supposed to mean something to us?" asked Rambler.

"That it will take him three minutes to get into place for a good shot," replied Kate.

"Barring her moving out of his line of vision," said Rambler.

"No plan is perfect. In fact, I'm sure this one has already been thrown out the window," said Echo.

"Why? What?" asked Clarissa.

"You know the old adage. The plan goes out the window the moment the first shot is fired, if not before. I'm hoping whatever on-the-spot changes Zeb has to make are to his advantage," said Echo.

Rambler glanced to the west and the setting sun. The high ground was already starting to become covered by the gray of dusk. Zeb had better step on it or he'd be no better off than an untrained outfielder looking into the west on a sunny day while trying to catch a fly ball. The mother nature advantage was being handed over to Bronya with each passing second.

"Do we want to fire on her again?" asked Rambler.

"Not yet. Just be ready. Zeb will come back down to the low spot in Dead Gulch if something changes."

Echo breathed. Rambler grumbled to himself. Clarissa prepped herself by praying. No sound at the minute mark. Still nothing at minutes two and three. Thirteen seconds later Zeb fired his first round. It either grazed Bronya or was close enough to her that she made a mad dash between two rock slabs that were ten feet apart. The distance took less than one second to cover. Echo, Rambler and Clarissa, anticipating her movement each got off perfect shots. Almost simultaneously Zeb fired a second round.

None of the three could tell if Bronya had been hit or if she lost her footing. What they could see was her body as it fell from the very top of the steep embankment, leaving a trail of blood on the rocks as it bounced and rolled. The air was silent except for the thudding of her body and the sound of her bones breaking into small pieces as it fell well over two hundred feet. Her killing days were done.

Chapter 45

TOWN TALK

THANKS TO A HEADS-UP call from Helen, Maxine had the table in the back of the Town Talk all set for everyone from the Graham County Sheriff's Office. The usual celebration of solving a big crime, in this case two murders, was subdued because one of the dead was one of the most successful Apache women to grow up on the San Carlos Reservation.

The death of Doctor Izdzán Gouyen was mourned not only by all on the San Carlos and by the locals who knew her, but also by the scientific community nationally and worldwide. She had been a pioneer whose work would eventually help bring an end to a devastating war. Her passing was especially mourned by the young girls and women who she inspired to be not only scientists but better people.

Clarissa, Rambler, Shelly, Kate, her husband Josh, Helen, Zeb, Echo, Elan and Onawa arrived as a group. Doc Yackley and his pal Doctor Zata were waiting along with Song Bird and his protégé, Sawni. All had downed some harsh Apache coffee much to Song Bird's delight.

Small talk, coffee, tea and the wandering away from the table of Elan and Onawa preceded Zeb clanging a knife against his water glass.

"I want to thank you all for a job well done. Each of you played a huge role in one of the most difficult double-murder cases that has ever crossed my desk."

His opening statement was interrupted by a round of applause. A smile crossed his face.

"Doc, Doctor Zata, without you two we would never have been able to figure out the type of poison used."

"One more in the books for Duck Watson and Sheer Luck Holmes."

Hearty laughter followed Doc Yackley's tongue-in-cheek statement. Everyone knew how he and Zata had been role-playing Watson and Holmes for over fifty years. The truth was it kept them young and at this moment youth shone from the old men's faces.

"And when is the county going to reimburse me for my helicopter ride?"

Helen got up from her chair, tapped Doc on the shoulder and handed him an envelope with a check in it for his joy ride.

"About time."

Helen kissed the old doc on the cheek. As she turned to return to her seat Doc feigned a pat on the fanny only to have his hand quickly slapped away. The mood turned downright silly. When things settled down Zeb once more spoke.

"Clarissa, Rambler if you hadn't come across the partially burned evidence in the caverns out by the cliff dwellings near the home of Doctor Gouyen we may never have come to closure in this case. Excellent work. I must admit when you found Echo's boonie hat in the cavern and her turquoise bracelet among the ashes I had a moment of doubt. For some reason, those items seemed harder to explain than her knife being found under Tavisha."

"Echo, I was certain you were guilty," said Rambler. "The evidence was pretty overwhelming. I mean your knife as the murder weapon, your missing bracelet story and you not even knowing your boonie hat was missing. The only reason I kept my faith in you was because everything seemed a little too convenient. I never figured you as one to make stupid mistakes."

"Rambler, I knew what you were thinking. I didn't care one bit for Zeb withholding the knife as evidence. He was covering his own ass as much as mine because he hadn't closed the safe. As to the bracelet, after thinking about it I remembered that I took it off in the bathroom when I washed my hands at the Community Center. Tavisha was there with me and I believe she took it. At that time I do believe Tavisha and Bronya were working together and Tavisha told her twin about it. After Bronya killed Tavisha she had access to my bracelet. As to the boonie hat, it had to be Bronya who broke into our house and took it. I think the knife was a bonus, as she couldn't have counted on the safe being open. It was just another piece of evidence to make me look guilty."

"Echo, why did they choose you as the one to pin the murders on?" asked Clarissa.

"They must have done their homework. Not only do I visit that area of the Pinaleños, Bronya must have been aware of my hand-to-hand fighting skills. What she didn't count on was that Zeb would not rest in proving my innocence until he found the real killer."

Helen raised a toast to her favorite red herring. Momentarily the mood lightened, at least until Zeb spoke.

"Kate, I can't say enough about your hard work and insight in this case. Without your excellent debriefing of Prioress Nichinka I wonder how long it would have taken us to figure out that Bronya had taken Tavisha's place at the Priory."

"We should all be thankful the Prioress has a keen eye," replied Kate.

"Regardless, your diligence and hard work makes it certain in my mind that you are going to be the next Sheriff of Graham County."

Stunned expressions covered everyone's faces. Was Zeb announcing his resignation? He carried on with a smile.

"Now everyone hold your horses. I'm running one more time for sure. Maybe two. Echo and I need to discuss what our futures hold. No one lasts forever in this position. I am just thinking ahead a bit. The next person in line for the job, in my opinion, is Kate."

Kate humbly observed everyone's reactions. There was no doubt she had their backing. Even Rambler, though once he reached his goal of becoming police chief of the Rez would no doubt have his eyes set on becoming the first Apache Sheriff of Graham County.

"I guess this is as good a time as any to tell you this."

The room quieted, curious about Kate's announcement.

"Josh and I are pregnant."

Her revelation was met with congratulations all around and a little bit of good-natured ribbing about Josh being pregnant. Josh in turn made several jabs at the others about them not understanding his unusual food cravings and fatigue.

"So I think it will be five years or more before I'm ready to run," said Kate.

"The timing is fine by me," said Zeb.

"One thing," offered Kate. "If for some reason I can't do it I'd like Rambler or Echo to consider running."

"Hell, yes," said Rambler. "But only after I'm PC on the Rez."

Echo's response was decidedly hesitant.

"We'll see. We'll see. I have no idea what my future holds in that regard."

Laughter came from the front of the café as Elan explained to everyone within earshot that he was getting a Mohawk haircut.

"Zeb, why do you think Bronya and Tavisha turned on each other?" asked Clarissa.

"I think I've talked a little with all of you about that exact thing. I've concluded that Tavisha truly fell in love with Doctor Gouyen. In doing so her loyalty shifted from her mission to her lover. There are certain things we can never be sure of. That being said, it is my assumption based on facts and timing that Tavisha explained her true feelings to Bronya. Bronya must have felt horribly betrayed. Being that Doctor Gouyen was such a high value target, the planning of this operation must have been in the offing for years. Tavisha's change of heart changed everything and likely destroyed years of planning."

"Do you believe Tavisha wanted out?" asked Kate. "Especially after she fell in love with Doctor Gouyen?"

"I do believe she did. And, with the stakes being as high as they were, there was no getting out. Bronya had no option except to kill Tavisha, who we now know was her twin sister."

"Plus, having extensively trained together and being identical twins, Bronya felt she could simply take Tavisha's place once she killed her," suggested Echo. "She was taking a chance that no one would be the wiser."

"Had it not been for Prioress Nichinka's attention to very minor details and Doctor Gouyen's ability to tell something was wrong, she might have gotten away with it," said Zeb.

"Zeb, you've repeatedly called this a mission," said Kate.

"Yes," added Clarissa. "Have you been able to learn from the Feds what their interest was in this mission or case or whatever you want to call it?"

Zeb was about to speak about the involvement of the Feds on another matter, but before he could Shelly grabbed the floor.

"I'll take that one," said Shelly. "I read all of Doctor Gouyen's published works. Her concepts are fundamental but brilliant in their usage of technology. The Russians saw that published material and linked the telescopes on the Mount to satellites that controlled drone attacks in Afghanistan."

"How so?"

"The telescopes signal satellites which in turn signal drones that can then fire with amazing accuracy at specific targets. I believe Tavisha and Bronya were sent to the United States to gain that technology for Russia so that those signals could be interrupted on the battlefield. If the Russians had that technology, not only could they stop U.S./Ukrainian drones but they could reproduce the stolen technology and use it for themselves. Clearly the effort was not successful, as Russia has lost many top generals in the past year."

"Not only did we solve two murders but we stopped a Russian spy from stealing the signaling information between telescopes, satellites and drones. Certainly for all of us, except perhaps Shelly, this is brand-new territory." said Kate.

"One more thing you all should know. I only learned of this right before our meeting this morning. I know you are all wondering how the highly toxic chemicals that make up the Novichok nerve agent were placed on Doctor Gouyen without her knowledge," said Zeb.

"And when did she return from her vacation and how long was she dead?" asked Kate.

"One thing at a time," said Zeb. "First of all the DIA in conjunction with the NSA had agents go over Gouyen's house and work it as a crime scene. What is now very obvious is that Bronya sprayed nearly every high-touch surface on the inside of the house."

"It was a damn good thing we never got a search warrant," said Rambler. "Or we might be deader than doornails."

"That's not a maybe," added Clarissa. "It's a for sure."

"When was Doctor Gouyen exposed to Novichok?" asked Rambler.

"The Feds were a big help with this one. Following the GPS tracker on Doctor Gouyen's car they discovered a couple of things. During her extended vacation she drove to California and hand delivered the letter to Doctor Erin Malvala's office. Obviously she did it on the QT as no one had any contact with her when she was there."

"Hence no cancelled stamp on the letter," said Helen.

"Right," said Zeb. "The GPS also showed that the day before Doctor Gouyen's body was found she went home and grabbed some things that were found in her vehicle. Sometime shortly before that the house must have been poisoned with the Novichok agent."

Zeb pulled a crumpled sheet of paper from his back pocket, opened it and began reading.

"This letter is to all of us."

"'The National Security Administration is thankful for the part the Graham County Sheriff's Department played in preventing the Russian Federation from stealing/interfering with current technology being used in the Russia-Ukraine conflict. Through your efforts thousands of lives have been affected positively and many lives have been saved. We owe you a debt of gratitude.' It's signed by the head of the NSA."

Zeb handed the letter to Echo so she could pass it around and everyone could have a look at it.

"From what I hear they have one of the largest budgets in DC," said Doc. "I hope it was their money that was used to reimburse Graham County for my chopper ride."

"It wasn't."

"But I'm going to send them an invoice anyway," interjected Helen.

"We won't hold our collective breath on that," said Zeb. "For now let us all be proud for having served not only Graham County, the San Carlos Reservation and the United States of America. We also did our own little part to help save lives in a far-away war."

Coffee and tea cups were hoisted. "Hear, hear," was shouted by all.

Echo's voice was the final word.

"Peace!"

Free Book from Mark Reps

I HOPE YOU ENJOYED this novel in the Zeb Hanks Mystery Series. If you liked NATIVE DECEPTION, you'll love NATIVE ROOTS, a prequel to the Zeb Hanks Series. This two-part novella explores Zeb's roots as a young man and his early law enforcement career as a border patrol agent and Tucson policeman. Click here to get NATIVE ROOTS for FREE.

Connecting with my readers is one of the best things about being an author. Occasionally I send out newsletters, free content, book reviews, and new book releases to my fans. I never use this list for any other purpose and never share it. You can unsubscribe at any time.

Get NATIVE ROOTS for FREE here.

https://dl.bookfunnel.com/jjk5j4wwpk

THE LOT 1961

Coming Summer 2023

A BASEBALL NOVEL BY MARK REPS

GRANDPA DALE'S LAST HOME RUN

A week after the big storm the town looks pretty much normal again. Only two old trees are knocked down by the storm and they were pretty much rotten on the inside anyway. People everywhere, especially at church and the coffee shop call it a 'miracle' or a 'blessing.' Sounds right by me. The town would look stupid without trees. By now everyone is back playing ball at the Lot. The Lot miraculously was left undamaged. Truly the work of the big man in the sky who I now know is most certainly a fan of the game. The baseball gods probably had their fingers in helping keep it safe as well.

It seems as though something weird happens as a result of the power of the big summer storm. A lot of kids are suddenly a lot stronger. A kid we call 'Brainiac' explains something called 'the lightning effect.' He claims this so-called 'lightning effect' does everything from greening up the grass to making everything that was near the lightning strikes grow faster and get bigger too. He should know. His dad is a physicist at IBM. Everyone in that family is a genius.

The proof in the pudding to his theory is that there are many more dingers and a ton of really high, high pop-ups. One of the major league pop-ups smacks me on the nose. The wind took it. Not my fault. I don't even give myself an error. I call nature interference and it is agreed upon by my pals. No error. My eyes water and Knothead claims I'm crying. I'm not.

It's August and the August heat is as bad as the July heat, only it rains more, at least this year it does. The farmers complain a little about too much rain. It seems as though the farmers never think they get the right amount of rainfall. It's always either too much or too little. I wonder if they'd know exactly the right amount if it fell on them.

We overhear the farmers talking at The Windy Place Café. I think they call it The Windy Place because everybody who goes there talks a lot. But I'm just guessing. The farmers sit in the Café from eleven in the morning until three or three-thirty in the afternoon. They can do that because the crops are all in the ground and they are just watching them grow. None of these guys have cattle or pigs. I overhear them say that.

The farmers tell stories, good stories and shake dice. They also like to play a game called liars' poker. Once in a while we kids get to shake dice with them, but never for money. Sometimes they take a break and go out to the empty lot next to the Windy Place Cafe and toss horseshoes. When they're done they leave the horseshoes in the pits and we toss them around. They're too heavy for us to throw the whole regulation length so we stand about half-way to the ringer pole. When we play a few times a week we get pretty good. I get more leaners than ringers. Lefty McNeil and Knuckles throw ringers all the time.

Like I said the storm damage has been cleaned up and we are once again playing baseball every day again at the Lot. During the third week of August something that has never happened, ever, in the history of the Lot happens. Well, it might have happened before but none of us ever heard about such a thing as this. Plus it seems unlikely that this kind of thing could have ever happened before.

Mac is at bat. Digger is pitching to him. He's firing the ball with all the heat he's got and that is a lot of speed. Today each team has nine players and some subs. I am playing second base so I see this whole thing happen, from start to finish. It happens like this.

Digger winds up and fires a high hard one right down old Broadway. Mac sees it as clear as day, lifts his front leg for more power in his cut, leans into the pitch and swings with all he's got. He catches it just right and the wind is blowing out toward left field. I spin my head just as the ball crosses over the baseline between second and third directly over the shortstops head. Right there it begins to rise like freshly fired fireworks on the fourth of July. It keeps soaring across the street over the top of the telephone lines and heads directly toward the house of the old man and old lady who live on the corner just beyond the imaginary left field fence which looks a lot like the Green Monster in Fenway Park, at least in our heads.

The ball is still soaring. I freeze in place. My mouth hangs open when I see the ball smash right through the top pane of a second story window where the old man who lives there is watching us play ball just like he does every day at this time. Just below him on the first floor, also staring out the window and doing the dishes is the grandma lady who sees the whole thing. What happens next is just plain crazy. It's the kind of thing you have to see to believe. And even seeing it, it's hard to believe it happens.

All eighteen guys that are playing plus the bench players split from the ballfield as fast as greased lightning once they hear the glass break. Some run into nearby bushes. Others dive into open garages. Still others climb trees or duck down behind cars. A bird's eye view would have shown us scattering like geese from a gunshot.

We wait for what feels like an eternity. No one even lets out a whisper. The first person to move is a kid named Ricky Dale. And the weird thing is, he doesn't run away like the rest of us had. He walks right over to the house and shouts something up toward the broken window. A second later the ball comes flying through the broken window. Ricky Dale barely has to move an inch to nab it in mid-air with a basket catch. He's a great outfielder any way you look at it. Someone shouts from the window to the street below. Then the broken window slides up and a head appears in the window. It's the old man! He speaks so softly none of us except Ricky can hear him. We only hear the wrap-up of their conversation.

"There ya' go then."

"Gotcha," replies Ricky. "I can do that."

The old man shouts a reminder.

"Right now."

"Right now?"

"Right now is good a time as any."

"Okay. I'll check on it with the guys."

"Do it now or you'll forget..."

"Yeah. Okay."

The old man points a finger at Ricky before closing the broken window.

Ricky tosses the ball up in the air and snares it behind his back with his glove a few times before firing it on a running jog toward the mound where Digger and Mac are standing. The rest of us start to come out of our hiding places by order of bravery and age. Ricky stops at the mound where he speaks to Digger and Mac while making a whole bunch of gestures with his hands. Both listen closely. After the exchange a glance toward the old man's house, a rub of the chin and a nod and a couple of return nods, Digger and Mac give an all clear signal that indicates it's okay for everyone to run back onto the field. Apparently we aren't in as big trouble as we thought we might be.

"Okay. This is good. It saves us from having to get money to pay for a broken window," says Digger.

We all lean in. Something big is happening. No, better than that, something completely unexpected is going to happen.

"That guy." Digger points to the house with the recently broken window. "He says he'll take care of the broken window under one condition."

We wait with bated breath. What the heck can bated breath possibly even mean? It doesn't matter because we've all got it.

I am so into what is happening in front of my very eyes that I don't even realize I ask the question out loud. Knuckles rolls the back of his fingers over my head. I guess he's call me a knucklehead in sign language.

"Oh. Oh. Hmmm?

I still don't get it so I ask Mac.

"What does an old man want from a bunch of kids?"

The old man had answered for himself. He told Ricky and Ricky told Mac and Mac told us.

"He said this and I quote," said Mac. "I want to bat one time and I want you whippersnappers to treat me like I'm one of your own."

A circular exchange of glances shot around us boys. What does the old man mean? One of us? Why would an old man want to be a kid? It doesn't make any sense. Mac notices our reaction.

"He wants to feel like a kid again. Get it?"

Not one of us did. It just made no sense at all. An old man can't be a kid any more than a kid can be an old man. I can't even begin to wrap my head around it.

"No," replied Knothead. "I don't get it."

"Doesn't matter," said Digger. "We're going to let him bat and run the bases. We will all treat him like we'd treat any one of us. If he hits a fly, catch it. If he hits a grounder, throw him out. Got that?"

That much we understood.

"He's Ricky Dale's grandpa, Ed Dale."

"Ahh."

Now we understand. Suddenly things were maybe starting to make sense. I think.

If I hadn't seen the whole thing with my own eyes, and only heard it said I might have called the storyteller a big fibber. I mean the ball going through the second story window right after it glided swiftly over the telephone wires and the imaginary Green Monster seems like a pretty tale in and of itself. Hah! Wrong!! That's only the first half of the tale.

Because just then Grandpa Dale comes walking out of his house using a walker. A walker! How is he going to bat? He can't even stand up without help. To make things worse for him, his wife is following two steps behind him in order to catch him if he falls, which it looked more likely with each step he takes.

We kind of just stop in our tracks and watch him cross the street. When he moves down the cement sidewalk which is heaved up in a lot of places from the winter freeze and spring thaw we hold our collective breath. But the old man makes his way good enough. I don't see that his wife really needs to help him at all. As he gets closer to us we can see he hasn't shaved in a day or three. Old men, when they don't shave and are all grey like that, look older than they really are. And Grandpa Ed is pretty old to begin with.

"Well?"

He barks when he speaks.

"Are we playing baseball or tiddlywinks?"

"Not tiddlywinks," says Knuckles.

Everyone laughs including Grandpa Dale.

Grandpa Dale may be old but he knows how to give us the raspberries. Still I am wondering if he can even lift a bat, much less swing one. Me, along with everyone else, well we just sort of stare blankly at the old man as he picks up a bat. He taps it a few times on the ground before he takes a really weak cut and then a second that has a little something, but not much, backing it up. Still I wonder if his wrists are going to break. He looks awfully weak and not a whole lot stronger as he takes a few more practice cuts.

I look around the field. All eyes are fixated on the old man. All heads shaking. Each kid feels sorry for the old man even before his first swing. Even though he's an old man he seems like the kid who wants to play but just doesn't have enough of the right stuff. Maybe he had it once, but it sure seems like it's gone now. The outfielders creep in and he hasn't even stepped in the batter's box. I feel kind of sad, especially when his wife yells in his direction.

"Edward don't hurt yourself. You're not a young man any-more."

We nod in agreement, that is every single one of us except Ricky. Grandma Dale is right. Edward could be in big trouble here. She pleads a second time.

"Edward please don't hurt yourself."

No one has ever died at the Lot before, at least that I know of. Today is not a good day for someone to break that tradition.

Leaving his walker behind Grandpa Dale shuffles slowly to the plate. We wince each time he puts one foot in front of the other. He stumbles slightly before he steps into the batter's box. Like all batters he taps the plate a few times with his bat. We collectively hold our breath when the old man leans forward and almost falls across the plate. He catches himself, lifts his head and gives us a nasty old man glare before he speaks.

"You little shits think you're better than me. Don't you?"

No one says a word. No one dares. And, no, we don't think anything like that. There's no need to.

Resting his bat on his shoulder he points a craggy old finger at Digger before running a hand across his letters. He spits a chaw of genuine tobacco toward the mound. I don't mind spitting on the field, in fact I dig it. If someone just randomly walked by and spit tobacco on the field I would be downright indignant. But Grandpa Dale was in the game.

"High and tight is how I like 'em, sonny."

"Yes, sir," replies Digger.

"You busted my window so toss me the pitch I like. You got that, young man?"

Digger nods. He's got it. Digger winds up but in the middle of his wind-up he slows down and tosses the first pitch under-handed. Grandpa Dale catches it in his bare hand, looks at it, spits a second chaw that arcs high in the air and lands on the edge of the pitcher's mound with a splat we can all hear. Then he stops and slowly rolls the ball on the ground back to Digger. I can't help but laugh.

"Good one, Mr. Dale," I shout.

Digger turns and gives me a look. I shrug my shoulders. It was pretty funny. Even Digger couldn't disagree about that.

"I've been watchin' you from my perch, Digger Torkelson..." The old man points the thick end of the bat toward the broken window. "...and that ain't the way you pitch."

"Yes, sir."

Digger winds up, rears back and sends it to the plate high and tight just like the old man has asked him to. I wince in fear that it's going to bonk the old man in the head and kill him dead right there in front of my eyes. But old Grandpa Dale has different ideas. He pulls his front foot out and takes a mighty cut. The thick wooden end of the bat cracks against the ball and explodes like a firecracker on the 4th of July. The ball shoots off his bat like a bottle rocket. Digger whips his head around as we all turn and watch as the ball soars over the power lines and our make-believe Green Monster as it flies across the street.

It keeps rising like some sort of voodoo magic was transferred from his bat to the ball. I can hardly believe my eyes as I watch it go right through and bust the lower pane of the window that Mac had just busted the upper pane of. What are the odds of that? A billion to one? A trillion to one?

Grandpa Dale keeps pointing one finger up and down like it's on a yo-yo string as he makes his way around the bases at a very slow trot. Grandma Dale stands by his walker smiling and proud of her husband but shaking in her boots. I imagine she is worried her husband might have a heart attack or a stroke from the stress of it all.

By the time Grandpa Dale reaches second his slow trot turns into an unsteady walk. We all, every single one of us, run in from our positions and walk along beside him as he rounds second and heads for third where Grandma Dale is anxiously waiting with his walker. As he huffs and puffs around third, missing the deep hole, he stops dead in his tracks. I can't see his face but I imagine it's as red as a beet. Grandma Dale struts right up to him with his walker.

Then to our surprise he reaches into a little bag that's under the seat and grabs his pipe along with a stick match. He runs a thumb along the sulfur end of the wooden match. It fires up and fades before it refires, just like all struck matchsticks do before it lights itself up big. Grandpa Dale takes the perfectly lit match and stuffs it down into his pipe, lights it up and takes a couple of puffs. A puff of smoke dances out of his nostril. I do a doubletake. I swear I see a smoke ring come out of each side of his nose and join together in an infinity symbol. Unbelievable! He watches the smoke drift away before he glances up at the sunny blue sky. In all my ten years on this earth I've never seen a smile quite like the one that covers his face. At that moment I figure out what my dad means when he says, "It's the kind of smile you can't wipe off with a rag."

Grandpa Dale hands the pipe to his wife and picks up the pace just enough to make it look like he actually crosses home plate at a pretty darn good clip.

We all burst into a cheer. When we gather around him and pat him on the back he sticks his arms straight out to his sides like their angel wings or something and says one word.

"Well?"

All I could think of was, 'Well, what?' But Digger and Mac understand exactly what he is talking about. It's Grandpa Dale's bottom of the ninth in the seventh game of his World Series. He expects us to lift him up on our shoulders and carry him around the bases.

I discover right then and there old men don't weigh much. It only takes four of the bigger kids to lift him up. He waves like there are 50,000 fans cheering him on. As a team we carry him around first, then second and we are all clapping, cheering and shouting out his name.

"Grandpa Dale. Grandpa Dale. Grandpa Dale."

When he's crossed home plate his wife is waiting with his walker. As we pat him on the back some more we can all see he has tears in his eyes. I'm confused by the tears. He just hit a monster home run and he is ten times our age. He's a genuine ballplayer. He's just proven that he's the real deal. That's nothing to cry about. It's something to celebrate.

We stand in a group as he heads back down the erupted sidewalk squares. Speed Limit quietly whispers the question.

"What is he crying about?"

Digger and Mac speak in a single voice.

"He just hit his last home run...ever."

I feel like crying. But I don't.

About the Author

MARK REPS HAS BEEN a writer and storyteller his whole life. Born in small-town southeastern Minnesota, he trained as a mathematician and chiropractor but never lost his love of telling or writing a good story. As an avid desert wilderness hiker, Mark spends a great deal of time roaming the desert and other terrains of southeastern Arizona. A chance meeting with an old time colorful sheriff led him to develop the Zeb Hanks character and the world that surrounds him.

To learn more, check out his website www.markreps.com, his AllAuthor profile, or any of the profiles below. To join his mailing list for new release information and more click here

bookbub.com/authors/mark-reps
facebook.com/ZebHanks
goodreads.com/author/show/2105996.Mark_Reps
twitter.com/markreps1
amazon.com/Mark-Reps/e/B00BYFEBQ4

Also by Mark Reps

ZEB HANKS MYSTERY SERIES
NATIVE BLOOD
HOLES IN THE SKY
ADIOS ANGEL
NATIVE JUSTICE
NATIVE BONES
NATIVE EARTH
NATIVE DESTINY
NATIVE WARRIOR
NATIVE TROUBLE
NATIVE FATE
NATIVE DREAMS
NATIVE REVENGE
NATIVE DECEPTION

NATIVE ROOTS (Prequel Novella)

OTHER BOOKS
HEARTLAND HEROES

BUTTERFLY(with Pui Chomnak)

Made in the USA
Monee, IL
10 October 2023

44340510R00144